DANNY
AND THE BOYS

GREAT LAKES BOOKS

DANNY

AND THE BOYS

Being Some Legends of
Hungry Hollow

BY

ROBERT TRAVER
author of ANATOMY OF A MURDER

 WAYNE STATE UNIVERSITY PRESS   DETROIT

TO

Annie Isabella

Manufactured in the United States of America.

98 97 96 95 94   8 7 6 5 4

Library of Congress Cataloging-in-Publication Data

Traver, Robert, 1903–
    Danny and the boys : being some legends of Hungry Hollow / by
Robert Traver.
        p. cm. — (Great Lakes books)
    ISBN 0–8143–1927–0 (alk. paper). ISBN 0–8143–1928–9 (pbk. : alk.
paper)
    1. Upper Peninsula (Mich.)—Fiction. I. Title. II. Series
PS3570.R339D36   1987   87–24415
813′.54—dc19   CIP

CONTENTS

Author

SOME REFLECTIONS
ON THE REBIRTH OF DANNY

For many years I have prowled the woods and fished the waterways of my native Upper Peninsula of Michigan, having been born in one of its scattered logging and mining towns around the turn of the century—though I suppose I should confess that of late years I sometimes get turned around about precisely which century.

Before I learned to spell cat without a k I began spinning yarns about the place and its heady mixture of peoples, once even winning a prize in sixth grade for a story entitled, of all things, "Lost All Nite Alone in a Swomp with a Bare." The prize was three green apples grown in the yard of our teacher, sweet patient Miss Fisher, though my boyhood pal Fritz Ludlow had other views. "After a title like that," he sniffed, "about all you really needed to add was 'woof!' "

Local characters have always fascinated me and that's what this book is all about. Perhaps my natural curiosity was aided by the privileged advantage of often being able to study them in a special research laboratory usually denied lads of my age, namely, the inner precincts of my father's busy saloon on downtown Main Street, especially on pay days.

In any case, it's well that I decided to write the book back when my memories were still fresh. They were also written, I might add, quite a few years before they ever got published. It's the second of my eleven books, as I recall, and ever since then local characters seem to be getting as scarce as passenger pigeons, passenger trains, and old passenger depots that haven't long since been bulldozed to oblivion or else converted into fancy gift or antique shops.

Today, alas, local characters and the way they talked have vanished as completely as traveling circuses, livery stables, and the volunteer fire departments around and near which the local bar flies once used to hover waiting to find—and maybe earn a volunteer buck or two—for whom the next fire bell might toll.

In this book I try to revive some of the local characters I remember most vividly as a boy growing up almost within fly-casting range of Lake Superior. Danny and his boys lead the nostalgic parade, of course, but their many antics, monkeyshines, and assorted shennanigans naturally brought them into frequent collision with many other local characters, all carried on in the diverse brogues, accents, and dialects now grown as obsolete as the vanished characters themselves, today replaced by a sort of bastard form of pidgin televeese.

The accompanying photo of "Danny" and "Timmy" was taken 'way back when and by whom I know not, but I thank my old friend and fishing pal, Chuck Kroll, for unearthing and letting me use it— though I'm still a little puzzled how the resourceful photographer ever managed to hit such a handsome photogenic home run while at the same time so slyly and deftly catching such a magnificent open fly!

FOREWORD

The following stories of Hungry Hollow mainly concern the fabulous doings of Danny and the boys who live there. Hungry Hollow lies on the rugged Upper Peninsula of Michigan midway between Lake Superior and the iron-mining town of Chippewa. Before Danny and the boys came to the Hollow it was the site of a white pine logging camp. Prior to that the Indians used to dwell there. That was before the heap big white man came and drove the Peninsula Indians away, nearly exterminating them for their bad taste in fighting for their homes and for their freedom. Before the Indians there were the glaciers.

These tales are written to celebrate and reaffirm the wonder and the glory of the individual man. Any shred of "social significance" that may have crept into this narrative is an accident for which I humbly apologize. If these stories must prove anything perhaps it is simply this: In our time there still dwells a group of men who live as they do because they choose to. Reflection may move one to conclude that this is no longer the common lot of mankind.

Finally, to vary the formula a trifle, the characters and situations in this book are as real as Santa Claus.

ROBERT TRAVER

Danny and Timmy
Tape recorders weren't invented back then, so one can only speculate that this ancient snapshot of "Danny" and "Timmy" taken during a bygone Thermos bottle coffee break was snapped during a pause in their discussion of Danny revealing new open-fly policy.

Author and Danny
Equally ancient snapshot of our aspiring young author evidently trying to interview "Danny" for this book. Yep. Yep.

1

HUNGRY HOLLOW

The log cabin of Danny McGinnis and the boys stands on the side of a birch-covered slope where the Mulligan Plateau abruptly sheers off into the valley of the Big Dead River. The front door of the camp faces west, and occasional gleaming patches of the river show through the dense tag alder thickets and spruce bottom lands which mark its winding course. A portion of this swampy lowland knifes into the slope just north of the camp. It is in this little swamp that Danny hides his moonshine still.

A quarter of a mile north of the camp stands the edge of the tall Silver Lake hardwood. Behind the camp to the east rises a series of rough wooded terraces to the top of the Mulligan Plateau. This plateau runs east as far as the eye can see, bounded on the north by the Silver Lake hardwood and on the south, a mile away, by the tumbling Mulligan Creek, beyond which looms the brooding Mulligan mountain range. The Mulligan Plateau, with its miles of charred white

pine stumps and lonely sentinel trees, standing amidst
the tangle of sweet fern and huckleberry bushes, looks
like a great unkempt burial ground. This is the home
of Danny and the boys of Hungry Hollow.

The manner in which Hungry Hollow acquired its
name has become lost in the mists of local legend.
Danny's place stands on the wind-protected side of a
hill, not in a hollow. As for the hungry part, the place
had once been the main Dead River camp of old Angus
Ferguson, one of the Upper Peninsula's fabulous lumber barons. Graybeards allowed that one winter in the
eighties the snow had been so deep, the storms so lash-
ing, and the cold so bitter, that for over a month supplies could not be brought in; the camp hunters found
that the deer had perished in their swampy winter
yards, and that when relief finally came not a single
horse was left in the camp. Dark rumor had it that
forever after that the lumberjacks of Hungry Hollow
had to be shod by a blacksmith.

Danny McGinnis, then a beardless youth, was one
of the survivors of that desperate winter. He was a
chore boy or "bull cook" for the camp cook. And he
was curiously loath to admit that he had ever partaken
of horseflesh. "Naw, we didn't eat no bloody horses,"
Danny scoffed. "What really happened was me an' the
cook run clean out a mushrooms! Would you believe it
—them bloody high-toned lumberjacks went into a
pout an' wouldn't eat their porterhouse steaks nor
nothin' 'thout they was smothered in mushrooms. It's
as true as I'm settin' here!"

Old Angus Ferguson . . .

This terrible red-bearded Scotch giant had dedicated
a lifetime to ravishing the Peninsula of its white pine.
He was called the King of the White Pine. People said
he leered ecstatically as he drove his team of prancing

bays through the dreary miles of his barren cuttings. At one time he was reputed to be a millionaire, although he had never owned more than forty acres of timberland. How did he do it? "Hm," Danny would say, spitting a rich stream of Peerless juice, "it was dead simple. All he done was buy forty acres at Hungry Hollow an' log all aroun' it fer seventeen winters. Yep, yep!"

But finally all the white pine had been cut, and Old Angus had gone broke while trying to log the Mulligan Mountains and sustain a menagerie of wives all at the same time. He had died penniless at the turn of the century, cleaning spittoons and cadging drinks in George Voelker's saloon in Chippewa—Chippewa, the iron-mining town which lay some seventeen miles south of Hungry Hollow. All that he left behind him was endless miles of charred white pine stumps ("a woodpecker'd have to pack his lunch to fly acrost it!" Danny said), a brood of red-headed children, and the tumbling ruins of the main camp at Hungry Hollow. Danny had appointed himself the sole heir of old Angus and had acquired Hungry Hollow and its ruined buildings by the simple expedient of moving in. He had lived there ever since.

Hungry Hollow finally reverted to wilderness. With the exception of Danny and the boys, only an occasional hunter or trapper or fisherman came along that way. No longer does the river valley echo with the tumult and shouting of the spring drive. The mighty torrent of the Big Dead River continues to spill out of Silver Lake and restlessly search its way eastward to Lake Superior, finally joining its icy waters just north of Iron Bay, the county seat of Iron Cliffs County. The Big Dead flows on and on as it did when the clan Ferguson foraged for food with the aid of clubs, and just as it will continue to flow when men have at length disappeared from the battered earth—have hurled their last bolts of hate and fear at each other across the screaming skies.

Hungry Hollow is, in its way, one of the most exclusive clubs in America. There are no officers or directors in the usual sense. Old Danny McGinnis is tacitly the president, king, treasurer, chef, imperial potentate, grand wizard, and official barkeep all rolled into one. Nor are there any rules or dues or membership committees; no ritualistic mumbo jumbo or secret handclasps or blackballs or any of the other dazzling paraphernalia of male exclusiveness. Decisions are arrived at in Hungry Hollow by a silent nod of the head.

"Well, it's Sat'day ag'in," Danny might observe. "Will we go to town tonight an' have a few snorts an' mebbe visit Big Annie an' the girls? What say, boys?" There is usually a brief period while the boys discuss the problem. Then comes the quick nod or a negative shake of the head. The majority rules. There is little debate and no appeal. Elementary democracy flowers at Hungry Hollow.

Big Buller Beaudin was the first to move in with Danny. That was the summer the first World War flamed over Europe. Big Buller, who drove a local dray, had devoted himself that summer to a vain attempt to consume all the alcohol in Chippewa. It was a losing battle. He finally sought the solace of the forest. The sun was going down as Buller, like a lone elephant going out to die, lurched along the river ridge, following the winding, sandy, two-rut road down the slope to Hungry Hollow. Danny met him at the door as Buller shambled up the knoll to the camp.

"Hello," Danny said, his darting gray eyes surveying the vast alcoholic wreck that swayed before him.

"Thinks I you're Buller Beaudin, ain't ya? What's left of him, I mean?"

Buller looked at Danny with his inflamed bloodhound eyes. His soiled clothes hung loosely on his great frame. "Look, Danny," he croaked. "Look—Jes' let me stay out here till I die. It won't take a hull lot of time. Please, Danny—I don't wanna up'n die in there with all them people watchin' me." Buller swept his arm vaguely to the south, in the general direction of Chippewa.

Danny folded his thin, powerful arms loosely across his sweat-stained suspenders. He raised his bald head and spat sightlessly into the sunset. "Hm . . ." he said. He looked at Buller. He spat again and then curtly nodded his head. Buller was in.

"C'mon in an' have a wee drink a moonshine before we eat," Danny said. "I jest run off a fresh batch this mornin'. I'm havin' Mulligan stew fer supper. Lucky fer you you happened along. Yep, yep!"

In his grotesque eagerness Buller stumbled across the threshold of the camp and nearly fell flat on his face. "Steady there, me lad," Danny warned sharply. "Don't rush. Don't crowd. The bloody moonshine'll keep! It allus has."

"Boy, oh boy!" Buller exclaimed huskily, falling into a chair at the oilcloth-covered table and rolling his red eyes up at Danny in an expression of deathless gratitude.

Gentle Timmy was the next member of Hungry Hollow to be taken in. Little, wiry, lean-wristed Timmy Pascoe, a timid pocket edition of old Danny. Timmy with the soft brown eyes, Timmy, the self-taught mechanical genius, who had once worked for a tinkerer called Henry Ford before the latter's name had become a household word. Proud Timmy, the gassed veteran of the first World War, who scornfully spurned his veterans' disability pay, and who had returned from overseas with the bitter resolve never to work again—"to punch a goddam clock"—as long as he remained on earth. He had lived in a crude log shack and trapped in the vicinity of Hungry Hollow for nearly a year before Danny and Buller were sure he was there. He moved through the woods like a wraith, canoeing the Big Dead and its tributaries, trapping and fly-fishing like one possessed, shunning all company, going into Chippewa only for necessary supplies and to dispatch his furs.

One morning at breakfast time he had appeared at Hungry Hollow with two shimmering rainbow trout. "Here," he said, presenting them to Danny. "I just caught 'em." He then timidly asked Danny and Buller if he could borrow an old newspaper or magazine with a crossword puzzle in it. Timmy took a boundless delight in working crossword puzzles. Danny found an armload of back copies of the *Hematite*, the Chippewa weekly newspaper. Timmy stood wistfully examining Danny's behorned and earphoned battery radio set.

"Does it play?" he inquired.

"Naw," Danny replied. "I dunno what in hell's the matter with the damn thing. Won it in town a year ago Christmas on a punchboard at Charlie's Place. Thinks I it's the battery's flat." Danny scowled. "Someday if I ever fin' the time I'm goin' to yank the Fallopian tubes outa that goddam cabinet an' make a tool chest! Yep, yep, if I ever fin' the bloody time."

"Do you mind if I look at it?" Timmy said.

In ten minutes, with the aid of a pair of Danny's ten-cent-store pliers, the camp was flooded with hillbilly laments and laxative ads. "How is your stummick?" the radio announcer bawled. Timmy had saved the little radio from its ignominious fate as a tool chest. "What you fellas really need is a wind charger for your storage batteries," he had ventured timidly, gathering up his newspapers to depart. Danny had looked at Buller and Buller had looked at Danny. "Do you have an acid stummick?" the announcer persisted.

What Hungry Hollow had needed for a long time was a first-class jack-of-all-trades. Not that Danny and Buller couldn't fix radios and wind chargers and simple things like that—but they were usually far too busy with more important concerns: making moonshine whisky and home-brew, or playing endless games of cribbage, or planning trips to Chippewa, or recovering from their last visit to town. Danny and Buller nodded at the same time. Danny cleared his throat.

"Don't be in no rush to leave, Timmy," he said, hospitably bobbing his eyebrows and mustaches. "Stick aroun' fer a while. Mebbe you kin help us to put up our goddam wind charger. Don't be in no bloody hurry."

"Do you suffer from bloat and stummick gas?" the radio shouted.

Timmy had not been in a hurry. He was back that evening with his packsack, his canoe beached at the Big Dead pool below the camp. Within a year Hungry Hollow had a towering new propeller-bladed wind charger. Timmy even built a brand-new radio ("outa ol' tin cans an' rusty button hooks," Danny liked to boast) and put a new tar-paper roof on the camp, spaded a potato patch, built a new log outhouse, and even soldered and repaired Danny's battered still. There seemed to be nothing he could not do. All he needed for inspiration was a constant supply of cross-word puzzles. He tied his own flies, repaired and wound his own fly rods, and kept the camp supplied with fresh brook trout and rainbows from the Big Dead.

"Yep, yep," Danny said to him one day, reflectively stroking his corded throat. "I've et so goddam many fish since you come here I—I'm developin' gill slits! It's as true as I'm settin' here!"

Nearly ten years had passed before any new members were taken into Hungry Hollow. A number of wistful candidates had appeared but they had somehow failed to win the nod. Danny was nearing seventy, and a strange tidal wave known as the Depression was engulfing the land. Borne upon its muddy crest were two bewildered refugees called Nicholas Vedder and Swan Kellstrom. "Taconite Nick" Vedder had been born in Chippewa years before.

They had landed in Chippewa from Minnesota, riding the rods of a freight train on the Lake Superior and Chippewa Railway. They had found their way to the local hobo jungle near the roundhouse on the edge of town. There they had partaken well but not too wisely of a hobo drink known as "canned heat." Under its mellifluous glow they had reeled and lurched about downtown Chippewa until one of Chippewa's dismounted police had tenderly guided them to the jail under the city hall. The next morning the local justice of peace, Judge Williams, had sentenced them each to pay ten dollars fine and three-fifteen costs or to serve thirty days in the county jail down at Iron Bay. It might just as well have been a million dollars.

"Ve vill goo to yail," Swan had gleefully told the judge, happy over the prospect of a month's freedom from cold and hunger. But the good judge had thought otherwise. The county jail was crowded. Men virtually waited in line to gain admission to the place. No, the judge would suspend the sentence if they would leave town immediately. "Move on," had become the order of the day, the byword of a bewildered and tramping nation.

Such was the home-coming of "Taconite" Nicholas Vedder whose restless wanderings about the mining camps of America had led him to Houghton, Ironwood, Chisholm, Coleraine, Hibbing, the Black Hills, Butte, Montana, then back to Taconite, Minnesota— where he had got his nickname—and finally back to Chippewa where his father had been an iron miner before him.

Dusk found Taconite and his chum, Swan Kellstrom, a native of Minnesota, trudging along the ridge toward Hungry Hollow. As a boy Taconite had heard of Angus Ferguson and had fished the Big Dead River. He even remembered Danny McGinnis. Perhaps the logging camp was still running? Perhaps they could get a job cutting white pine?

"But it's all yust stumps!" Swan said, skeptically surveying the ravaged Mulligan plain. "Do you know even if da camp vere still dere?" Swan had learned to be watchful of Taconite's judgment. He had discovered that his mental processes were inclined to be a little slow.

"See!" Taconite exclaimed in his gobbling, extravagant voice. "See the light in the window! Ol' Ferguson'll sure give us a job! Gee whiz!"

But old Ferguson had been dead for over thirty years. It was Danny McGinnis who met them at the door, who served them steaming helpings of Mulligan stew out of the big iron kettle and, after glancing at Buller and Timmy and getting their nods, pointed out the empty upper bunk where they might spend the night. For there were jealously guarded temporary admissions to Hungry Hollow for the lone trapper, the hungry wayfarer, for the down and out.

The next morning grateful Swan and Taconite had sallied forth with saw and axes and cut and sawed and chopped enough hardwood firewood to last a month. They had the whole Silver Lake forest to work on. It was so late when they had finished that they naturally had to be fed and given another bed for the night. The next day Taconite and Swan were so grateful that they again cut wood all day. Danny and the boys didn't have the heart to turn them out. And so it ran, day after day, week after week, until the camp woodshed and temporary lean-tos were bulging with firewood, after which neat piles of wood began to dot the hillside like eccentric fortifications.

The word finally got around Chippewa that Danny McGinnis had a wonderful store of firewood out at Hungry Hollow. Could he be persuaded to sell some? He could. "Choice firewood for sale dirt cheap at Hungry Hollow," ran the ad in the *Hematite Weekly* composed by Timmy, whose crossword puzzles naturally made him the camp's undisputed intellectual. "Come and get it! D. McGinnis, Prop." the ad concluded.

Danny's buckskin purse began to swell with the proceeds from the sale of wood. Taconite and Swan toiled on and on, cutting wood like avenging angels. Verily, they would hew their way to economic security. During their absence one Saturday, Danny and Buller and Timmy had a formal meeting. To nod or not to nod? When tired Taconite and Swan dragged themselves back to camp that night, Danny met them at the door and made the announcement. He held an open quart of Hungry Hollow moonshine in his hand.

"Welcome to Hungry Hollow, boys!" he proclaimed, genially rubbing his bald head. "C'mon in an' stay as long as you like!"

They had already been there six months.

2

DANNY AND THE BOYS

Scotch-Irish Danny had catapulted out of Canada when he was seventeen, reputedly chased by a bailiff who sought to find a husband for a country lass who needed one badly. Eventually landing in Chippewa, he went to work in one of the iron mines. Child labor laws were then the wistful dreams of long-haired eccentrics. After a few months underground, Danny quit the mine in disgust. For Danny was a natural-born sun worshiper. "I'd sooner be in hell with my back broke!" he told his boss one day. "But when I git there I don' aim to dig my way down!" He abruptly threw down his tools, snuffed out his candle, and walked away. He never mined another pound of ore. Instead he went to work for old Angus Ferguson and nearly starved to death; and when Angus died he moved into the old camp at Hungry Hollow, got himself a moonshine still, and permanently retired from all forms of gainful employment.

Danny, who constantly maintained a miraculous two-day growth of beard, had lively, darting little gray eyes, the permanently flushed countenance of an erring Santa Claus, and a remarkable set of tobacco-stained teeth which he evidently thought had been given him for the sole purpose of removing beer-bottle caps. "Them bloody newfangled bottle openers is always slippin'," he complained. Danny was one of those singular persons who seemed to have been born to be bald, who indeed would have looked ridiculous with a head of hair.

He was never still. Nature had installed a great spring in the man and coiled it tightly for a long run. When animated, his eloquent eyebrows bobbed in synchrony with his mustaches; he blinked his eyes, ground his teeth, whinnied, sighed, shrugged, grimaced, protruded his chin, stroked his wire-haired whiskers, tugged at his mustaches, puffed out his cheeks, pulled them in, licked his lips, scratched himself, protruded his tongue, twisted his bald head, rubbed it, craned it, tilted it, and occasionally fell on it. Even in repose he was never still, loosely kneading his palms with his gnarled fingers, thumbs up, as though he were milking an invisible cow. And, of course, he talked to himself.

"How come you're always talkin' to yourself?" Buller asked him testily one day, coming upon the old man mumbling to himself. Danny stroked his wire-haired chin reflectively.

"Fer two reasons," he replied. "In the first place, I likes to hear a smart man talk—an' in the second place, I likes to talk to a smart man! Yep, yep."

In his way, Danny was one of the most articulate men who had lived since Shakespeare. With a vocabulary limited to a few thousand words, a generous part of which was profanity, he nevertheless managed to communicate the most original ideas and subtlest emotions. He was a natural master of the rhythm and nuances of speech. He talked rapidly for the most part, constantly punctuating his words with his staccato and peculiarly expressive "yep-yep-yeps." In short, Danny was a man of few words but he used them over and over. He was also the poet laureate of invective. He could inject more feeling into a single "goddam" than most poets could into an entire sonnet. He was a rustic genius, an illiterate spiritual offspring of Walt Whitman, an aging goat, a disorderly Pan, the last Adam, a one-man band. He was old Danny McGinnis of Hungry Hollow.

Danny never tired of telling the boys about his brief experiences as an iron miner. The miners had then toiled long hours each day. "Eleven hours of savage amusement!" he snorted. That was in the days before laborers grew soft and plaintive and began to think that perhaps eight hours might be long enough for men to remain out of the sun. He invested the few months he had spent "in the goddam bowels of the earth" with the dignity of a saga. He embellished his experiences until one marveled that he had survived. He had lived at a Cornish boardinghouse in Chippewa.

One of his favorite stories about his earthy and rugged Cornish mining mates was the " 'Anging of Jan Tregembo." Jan was the husband of his boardinghouse lady. With Jan, fits of melancholia regularly supplemented fits of drinking. The Sunday pasty dinner—the proverbial Cornish meat and suet pie—was served, but no Jan appeared for dinner. He had spent a bad Saturday night. Long-suffering Mrs. Tregembo wearily dispatched Dicker Matthews, her star boarder, to go out and find her missing husband. After a spell Dicker returned and thoughtfully resumed eating his pasty. He seemed to have lost his appetite.

Mrs. Tregembo emerged from the kitchen and asked Dicker if he had searched for her spouse.

"Yes'm," Dicker replied, "Hi searched in the aout 'ouse an' in the bloody woodshed."

"Did yew find un?" Mrs. Tregembo asked.

Dicker looked up at Mrs. Tregembo. "'E's 'anging in the woodshed with a rope aroun' 'is neck."

"Did yew cut'n daown, Dicker?" Mrs. Tregembo inquired.

"Cut'n daown!" Dicker replied. " 'Ow could Hi cut'n daown? The bloody booger weren't even dead yet!"

"Yep, yep, yep," Danny usually concluded this account, "the Cousin Jacks is a mighty fine people— the greatest people on the face of the earth. Yep, yep!"

But 'Arry Penhale was Danny's favorite Cornishman. 'Arry was Danny's working partner down in the mine. Along about midnight on the nightshift 'Arry liked to slip secretly up the ladderway and scamper home and pay a brief visit to his young wife. The trick was not to be caught by the mining captain. In this way 'Arry's pay was not docked and the interlude made a fine break in the long evening's toil. He would surely have been discharged had he been discovered.

One night 'Arry had returned from his nocturnal visit quite thoughtful, if not downright depressed. This was contrary to experience, as he usually regaled Danny with the glowing details of his truancy. Danny pondered the problem. What had happened?

"C'mon, ol' boy," curious Danny finally said. "Buck up! What's ailin' you, lad? She mad at you?"

'Arry broke down and confessed. "W'en Hi got 'ome Hi tiptawed hup the bloody stairs, an' guess wot?"

"What happened?" Danny brightly inquired, licking his lips in vicarious anticipation.

"Wot 'appened! Would yew believe un—there was the captain of aour bloody mine in bed with Sarah," 'Arry replied in an awed voice.

"What did you do to the bastard!" Danny demanded, his hackle rising.

"*Do to 'im!*" 'Arry replied. "Lucky me snuck right back daown the stairs an' aout the side door—an' so 'elp me, Danny, Hi don't really think 'e heven seen me!"

Buller Beaudin was born in Chippewa, of French-Canadian parentage. Until he had come to live with Danny he had spent most of his life around horses and livery stables. He was a tremendous hulk of a man, splendidly equipped with a set of appetites to match his bulk. There were those hapless persons who had dared to call him fat. Retribution had been violent and swift. For Buller was as strong and hard as a blooded bull. "All over this goddam Peninsula," Danny said, "there's men roamin' aroun' on crutches, mumblin' to theirselves an' sleepin' in depots an' boxcars, what's called Buller 'Fatty'! Yep, yep." His girth was so great that Danny disciplined the boys at Hungry Hollow by threatening to make them run around Buller ten times.

"Either that or run clear down to the Mulligan Creek an' back! Take your bloody pick, now!" Danny would warn.

Slender little Timmy was of Cornish ancestry, with dark reddish hair and burning dark brown eyes. There was something indefinably genteel about him. Even dressed in his woods clothes he somehow managed to suggest an aristocratic courtier. In him there was more than a little of the trace of the Spanish invaders who had long ago overrun Cornwall. Danny used to chide Timmy about his refined and gentle nature—especially when he refused to join the boys in their Saturday night excursions to Big Annie's. "The trouble with you, Timmy—hm—I'm damned if you ain't afflicted awful with character! It's horrible an' torrible."

Taconite was part German, part Indian, and, according to Danny, part Norway pine. The man was gently mad about trees and wood-cutting. He would crouch on all fours to inhale the odor of the stump of a freshly cut tree. "Ain't that a gran' smell," he'd sigh, shaking his dark cowlick from his eyes. Taconite took an inordinate pleasure in small things. After he and Swan had cut acres of hardwood barehanded, raising great callouses, Danny finally relented and bought each of them a pair of buckskin mittens. Taconite proudly wore his all the year round.

"Gee whiz, these is swell mitts," he'd confide to the envious beholder. "They's warm in winter an' cool in summer. Gee whiz!"

Taconite had a large, pendulous goiter which gave his gobbling talk a breathless sort of quality. The night Danny presented the new mitts he stood closely watching Taconite as he postured before the little camp mirror, clapping the mittens delightedly before him. "That Taconite's a mighty fine-lookin' fella," Danny mused aloud. "Yep, yep. He coulda been in moom-pitchers if his forehead wasn't all used up by his hair."

Swan Kellstrom had turned out to be a golden find for Hungry Hollow. It had developed that he was a marvelous cook. Sometime in his restless drifting about his native Minnesota he had been—among many other things—a baker in Duluth. Though he hadn't been in a bakery shop in years, Swan's face and hair and general aspect somehow forever bore the dusty, floury look of a journeyman baker. A thin mist of falling flour seemed to surround him perpetually, like a halo. Swan insisted it was simply dandruff.

Swan was the lady-killer of Hungry Hollow. His nostrils flared and twitched if he saw a woman a block away. He had a horror of getting bald, despite his wild thatch of blond hair which, when it was uncurried, might have afforded refuge to a flock of carrier pigeons. He constantly shampooed his hair with all manner of soaps and toilet preparations and then reverently anointed it with various aromatic decoctions. He hung over the little camp radio avidly listening to the extravagant claims made for each new miracle shampoo and lotion. After washing his hair he sometimes resembled a blue-eyed Zulu. After perfuming and plastering it, Danny had a more pungent description for him.

"Swan, me lad," he would often say, dolefully wagging his head, "I'm damned if you don't smell exackly like one of Big Annie's girls on a Sat'day night! Yep, yep . . ."

An unspoken but basic requirement for admission to the Hollow seemed to be that one should not be gainfully employed nor possess any discernible ambition for any form of permanent toil. In theory Danny and the boys were supposed to take turns working in Chippewa when the funds ran low. But like many fine theories of men, its beauty lay in the wonder of its contemplation.

Danny was king, and the king couldn't work, and besides he had stomach ulcers, which flared dangerously when any form of toil impended. In addition he had his hands full distilling his moonshine and bottling his home-brew and shooting an occasional deer. No, Danny was out. Timmy scornfully shunned the town, and somehow nobody cared or dared to press the point. Timmy just fished and trapped and sold his furs and kept the camp radio and wind charger going. During his leisure he got out a stub pencil and worked crossword puzzles. He knew the names of all the Egyptian sun gods and extinct birds by heart.

Lovelorn Swan was a good and willing worker, but when he worked in town he had a grave tendency to leave all the money he earned at Big Annie's—that is, the part he didn't spend on the latest shampoos and lotions. And besides, the boys needed him at home to bake bread and to cook. No, it was far better to keep Swan tethered at the Hollow and let him out only to cut firewood.

Taconite was childishly willing to work whenever and wherever he was told. But he always came home broke, even when he hadn't been tossed into the Chippewa jail. The last time he'd been allowed to go to town and work, the Easter before, he had come back dead broke lugging a huge velvet rabbit.

"L-look," he gobbled excitedly, proudly thrusting the stuffed rabbit at Danny. "It on'y took me seven hours to win dis on Charlie's punchboard. Hully gee, am I lucky!"

Danny stood uncertainly, holding the enormous rabbit as awkwardly as a father holding his first son. He blinked thoughtfully.

"Hm," he said slowly, sparring for time. "Well. My, my! Jest what we need. Sure. Thinks I we'll set this here rabbit down in the swamp fer a decoy. Yep, yep!"

"Gee, y-you think it'll really work?" Taconite said eagerly.

"Hell's fire," Danny replied gently over his shoulder, carrying the rabbit out the door, swamp bound. "It'll make the finest rabbit bait in the hull worl'! The other rabbits'll come fer miles aroun' an' jest set an' stare, dyin' with envy. Then all you gotta do is sneak up an' pick 'em off while they's settin' there moonin', like shootin' fish in a rain barrel. Yep, yep, this here present was mighty fine of you, Tack. Mighty pracktical an' mighty fine."

Taconite's eyes glowed. "Aw, gee whiz—thanks, Danny," he breathed rapturously. "Dat's swell. Hully gee!"

Buller was Hungry Hollow's main economic hope. When he made up his mind to work he could move mountains. He could drive any horse on four legs, or carry it if the going got rough. He could do anything that involved a horse: shoe it, curry it, doctor it, bury it. Aging Wink Vivian, who ran the Chippewa dray, occasionally summoned him into town to relieve him. Buller nearly swooned with perverse pleasure when he could wrap his great arms about a piano.

There was one fly in the ointment. This fly—or rather the ointment—was dispensed under the trade name of Old Cordwood, the Peninsula's favorite whisky—a fantastic blended firewater which gentler souls insisted was the by-product of an avaricious lye works. Buller could drink Old Cordwood as an elephant gulps water. After an interval, however, he would begin to trumpet and wander about like the same elephant looking for mischief. These Old Cordwood bouts generally landed him in the toils of Judge Williams, which usually meant a hurried financial sos to Hungry Hollow or Big Annie or Charlie Jokinen, the Finnish proprietor of Charlie's Place. Sometimes it even meant an involuntary rest cure in the county jail at Iron Bay. Buller worked hard and played hard. When he could be coaxed into Chippewa to go to work, Danny and the boys would engage in meditation and silent prayer for days.

At times Danny and the boys grew vaguely uneasy over their freedom from regular toil. From boyhood on they had been taught to work, to regard it as a sort of social and moral obligation. They had been taught that they had been born to work; unfettered leisure was only the lot of drunkards and fools. When this strange feeling of unease, this curious sense of guilt, grew too oppressive, they usually resolved it by piling into the old Model A Ford which Timmy had miraculously contrived out of odds and ends of other Fords, and rattling into Chippewa for a celebration.

When little Matti Hunginen the Finn moved down from Nestoria and bought his new farm on the road between Chippewa and Hungry Hollow, he could not fathom why Danny and the boys were reluctant to help him with the fall harvest.

"W'at's matter, you great big lazys!" Matti said. "Why you no help dat Matti wit dat hay an' potato? You fellas not crippled. I pay you vell—Matti's no seap-skate. Look, lazy-pones, if you come help it me maybe someday I vill give it you one fine milking cow. W'at you poys really need is fine big cow for dis place —not all dat time drink it moons'ine, moons'ine, moons'ine."

The prospect of a cow for Hungry Hollow was not to be sneered at. Matti's offer so disarmed the boys that they gladly went to his farm and stayed until all the fall crops were harvested. Even Danny went, flaring ulcers and all.

3

THE COW JUMPED
OVER THE MOON

Bessie was her name and she had a crooked horn and
five teats. Her breed was difficult of diagnosis. It was
safer simply to call her an American cow, though
Jersey, Holstein, and a dash of Guernsey clamored
loudest for recognition. She had large, wet, ruminative,
slate-colored eyes which she blinked as languidly as
any Hollywood siren. Functionally she was something
of a failure as a cow—she did not give much milk. For
lean Bessie was not a chesty cow. She was more the
racing type. If she had been a woman of vanity she
would have had to wear an uplift.

Bessie came jolting out to Hungry Hollow from
Chippewa late one June night in the back of a Ford
pickup truck driven by Tauno Taskila. Tauno was a
husky itinerant Finnish butcher and dealer in hides
who drove about the Peninsula trading with the Finnish
farmers and iron miners. Asleep in the cab and leaning
against Tauno was little Matti Hunginen. Of the three

occupants of the pickup, Bessie was the only one that was strictly sober. The pickup slid to a stop before the camp.

The camp was dark. A thin moon showed a ghostly lake of mist down by the river. The frogs and crickets vied shrilly in their timeless rivalry. Swearing softly in Finnish, Tauno stiffly got out of the pickup. With a contented sigh Matti slumped over in Tauno's seat. Tauno stood by the side of the car and relieved himself. Bessie, not to be outdone, proceeded to do likewise. Tauno came over and surveyed Bessie's handiwork. He again swore in Finnish, this time not so softly. He reached down and picked up a length of stovewood and, standing behind Bessie, whacked her where she had offended most. *"Moo!"* bawled Bessie.

"Halloo!" came from the camp. It was old Danny, emerging in his nightshirt and cap, holding aloft a kerosene lamp. "Take for dat, you crazy son-a-bits!" Tauno grunted as he again wielded the stick against Bessie. "Moo!" Bessie called. *"Moo-oo!"*

"Boys! Boys! Git up! Quick!" Danny was hopping about on his skinny legs, balancing his lamp. "Somebody's bein' assassinated out here!"

"Moo-oo!"

"Hurry! Fer Gawd's sake—they're like to git kilt!" Danny shouted, tugging at his long mustaches.

Buller came first, charging wildly out of the camp, pumping a cartridge into the old Winchester .44. "Where're they at?" he shouted, plunging down the trail toward the truck, followed by Timmy, who played the beam of the big camp flashlight in Buller's wake. Then came Swan and Taconite, sleepily hitching themselves into their breeches as they ran. With the wisdom born of his many years, Danny remained discreetly by the camp, still holding the lamp aloft and shouting into the night.

The boys gathered around Tauno and Bessie at the rear of the pickup. Bessie craned her neck around and looked at the boys. The boys stared back at Bessie.

"Is he dead yet?" Dan called from the camp.

"She ain't no he," Buller yelled back to him.

"What! They've ain't gone an' murdered a woman on my place? Oh, my Gawd!"

"Tain't no woman—it's a goddam cow. Come on down here an' see for yourself!"

By the time Danny pattered down to the truck in his bare feet, Matti had bestirred himself. He suddenly popped out of the car, took three reeling steps like a man going downstairs, and subsided on his face in the dewy grass. Timmy coolly played the flashlight on little Matti, who propped his head on his elbow and grinned engagingly into the light. "Hallo, poys—what you t'ink for dat nice present I bring home for you?"

Timmy played the flash back on Bessie and the truck. "Looks O.K.—what's left of her," he said. Stepping gingerly in his bare feet, Danny held the lamp near Bessie for closer inspection. "Hm," he said, spitting judiciously, "looks like someone's knocked the stuffin's outa her."

"You not mad for me, poys?" Matti anxiously inquired from the dark. Timmy shifted the beam back to Matti.

"No, we're not mad at you, Matti," Dan said. "But where in hell did you git her?"

Matti pondered for a while, lying on his elbow, dreamily blinking his eyes. "All I 'member I goin' Sippywa on yesterday for sell it dat milk an' dat egg for ol' voman." He grinned. "I get little 'runk for me, you know, an' tonight—dat's really on las' night, I guess—I play little poker game wit' Tauno in back room for Sarlie's Place." Matti grimaced, groping for recollection. The effort was not fruitful. " 'S better I guess you ask it my frien' Tauno dere how I come get dat cow. Tell for dem, Tauno, how I get dat cow. Matti's be tired now—an' li'l 'runk, too." Matti yawned prodigiously. "Now where in godtam hell I, Matti Hunginen, get for dat lady cow . . ." With this brief soliloquy Matti's voice trailed into nothing as his head slipped from his elbow and he relapsed into a profound sleep.

"Tauno," Danny asked, "where did Matti get this here animal? There ain't been no trouble, is there?"

Tauno grinned and looked at the ground, shame-faced, as Timmy swung the light on him. "No, Mister Danny," he said, "dere's no troubles for dat cow business. All dat happen was dat little son-a-bits Matti he beat for me in studs poker—an' won dat Bessie cow." Tauno looked over at Matti with grudging admiration. "Dat godtam lucky Matti."

Danny pulled off his tasseled nightcap and slowly rubbed his palm over his bald head. "You mean, Tauno, that Bessie's fer us—we kin keep her here at the Hollow? Fer good?"

Tauno nodded as he spoke. "Dat's right, Mister Danny, Matti he say dat Bessie cow's goin' belong for his bes' frien's. He's 'fraid to take her home for his ol' voman—an' anyvay he say he like have dat cream for his coffee when he come here for visit you peoples. Yes-sirree!"

Danny looked around at the boys. One by one they slowly nodded their heads. Bessie was in.

"Whoopee!" Danny shouted, thrusting the lamp at Swan, twirling his nightcap, dancing a barefoot jig. "Yippee! 'She's the cream in my coffee . . .' A bloody cow for Hungry Hollow, boys! Let's feed her an' then celebrate! I got a gallon a three-year-ol' stuff—I jest run her off 'n the still yesterday. Whoopee! Wrap her up an' drink her down! Jest think! A cow for the Hollow. They called her Messy Bessie! Ol' Danny's wanted to milk a goddam cow ever since he left Canadee!" Bessie was gazing back at Danny with her big soulful eyes.

"Moo," called Bessie very softly. It was love at first sight.

Danny triumphantly led the way up the trail to the camp, executing a skinny clown dance, this way and that, daintily holding out the tails of his nightshirt. He was followed by Tauno and the boys, who had gently retrieved Matti. Shafts of colored light were showing over the birch ridge to the east. A late-carousing whippoorwill made its bubbling noise from the birches. Another dawn had come to Hungry Hollow.

"Moo," lowed Bessie. It sounded as gentle as a lullaby.

In the weeks that followed Bessie completely captured the hearts of the dwellers in Hungry Hollow. The boys reverently installed her in the woodshed, throwing Taconite's neatly piled firewood out to the weather. Nothing was too good for Bessie. Matti augmented his original gift with a load of clover hay hurriedly stolen from his farm when his "ol' voman" was in Chippewa. On every trip to and from Chippewa the boys raided the gardens of the Finnish farmers along the way for tidbits for their Bessie. Young carrots on the stalk were one of her favorites. But Bessie was not choosy—she'd even eat cedar boughs if Danny or one of the boys gave them to her.

One day Taconite, smitten by inspiration and thinking to vary her diet, fed her a bushel of pilfered green onions. The next evening Danny sat down to supper to drink Bessie's afternoon stint of milk. This was calculated to soothe his ulcers. Each day Bessie's milk was carefully cooled in the spring down by the river. It had become a daily ritual. Danny deftly combed out his mustache with one hand and took a long draught of the milk. "Ah!" Presently his eyes grew large with astonishment, and he sat gulping like a dog that had swallowed a fishbone. The boys glanced at each other apprehensively, fearful that Danny's ulcers had finally broken their moorings.

"Wah—wah—what in Christ's name is that there vile concoction?" Danny finally gasped. He fixed his horrified gaze on his bowl of milk. "I bin poisoned. In my own bloody house I bin poisoned." He glared fearfully about the room. Taconite sat looking sheepishly down at the palms of his big calloused hands. "*You* done it, Tack!" Danny shouted hoarsely, clutching his stomach with both arms and hopping about the room. "My ol' chum Taconite poisoned me," he wailed. His eyes rolled upward in his head. He was sinking fast and making ready to die. "Oh, why did you poison a feeble ol' man like me, Tack!"

Taconite looked up at Danny with glistening eyes. "All I done, Danny, was to feed Bessie a coupla few green onions, that's all," he gobbled in a husky voice.

"*Onions*, man!" Danny demanded, rallying swiftly. "How many did you give her?"

"Only about a bushel."

"Oh, my Lord! My poor Bessie, my poor belly! Lissen, Tack, you never don't want to give no cow no onions. You gotta be awful careful what you feed a high-class cow like Bessie." Danny glared around the room. "Jest to make sure, I'm goin' to draw up a list of grub what Bessie can eat an' nail it on the woodshed door. After this nobody don't give her nothin'

what ain't on that there list. Do you understan'?"
Thus spoke Danny, the authority on animal husbandry.
"Yessir, Daniel," Taconite said meekly.

"An' as fer the rest of this goddam milk, if you'll
take an' heat it an' add salt an' pepper—we'll all of
us have onion soup!"

So Bessie was placed on a selected diet. But nothing
seemed to be able to make her give more milk. The
more she ate, the leaner she got and the less milk she
surrendered. Aside from this minor circumstance she
enjoyed perfect contentment, freely ranging the clear-
ings and woods by day, her bell softly scraping and
tinkling, and returning in the evening to her woodshed,
mooing for her milking by Dan.

Then tragedy struck, swiftly and savagely.

One evening in late August Bessie did not appear.
Dusk came, and then darkness fell, but no Bessie.
Danny was beside himself, pacing restlessly in and out
of the camp, "hallooing" for wayward Bessie until he
croaked like a frog. Then he hung a lantern over the
door of the woodshed for the missing prodigal. Torn
by anger and concern, he was like a father whose
young daughter was running around with the horsy
set. "I'll whack her rear end all over this goddam
forty acres!" he threatened darkly in one breath.
"Oo-oo-o, my poor lost Bessie," he wailed in the next,
on the verge of tears. Danny slumped to a chair at the
table and held his bald head in his hands.

Finally the boys, to ease Dan's and their own concern, took the long flashlight and started from the camp
to find Bessie. They had no more than left the camp
door when there was a sudden crashing in the tag
alders down by the river. Timmy flashed on the light.
There came dripping Bessie, her eyes glowing like
twin headlights, her bell clanging wildly, her tail
straight up in the air, plunging madly up from the river

bottom. Behind her, close on her heels and gaining, was a huge ball of rolling black fur.

"It's a bear, Danny!" Timmy shouted. "Git the .44!"

The bear heard Timmy and slid to a grunting stop. Then it reared up on its hind legs, slowly rocking its huge slavering head, scenting the air, looming up in the dark background like the charred stub of a white pine. Meanwhile Bessie had gained her woodshed, taking part of the door with her. Danny burst from the camp with the rifle. He knelt on the ground on one knee, pulled back the hammer and took steady, careful aim. Timmy quickly got behind him and sighted the rifle in the beam of the flash. "Now," Danny breathed, pressing the trigger.

"Click," went the rifle. Danny pumped frantically and aimed again. "Click," went the old .44. The gun was empty. Danny seemed to be praying to some unknown god. "In all my seventy-four besotted years on this goddam planet," he whispered savagely through clenched teeth, "I never laid eyes on a dumber lout than Daniel Wellington McGinnis!" With that he stood up and, whirling the empty rifle around him like a drunken discus thrower, hurled it at the bear, scoring a bull's-eye. "Woof," went the bear, and in a few leaping dark bounds he was crashing down through the tag alders and across the Big Dead River.

Danny dusted his hands in front of him as though they were full of sand. "Good night, gentlemen," he said to the boys, turning away with great dignity. "It's time for seenile ol' men to be hittin' the hay."

The next morning Danny, with his loaded rifle in one hand and a bunch of carrots in the other, tugged and coaxed Bessie from the woodshed. Once out in the open she rolled her eyes toward the river, distending her nostrils and sniffing like an asthmatic dowager scenting a peasant. Terror filled her big eyes, and she broke away from Danny and lurched back into the woodshed, banging the flapping door.

Danny turned to Timmy. "Git out your bear traps, Thomas," he said quietly. "There ain't no goddam bear's gonna devour our Bess."

Timmy took his three clanking bear traps down from the rafters of the camp, got out his rubber gloves, de-scented the traps, and, accompanied by Danny with the .44, carefully set and baited the traps with chunks of deer meat at strategic spots about the camp.

Danny and the boys clearly realized that an unmolested bear will never attack a human or another animal unless it is very hungry. Unfortunately for Bessie, there had been a series of killing frosts that spring, nipping the cherries and berries in the bud. There were virtually no wild fruits in the woods that fall. Since these items form a large part of a bear's normal autumnal diet, Bessie's bear was naturally gnawed by hunger. It was hideously plain to the boys that Mr. Bear coveted poor Bessie.

That afternoon it looked as though the bear had given up and gone away. Danny again enticed Bessie from her shed. This time her sniffs were unrewarded, and she gratefully licked her salt from Danny's hand and even took a few tentative steps toward the river. Danny went into the camp and proceeded to clean and oil the .44. There was not going to be any monkey business the next time.

"Moo! Moo-oo!"

Danny darted from the camp, brandishing the rifle. He spied Bessie down by the river, her head bent to the ground as though she were goring something.

"She's got the bear!" he shouted. He raced down the trail, the rifle ready. Just as he got up to Bessie he heard a crashing and grunting in the tag alders. Danny peered into the dense thicket but could not see the bear. "That bloody bear must be part ghost," he muttered. He looked over at Bessie. Her head was still bent to the ground, and she was rolling the whites of her eyes up in her head like a roped steer. "Well, I'm a goddam rooster!" Danny said aloud. Bessie's crooked horn was firmly clamped in the jaws of one of Timmy's sprung bear traps. She had been about to add venison to her restricted diet.

That night after supper, Danny and the boys held a table-thumping council over Bessie and the bear. What to do about Bessie? They couldn't let the savage bear traps remain around for her to wander into, could they? No, they couldn't do that. If they couldn't shoot this wraith of a bear, which seemed likely, or chase him away, what then? Should they keep Bessie locked in the woodshed twenty-four hours a day? No, it was not fittin' nor human to trammel Bessie's free spirit that way. Death would seem infinitely preferable to such ignominy. Death? Did some fiend suggest taking the life of their Bessie? Oh—simply for her own good. Perhaps they should lovingly butcher her before the bear did?

"Who's goin' to do it?" Danny asked in an anguished voice. He shook his head dolefully. "I—I can't, boys. I—I'm too goddam attached to her. It would be kinda like—like a fella hittin' his own maw." He sniffed and blew a mighty trumpet blast into his blue bandanna.

Who was going to dispatch Bessie? Timmy? No. Taconite? No. Swan? "Ay tank not." Buller? "Hell, no." Bessie was to be spared. Nobody would lay a hand on Bessie. Love had come at last to Hungry Hollow. In the meantime they'd let her have one last fling, like a condemned queen—lift the ban on her diet and feed her all and everything she would eat. "Even onions," Danny added, winking dolefully at Taconite. Taconite grinned his slow grin and stared down at his hands.

"Well, that's that," Danny said. "Mebbe we can nail that goddam bear in the meantime." But Danny and the boys were glum and depressed. They rolled in that night without even drinking their nightly hot toddy.

Bessie sulked in her woodshed the next morning. Danny tried to lure her out with handsful of salt. She gulped the salt gratefully, but she would not budge. Taconite, beaming with pride, gave her a peck of wilted green onions. Buller fed her a chocolate almond bar. Timmy dutifully scratched her head between her horns. Swan tried giving her a chew of Copenhagen snuff, but Bessie evidently concluded that, bear or no bear, she must stop somewhere.

And bear or no bear, too, there was work to be done at Hungry Hollow. Taconite and Swan got out the crosscut saw and the axes and left to cut winter firewood down beyond Mulligan Creek. Buller and Timmy packed a lunch and hiked away to fly-fish the beaver dams up at the headwaters of the Big Dead. Bustling Danny got a hammer and nails and fixed the broken woodshed door. Then he patted Bessie and gave her an extra helping of salt. He scratched her head for a spell, gently whispering to her all the while. "There, there, Bessie. Danny's got to go over to his still an' run off a batch of moonshine. Now don't you worry none about that goddam bear. Ol' Danny'll lock you in here good and snug an' be back in two-three hours. That's a good girl. Good-by, Bess."

"Moo," Bessie answered, gratefully lapping her salt.

Danny locked the woodshed door and, glancing stealthily behind him to see that he was unobserved, made his way to the still beside the little creek in the dense cedar swamp just beyond the birch ridge. He had trouble with the fire under the still and he took longer than he had expected. In the meantime he sampled his last batch of moonshine generously. At length he ran off the last of the new batch and hid the warm gallon jugs of fresh moonshine under his favorite stump. By this time Danny was gently drunk. He was about to dump the distilled corn mash into the little creek when he was struck with a sudden inspiration.

"Hell's fire, why don't I give this here nice cracked corn to Bessie?" he asked himself aloud, surveying the buckets of mash he was about to throw away. "If that goddam bear's goin' to git her, she might jest as well have a belly fulla corn."

Bessie was clamoring and mooing at the door of her woodshed when Danny got back with the buckets of fermented mash. Danny was all sympathy. "Poor ol' Bessie. Sure, she's a thirsty girl after eatin' all them there onions an' all that salt. But ol' Danny's got a real surprise out here for her."

Bessie's parched tongue was dangling like a rope when Danny opened the woodshed door. A little wild-eyed, she spied the buckets of wet mash and made for them like a homing pigeon, greedily sluicing down the damp mixture. Danny scratched her bobbing head and then consulted his big silver watch. It was time to go to camp and brew himself a pot of tea. An old man had to be mighty careful of his ulcers. Bessie rolled her eyes up gratefully at departing Danny, but did not pause in her mighty gulping and lapping.

Danny had himself another good hooker of moon, with a small one for a chaser. "Ah!" He clattered the rusty stove lids about as he lit the fire for his tea. Soon he had a crackling pine-knot fire going under the tea-kettle. Danny discussed his problems with himself aloud, as he always did when he was alone. "I wonder how in hell we kin save our Bessie from that there goddam bear? Yep, yep . . . Guess we'll all of us have to surroun' that bloody tag alder swamp an' root him out."

He deftly poured the tea into a thick cup, transferred it to a saucer and blew into the saucer, combing out his flowing mustache with his fingers in an expert crisscross motion. The way he did it made it all seem one continuous operation. He raised the saucer to his lips. "I wonder how Bessie's makin' out with her corn?" he said.

"Moo! *Moo! Moo-oo! Harrump!*"

Danny ran to the doorway just as blazing-eyed Bessie rounded the camp for the first time, snorting and bellowing like a rodeo steer, head down, neck hunched, back arched, her tail lashed out behind her. She was headed straight for the tall wooden sawbuck. Danny closed his eyes. "Harrump!" went Bessie. Danny opened one eye. "My Gawd, she made it!" he breathed in an awed voice. Bessie thundered on around the camp, rattling the dishes in the cupboard and quaking the very ground. "There she goes ag'in," Danny whispered.

"Two," he said as bellowing Bessie came leaping around the camp on the second trip, clearing the sawbuck by a good three feet. As she flung herself into her leap she went "harrump" in a strange sort of bovine belch.

"Three," Danny counted very faintly, leaning against the doorjamb.

He grew slightly dizzy turning his head as he watched Bessie pitching and leaping past the windows in her mad progress about the camp.

"Harrump!" went Bessie, soaring over the sawbuck.

"Four," Danny counted in a small voice.

Thirteen times a horrified Danny watched Bessie make the circuit. Thirteen times by actual count wild Bessie went careening drunkenly about the camp and "harrumping" over the sawbuck. Danny vaguely felt that he had died and gone to hell. On the last lap Bessie alcoholically veered away from the sawbuck and staggered uncertainly for a sagging moment. Then she sighted new worlds to conquer—and she was away again. "Harrump!" she rumbled, this time charging straight down the river trail, tail up, leaping and bellowing madly, finally crashing into the tag alders. Danny passed a palsied hand across his eyes, still holding the saucer of cold tea.

"Woof! Woof!"

"Harrump! Moo! Moo-oo!"

The bear broke out of the alders with head-lowered Bessie right behind him and gaining. "Harrump!" Bessie butted at the bear. "Ow-woof!" cried the bear, making a frantic burst of speed as he raced down the road toward Chippewa, drunken and leaping Bessie keeping tight on his scrambling heels. As the two disappeared around a dusty curve in the road, the saucer of tea dropped from Dan's nerveless fingers, shattering on the floor.

"Gotta quit drinkin', gotta quit drinkin'," old Danny kept muttering to himself in a sort of litany, over and over.

Bessie returned on the evening of the third day, penitent, red of eye, covered with burrs and brambles, her udders swollen with milk.

"Moo," she lowed outside the camp door.

"Bessie!" Danny and the boys cried in unison,

crowding pell-mell out of the camp. Danny was the first to regain his composure. He swung on the boys, menacingly shaking a gnarled finger at them, the cords of his neck distended with the earnestness of his edict.

"Henceforwards an' from now on, boys, no bloody man in this goddam camp is gonna feed her 'cept Danny," he shouted wrathfully. "It's jest like I tol' you—you gotta be awful careful what you give a high-class cow like Bessie!" Danny turned tenderly to Bessie. "Ain't that right, Bess? Ol' Danny knows best. Good ol' Bessie."

"Moo," said Bessie, lowering her eyes and running her tongue up over her nose.

4

THE VOYAGE

Next to playing practical jokes, Danny loved best to argue. He would take any side of any proposition, and, if the bases of dialectic were loaded, would swiftly occupy a new corner from which to hurl his dissident views. And he would go to extravagant lengths to prove his point.

There was the unhappy Saturday afternoon that October, when Swan came in from wood-cutting. Muttering hello, he immediately busied himself at the washstand, surrounded by his precious perfumes and ointments, where he proceeded to anoint himself for the prospective Saturday night trek to Chippewa. Danny was sipping his hot tea and quietly reading Dr. Miles' Almanac, of which he was a constant and advanced student. He looked over his glasses and casually observed to Swan that on that very day, over four hundred years before, an Italian adventurer called Christopher Columbus had discovered America.

"No, Dannay," Swan spoke up through waves of

cologne. "It vere Leif Ericsson who ver da first vun to discover America!"

Danny carefully placed his steaming saucer of tea on the table and removed his glasses. Buttressed by such unimpeachable authority as the editorial staff of Dr. Miles' Almanac, he immediately rose to file his firm dissent.

"You mean, Swan, you actually believe that this Norswenskin what's-his-name was the first fella what discovered America?" he demanded.

"Dat vere certainly true," Swan replied emphatically.

Danny could scarcely believe his ears. When quiet Swan contradicted any of the boys, let alone Danny himself, it was little short of rebellion. But this was sheer open revolt. Possibly Swan was suffering from wood ticks or something. Danny'd give him one more chance. He'd appeal to Swan's reason.

"I tell you, goddamitt, it was too Christopher Columbus what discovered America!" Danny shouted, just as Buller and Taconite quietly filed into camp to witness the argument. "The almanac here says so. Everybody says so. The hull worl' says so. Even the bloody history books say so. Who the hell ever heard tell of this Scandahoovian Leif Ericsson!" Danny turned and winked at Buller, then again wheeled upon poor Swan. "Now do you still believe Leif Ericsson discovered America?" he demanded.

Swan stood by his array of lotions, staring at Danny, grim and unblinking. He gripped and strained at the improvised wooden washstand as though by main strength he would lift Leif Ericsson from slanderous obscurity onto the pedestal of fame where he rightly belonged.

"Do you still believe Leif Ericsson discovered America?" Danny gently prodded.

"Dat vere certainly true," Swan replied hotly. "Ay tell you, dis hare great Leif Ericsson landed on Wineland by America y'ars an' y'ars before dis goddam Dago vere even t'ought of!" Swan was shouting by now. "Pret' near t'ousand y'ars ago, Ay tell you! Dat vere certainly true!"

"O.K. then. What'll you bet?" Danny said, closing in for the pay-off.

"Me, Ay bet anyt'ing—" Swan began, carelessly laying himself wide open.

"Two quarts of Ol' Cordwood, then," Danny said, smacking his lips in anticipation.

"Tew quvarts of Ol' Cordwood it vere," Swan agreed, doggedly accepting the stakes.

"Who's goin' to decide this here bet?" Danny asked. "Le's see, what smart folks do we know in Chippewa beside Charlie Jokinen?" He pondered. "Shall we go an' ask one of the perfessors in the high school?"

"No, no," Swan replied. "All dem crazy teachers and hist'ry writers vere all foolish an' blindfolded over dis hare faker, Christopher Columbus."

"Hm, now who'll we git, then?" Danny mused, biting his lower lip. "Big Annie? No-o-o, she'll be too busy tonight. My, my! Now le's see . . ."

"Ve will get Sharlie Yokinen to seddle da bet," Swan replied, innocently swallowing Danny's prepared bait. "Sharlie vere educated in Finland—an' dose people from da nordern parts of Yurope dey don't belief all dose lies about dat faker Christopher Columbus."

"O.K., O.K., have your own way," Danny resignedly agreed, again winking at Buller. "We'll go to town tonight right after supper an' let Charlie Jokinen himself decide fer who really discovered America. Let's shake hands on it."

Danny arched his neck. He would disarm all suspicion. "Now you're sure, Swan, that you ain't already heard what Charlie's answer will be? All bets is off if they's any shenanigans like that. Is it a deal?"

"Dat vere certainly true," Swan said, grasping and wringing Danny's gnarled fingers. Thus it was decided that Charlie Jokinen, the Finnish proprietor of Charlie's Place, would resolve this latest crisis growing out of the age-old issue of Nordic versus Latin supremacy.

Crafty Danny didn't tell poor Swan that he had himself paid a flying visit to Charlie's saloon during the week, at which time Charlie had just happened to announce his belief that Christopher Columbus had discovered America. Danny hadn't forgotten this salient fact. It had come about this way:

Arriving in town, he had heard a dark rumor that his old friend, Charlie Jokinen, had been arrested for committing assault and battery upon the person of the Chippewa fire chief, an amiable Irishman called Barney Langley. It appeared that Barney had gone to Charlie's saloon and announced to Charlie, a member of the Chippewa Volunteer Fire Department for years, that after his birthday on Columbus Day he. Charlie, would henceforth be an honorary fireman, because of over-age. Barney had smilingly presented Charlie with a scroll containing an elaborate resolution of gratitude from the entire fire department. He then offered to shake hands with Charlie, whereupon Charlie had hauled off and slugged the fire chief with his fist. Nursing a black eye, Barney had then gone over to Judge Williams' court and demanded a warrant.

Danny wanted to get to the bottom of this ugly

rumor, so he marched over to Charlie's Place and accosted his old friend.

"Charlie, what's this talk I hear about you gittin' pinched for hittin' the fire chief?" he demanded.

Charlie craved a sympathetic audience. He was more than willing to tell his side of the harrowing story. He shook his head sadly. "Danny, wat you dink for dis funny kind cases. Nex' Saturday, October twelve, he's being my birt'day, sixty-five years ol'. Dat vere also 'Lumbus Day—same day what 'Ristopher 'Lumbus discover America."

"Hm . . . What happened?" Danny demanded.

"Vell, I bein' member Sippywa Fire 'Partment dirty years—gettin' up all kinds hours an' all kinds col' vedder an' vet. Den vun day las' week dat fire sief— he's yust be dat big Irish pullsitter—he come my place an' say real sassy for me, 'Sarlie,' he say, 'after you birt'day nex' veek you's to be no firemans no more! Las' meeting ve reading over dem rules an' reg'lations an' ve sad to find you's soon to be age to be 'tired firemans. After 'Lumbus Day you's to be too ol' man for fight it dat fire.' "

"What'd you say?" Danny demanded, rallying to the cause of his old friend.

"What Sarlie say? Hm! Sarlie s'ake finger his nose an' he say, 'Lissen, s'it pants! Maybe I's be too ol' man for fight it dat fire. Maybe it's true I's to be 'tired firemans like you say for dat. But it's not already 'Lumbus Day yet, an' Sarlie not too tired for knock s'it *for you!*' So I vind up my fist like for dis an' give dat son-a-bits sief good smash for puss. Den wat you dink?" Charlie threw out his hands and shook his head, the picture of a broken old man. "Ol' Sarlie goin' for Yudge Villiams' court and pay den dollars fines and t'ree-wifteen costs. Hm!" Charlie drew himself up in scornful contemplation of the perfidy of human nature. "Dat's Sarlie's danks from Sippywa people for fight it dat fire dirty years!"

Charlie threw up his hands in mystification. "Now, Danny—wat you dink for dat funny kind cases?" he concluded.

Thus it came to pass that Danny already knew that Charlie was on the side of Christopher Columbus. A man could scarcely help being, when his birthday fell on the same day as that on which the great Christopher had discovered America. And so immediately after supper that Saturday, Danny and Buller and Swan and Timmy and Taconite piled into the old Model A and headed for Chippewa to let Charlie Jokinen resolve the burning issue.

Charlie's saloon stood on the west side of Main Street in Chippewa. The entrance door was in the middle, and in the tall windows on either side of the door, in front of suspended cloth curtains, there loomed tall potted ferns, supported by sticks. Just inside the door there was a broad standing mirror, framed in ornate mahogany and serving to help screen the iniquities within. On this mirror, in gold leaf, was printed the following:

Charles Jokinen—S A L O O N

Fine Wines and Choice Liquors
BEER—FREE LUNCH

North of the saloon, on the corner next to the town square, stood the brick Miners' State Bank. Kitty-corner from the bank stood the brownstone city hall. In the center of the triangular town square arose a large cast-iron drinking fountain, from the sides of which sprouted four little cast-iron drinking troughs for dogs, one big trough for horses, and two bubbling troughs for the townspeople. That dogs, horses, and people occasionally used the wrong troughs, especially late on Saturday nights, never seemed to bother anyone.

On top of the fountain stood a tall cast-iron statue of a hawk-faced Chippewa Indian chief, his bow and arrow sighted for a shot never to be released this side of eternity, his fine-etched eyes peering into the northwest, as though vainly searching for some survivor of his lost tribe which had fallen away before the avid, pushing, ore-digging whites. By common consent nearly all of the townspeople irreverently called him "Chief Booze-in-the-Face."

There were fourteen saloons on the town's Main Street and many more on the side streets. On Saturday nights and on paydays all of them were busy, for then hundreds of miners surged downtown, cashing their vouchers from the iron mines, paying bills, mingling with the lumberjacks and farmers, buying new boots and socks and heavy miners' underwear and, most of them, to the dismay of the local temperance workers, "sneakin' a few dollars on the ol' woman for a bloody drink or two!"

Danny and Buller and the boys had arrived in town and installed themselves at the far end of Charlie's bar, busily working on a bottle of their favorite bourbon, Old Cordwood. So sure was Danny of winning his bet that he had ordered one of the two bottles in advance. The loser was to pay. Charlie Jokinen, the proprietor, stood up at the front end of his bar, near the cigar counter, playing smear for drinks with three

Finnish miners. Charlie was a heavy, blue-eyed, florid, wispy-haired, big-boned man in his middle sixties. In fact, he was sixty-five that very day, and an honorary fireman to boot. Charlie had migrated to America from Finland in his teens. Coming directly to Chippewa, he had early discovered that he possessed a constitutional allergy to all hard work, including iron-mining. Being endowed with an alert mind and an affable manner, he was now the sole proprietor of Charlie's Place.

Occasionally Charlie looked up from his card game, casting a shrewd, appraising glance the length of the smoky bar at his two perspiring bartenders. He smiled to observe old Danny McGinnis and Swan Kellstrom at the other end of the bar engaged in a hot argument. "Poys vill be poys," tolerant Charlie often said. And anyway, today was his birthday, Columbus Day.

The big Swiss music box against the opposite wall was working overtime, obedient to nickels, the shuddering metal disks creaking up and down between each selection. Years before some forgotten traveling saloon artist had filled the entire wall opposite the bar with his alcoholic visions: a sinister, dank, malarial woods scene at night, dripping gloom, of no forest which ever grew in Michigan—a forest inhabited by ghostly creatures faintly suggestive of prehistoric deer. The entire panorama was relieved only by a troubled moon which peered from behind racing, troublous clouds.

Charlie's worn mahogany bar ran nearly half the depth of the long, high room. At the far end of the bar, near hotly debating Danny and Swan, stood the free-lunch counter, covered with cheesecloth against the droning flies. On the wall was a neatly printed sign: "Free lunch—25¢." The counter was flanked by a massive icebox. Beyond that was the partitioned, green-tabled poker room. At the back of the saloon was a small kitchen and the "Sunday door," leading out to the alley in the rear. Over the entire establishment there hovered a delicious, stale, boozy smell—a subtle combination of stale beer, mustard, cold ham, old cheese, brine of pickled herring, spilt whisky, overloaded spittoons, sweating men. This was Charlie's Place.

"Ay tell you vunce more, Dannay, dis hare great Leif Ericsson landed on Wineland by America y'ars an' y'ars before dis goddam Dago vere even t'ought of!" Swan Kellstrom shouted at taunting Danny McGinnis, pounding Charlie's bar with his fist. "Pret' near t'ousand y'ars ago, Ay tell you!"

Charlie stole another glance from the card game. He could see that real trouble was rapidly brewing. He'd have to step in pretty soon. He glanced back at a printed sign on the wall behind him. "Join the Army if You Want to Fight!"

Charlie was a slave to the magic of the printed word, especially to mottoes and bright sayings. He had a passion for such little signs, which he lovingly tacked at odd points about the saloon. One sign hospitably warned his customers not to spit on the ceiling; another neat sign, over the cash register, read as follows: "Glass of beer 5 cents—black eye for nothing." There were many others. The doorway to the cellar stood next to the entrance to the men's toilet. On the cellar door was a sign: "This Ain't It!" On the toilet door the companion sign read: "This Ain't the Cellar!"

The only place where Charlie wouldn't tolerate pictures or signs was in the little room marked: "This Ain't the Cellar!" Yet ironically enough, this was the place where his customers seemed determined to express their own innate craving for poetry and the linear arts. Every spring Charlie patiently redecorated his deflowered walls, only to provide a new working surface for those sly, secretive folk, that race apart, the toilet muralists of the world. Charlie muttered annual threats of the garroting and mayhem he would commit if he ever discovered one of these artistic adolescents during a creative moment.

Uno Niemi, one of Charlie's toiling bartenders, edged up to him and whispered in his ear. "Better you go talk for dat Danny an' Swan. Dey all time hollering loud 'bout whose name dat first man find it America. Pretty soon Uno's 'fraid dere's going to be one big son-a-bits fight."

Charlie Jokinen nodded and quietly finished his card game amid a crescendo of shouts and knuckle-rapping plays. "Vun more, Sarlie. Yust vun more game!" his opponents vainly pleaded. Charlie grinned and shook his head. "Vait li'l bit, poys. I going now an' give for Danny and Swanny dat 'traight dope for what man's really find it America. I be back an' play nudder game, vun minute."

Charlie took a dignified pride in his scholarship, particularly in his knowledge of American history. With the slightest encouragement he could be persuaded to admit that when he was a child in Finland he was the favorite with his schoolteacher. Whenever the provincial school inspector visited the school, the teacher proudly called upon Charlie. So Charlie moved down to the far end of the bar and stood before Danny and Swan.

"Hello, poys. What's da troubles dis place?" he said.

"Swan here wants to know who really discovered America," Danny said gleefully.

"O.K., O.K., I tell you for dat," Charlie said. He

would now not only end a noisy argument between two good customers, but at the same time remove the blight of ignorance as well. He was something of a pedagogue at heart. He loved to shed the soft glow, the cool light, of reason. He stood smiling before teasing Danny and a sullen Swan. Without further ado Charlie launched into his definitive explanation of just how, when, where, and by whom America was really discovered. A hush fell over the place. Drinks were held poised in mid-air.

"When I be yust a li'l kid in ol' country I's to be favorite pupils for my schoolteatser," Charlie said. "So whenever dat school 'spector come for our place, dat lady teatser put on good face an' call for Sarlie. One day dat school 'spector come our school on 'Lumbus Day—dat's my birt'day—an' 'dat teatser she put on smiling face an' she say, 'Sarlie, today's you birt'day so you tell for school 'spector all 'bout dat 'Ristopher 'Lumbus.' So I, Sarlie, get up front for dat class of dumb kids and tell 'spector for dat."

"What did you up an' tell the school inspector about Christopher Columbus," gently prodded Danny, the perfect interlocutor.

"Who, me? Oh! Vell, I tell dat you. One day dat 'Ristopher 'Lumbus he's to be out of vork—dere veren't no WPA dem days—an' he's just hanging roun' poolrooms an' tavern places, drinking like a fish an' going on da rocks. One day frien' for him say, ' 'Ristopher, you no got yob, why you no wisit America? Dere's lotsa vork dat place: Henry Ford, Yenral Motors, Cokey-Colas an' many udders.' So 'Ristopher he say, 'Py golly, dat's svell idea—but who's goin' to pay dat fares?' An' frien say, 'Go to king, 'Ristopher, he's good scout. He pay dat fares.' So 'Ristopher go wisit King an' ask it fares for America, but King he vink his eye an' yingle his pants an' say, 'I only got few bucks my pockets, 'Ristopher, better you ask Queenie. She vear da pants my house.' So 'Ristopher goin' ask Queen Isabellies and Isabellies say, ' 'Ristopher, how muts money you vant?'

" 'Ristopher he smile for Queenie real nice an' say, 'Oh, anyting what you like give it. Any loose change you can spare. I don't care. I pay you back some udder days. You got any sailing poats?'

"So Isabellies she lifting her skirts an' take it money her stocking an' give it money for 'Ristopher. 'Good luck, 'Ristopher—you find couple or tree poats down by dose docks.'

" 'Ristopher he real glad an' he run for taverns an' poolrooms an' get all his frien's—an few bums, too— an' dey holler an' yump on sailing poats an' head for America singing like dis: 'Happy days vere here some more!'

"Many many days 'Ristopher an' his frien's dey sail dose poats an' never find it America so quick dey stop singing. So some his frien's get real mad for 'Ristopher an' dey start picket his room, marching up an' down hollering: ' 'Ristopher, you sure you know dat roads for America?' 'Ristopher he's real proud man an' he finally say, 'Any day, now, we goin' lan' America. Go back to vork. Don't be 'ream puff!'

"Vun day cook he come 'Ristopher's room an' say, ' 'Ristopher, I no like to kick it, but grubs he's gettin' low—no more grub in basements. Maybe we all starving before we seeing America.'

"Just den one man he be vay up on flagpole for ship looking all over vit dat vun-pipe spy glass an' all of a sodden he holler, 'I see lan! I see lan'!' 'Ristopher he got real mad an' he holler back, 'Pullsit!' 'Ristopher no vant Iceland—he look it America!

"Pretty soon 'Ristopher an' his frien's dey steering near for some lan' by a helluva big river, an' dere's all kinds of Indians an' even Yimmy Durante on bot' banks, and dey all yump an' dance an' holler, 'Hello, 'Ristopher! How's da bucko? 'Ristopher come wisit America!' "

"An' where did Christopher land, Charlie?" Danny asked softly.

"Where he lan'?" Charlie repeated. "Oh, dat! 'Ristopher he lan' between Bostons an' Massatusitts seven-dirty o'clocks Vensday morning, s'arp on da dot. Dat's how 'Ristopher come to discover America. Yes-sirree!"

Triumphant Danny wheeled upon white and shaken Swan. "Well, there you are, Swanny, me lad. You just heard Charlie here tell how Christopher Columbus was the fella what discovered America. You lose the bet. That makes a quart of Ol' Cordwood I still got comin', beside the one we're drinkin' here. Hey Charlie, fix me up a bottle fer to take home. Swan'll pay fer both of 'em. Wrap it up careful-like. It's to be used strictly fer medicinal purposes only." Danny was flushed with victory.

"O.K., O.K., Danny," Charlie said, turning his innocent faded blue eyes on Danny. "But vy for you going ask me to decide your bets on 'Ristopher ven you know very well I tell you only las' Vensday already dat 'Ristopher he discover America?" Charlie paused as sagging Danny caught and clung to the bar. "An' py the vay, Danny, you owe me da price for dis bottle you poys are already drinking here. My bartender, Uno, he tell me you vere dat vun dat ordered it."

5

DANNY GETS RELIGION

The boys were getting worried about old Dan. Ever since he had stolen the Gideon Bible the previous New Year's morning when he had awakened to find himself lying across the old brass bed in the bridal suite of the Chippewa House, it had been evident to them that a profound change had come over him. For one thing, the old man had become more thoughtful, he talked less, and, even more remarkable, he had cut his drinks to a pint a day. He also used God's last name much less often. The boys grew fearful that Danny was getting religion. Alas, it was true.

Danny craftily read his stolen Bible in secret, disguising the volume between the covers of Grover's *Diseases of Horses* which he had stealthily wrenched from its deathless contents. It was Buller who had discovered this deflowering of Grover, and who finally found the camouflaged Bible hidden over a spruce rafter in Bessie's woodshed. But that was not the whole of it. Danny had taken to spending inordinate lengths of time in the little one-man log outhouse, to which he briskly repaired every morning promptly after breakfast. There he pored for hours over his pilfered Testaments.

Since it was midwinter, and generally below zero every morning, this circumstance naturally caused a measure of discontent and distress among the boys. The thing could not go on. The boys played a series of cribbage games to see who should tie the bell on Danny. Buller lost. So Buller was delegated to speak to Danny about this minor crisis which had come to the inhabitants of Hungry Hollow.

"Danny," Buller said the following night at the supper table, during the hush over the second cup of coffee, "Danny, we don't like to interfere with any man's readin', 'specially when he does it in his own can. But we was wonderin' if you couldn't read your Bi——I mean your horse book somewheres else? Or else let us get a crack at the place first," Buller continued hopefully. "Or maybe we should build us a bigger one, don't you think?" Buller was perspiring with embarrassment. "We was just wonderin', that's all, Danny."

Danny thoughtfully puffed on his corncob pipe. He tamped the bowl gently with a gnarled finger. Piety had lately brought him a certain benign quality of temper, a mellowed and philosophical outlook on the mundane concerns of man. Biblical quotations had likewise begun to flow from him like sap from a girdled maple in May. Danny's quotations were not necessarily appropriate to the occasion, nor yet always accurate. He flitted gaily from the Old Testament to the New, occasionally drawing from both for a single quotation.

Buller's plumbing inquiry had unwittingly opened the floodgates. The boys had learned the signs and they now averted their eyes in shuddering dismay. Danny took a few quick puffs on his corncob and then propped it against the side of his coffee cup. He locked his hands behind his bald head and, leaning back in his chair, rolled his eyes up to heaven. Sonorously, he began to speak to the ceiling of the camp. There his rapt gaze met the labyrinth of woolen socks, shirts, and drawers which dangled from the rafters. So the boys wanted a new outhouse, did they?

"Boys," Danny began, in deep and unnatural accents, " 'is it not lawful for me to do what I will with mine own?' "

"We'll be glad to build us a new one—" Buller began, laughing nervously.

Danny glared briefly at Buller and again contemplated the ceiling, continuing in sepulchral tones. "That there's from Matthew. Lissen to this one! 'Man shall not live by bread alone.' That's Dootrunnyme talkin' —a real smart fella. An' mind this, boys. 'A prophet is without honor' "—Danny groped for words—" 'in his own back yard.' " His voice quavered a little. "Ol' Luke must a made up that one special for me."

"Or shall we enlarge the old one an' put in partitions?" Buller blurted out.

" 'If a house be divided against itself, that house cannot stand,' " Dan intoned.

"Then shall we build a brand-new one, like I said, Danny—" Buller began.

" 'Peace be on this old house,' " Danny said. " 'Set your affections on things above, not on things of the earth.' "

"We could use some of Matti's cedars—" Buller went on anxiously.

" 'Which of you, intendin' to build a tower, sittith not down first an' counteth the cost?' " spake Danny.

"—an you can have the old place all to yourself."
Buller continued in growing desperation.

" 'He that is not with me is ag'in me,' " Danny
rolled on.

"Then maybe we could tear down the ol' one and
build a new one big enough for the hull of us." Buller's
voice was getting shrill.

" 'What we fellas here have put together, let no
man put asunder,' " misquoth Danny.

Buller was getting a trifle frantic. His voice rose to
a shout. "Danny, lissen to me! Please! You name it
an' we'll do it, man! *Do you want a new can or don't
you want a new can!*"

There was profound silence. The boys coughed and
shifted their chairs. Danny blinked innocently over at
Buller as he leaned forward for his cold pipe. "Oh,
that," he said brightly, in his own voice again. "It
ain't necessary a-tall, it ain't." He sighed. "Boys, I'll
tell you what I'll do. I'll give up my seniority rights.
Yep, yep! You laddie-bucks can use it first—right after
breakfast. Say, whose bloody turn is it to wash the
goddam dishes?"

Thus was one crisis met and averted. But it was an
uneasy winter in Hungry Hollow. By the end of Febru-
ary Danny had noisily cut down his drinks to three
small shots a day ("arkohol is the curse of the worl',"
he began to proclaim) and he was talking darkly about
giving up smoking his beloved Peerless. He had finally
abandoned any pretense of appearing to read the horse
book, and he kept his Gideon right out in plain view on
the little shelf where the clock stood, under a mangy
wolf pelt he had tacked to the wall.

Late at night after the others had gone to bed, Dan
would sit by the oil lamp, wearing his ten-cent-store

glasses ("the best goddam specs in America—I kin even read the fine print on a bill of lading by candle-light!") laboriously muttering and whispering out the ancient words. The boys lay rolled in their blankets pretending slumber, yawning elaborately, indulging in fusillades of faked snorings, listening to the wind searching and prying at the stout logs of the old camp as Dan read on. Then one night Dan knelt and prayed before he finally climbed into his bunk. He whispered his prayer, but every ear in the camp strained to hear him. It was a personal prayer, brief and to the point, direct from Dan to Heaven, in which Dan, in return for several months of rectitude, peremptorily invoked divine intervention to relieve his flarin' ulcers. The experiment didn't work very well because the next day Dan's ulcers were worse than ever. That was the last of the praying.

In May month it was Buller's turn to go to work. By this time the boys were so oppressed by the ecclesiastical atmosphere prevailing at Hungry Hollow that they were bidding against each other for the privilege of taking Buller's place. But Buller wouldn't sell his turn, and one morning he and Timmy left in the Model A for Chippewa.

"Mind you be back tonight, Timmy," Danny warned sternly. "An' avoid the demon rum."

Timmy returned in three days, quaking and red of eye. Danny not only wouldn't talk to him but wouldn't even look at him. After supper Timmy addressed Danny. Danny leaned back in his chair with folded arms, disdainfully blowing Peerless smoke at the ceiling.

"Danny," Timmy began. "I gotta tell you—Buller's in trouble again." The old man stared at the ceiling in stony silence as Timmy went on. "You see, Dan, you see—it's this way—Buller went an' got drunk," Timmy blurted. "Claims he was so goddam full a religion he just had to. S'matter of fact I got drunk too. But they run Buller in. They got poor Buller." Timmy gulped. "Ten dollars fine and three-fifteen costs. We got to have it in town by tonight or they take him to the county jail in the mornin' for thirty days."

Danny blew a vast cloud of smoke at the ceiling.

"How about it, Danny? Kin the treasury stand it?" Timmy asked anxiously.

"Let him rot in jail," spoke Danny. The prophets of old never dealt out justice with a firmer hand.

"But look, Danny—"

" 'As ye shall sow, so shall ye reap.' 'The wages of sin is thirty days.' "

"But Danny, it's our Buller," Timmy persisted.

Danny rocked forward in his chair and pounded the table so that the dishes danced and rattled. "Not a goddam red cent! That there's final!"

That night after the dishes were done and Danny was muttering over his Gideon Bible, the boys filed out one by one and met behind Bessie's woodshed. Fumbling in the dark, among the three of them they pooled exactly twenty-five cents over the required $13.15. "Buy dat yigger Buller vun gude shot vidt it," Swan whispered hoarsely, in a burst of unexpected generosity.

The boys helped Timmy push the Model A down the road out of earshot of Dan. Timmy finally slid her into shuddering gear and shot away toward Chippewa to rescue Buller.

In three more days a bearded and inflamed Buller showed up in the Model A, alone. It was a beautiful Saturday morning in May.

Danny ran out to meet the car. "Where in hell is

Timmy?" he thundered. "An' where have you been at?"

Hunched over the driver's wheel, Buller leered scornfully at Danny and jerked a thumb toward Chippewa. "Thirteen-fifteen fer Timmy, ol' man, an' you're payin' up this time." Wearily. "An' we're all goin' in town fer him together—this goddam thing is got to stop somewheres! Either that or we might's well break up."

This was the greatest crisis that had ever come to Hungry Hollow. Buller and Danny glared stonily at each other. Swan and Taconite exchanged fearful glances. Were they to lose their happy home? Danny gave ground first. "O.K., O.K.," he mumbled.

Sorrowfully Danny bowed his head and reached for his buckskin wallet. " 'A good man is merciful an' lendeth,' " he said. He looked up. "Forgive them, Chief, fer they know not what'n hell they's doin'."

The finale came that same Saturday night in Chippewa. Danny and the boys, augmented by a shaking Timmy, were standing by the fountain in the square next to the iron Indian, Chief Booze-in-the-Face. The boys were trying to coax Danny and his buckskin wallet into Charlie's Place. Danny was trying equally hard to herd the boys into waiting for the Salvation Army to appear for their Saturday night public service in the square. Things had come to a pretty pass.

"There they come now!" Danny exclaimed, sighting down the street, his eyes lighting up with fanatic zeal. "There comes Diddidum an' his big drum. Look, you boys wait through the—the service with me"— he paused—"an' I'll buy all of you a roun' of drinks. Mebbe two!" He was going to bribe the boys into salvation.

"Boom, boom, boom!"

Down Hematite Avenue marched the Salvation
Army, led by little "Diddidum" Couch, a becowlicked
and bowlegged Cornish miner. *"Boom, boom!"*
Diddidum was securely harnessed into his big bass
drum, a drum higher than himself. He had to peek
around the sides of it as he led his valiant little band
of men and women across Main Street where they
took up their stand at the side of the Miners' State
Bank in the town square.

"C'mon, boys," Danny said solemnly, leading the
way. "C'mon over an' lissen to Diddidum preach the
Word."

This was the same Diddidum that Danny had insulted years before on the occasion of Diddidum's first
public appearance as a member of the Salvation Army.
Diddidum had marched proudly into Charlie's Place
on a Saturday night, glistening and aglow in his new
Salvation Army uniform, and had thrust a rattling
and coin-littered tambourine under Danny's nose.
Choking, Danny had gulped down his waiting drink
and had wheeled on little Diddidum.

"My Gawd," he said, "I scarce knew you in your
handsome new soldier soot! When'd you join Teddy's
Rough Riders? Where's your rifle?" He pointed
at Diddidum's tambourine. "Hell, man, I'll *buy* you
a drink before you leave town. My, my! Any soldier
in Uncle Sam's Army don't never need to go aroun'
panhandlin'—'specially a fine figure of a man like you.
When'd you join the Army?"

Outraged Diddidum had drawn himself up to his
full five feet. "Hi'll 'ave yew hunderstan', Mister
Danny," he had piously declaimed, "Hi now belong
to the Harmy of the Lard!"

"Hm," Danny had mused. "Army of the Lord, is it? Then you better scoot, mister, before you gits arrested for desertion—'cause you're sure a hell of a long ways from headquarters. Yep, yep!"

Tonight the town was thronged with people—miners, railroaders, lumberjacks, and farmers in from the surrounding country. Danny and the boys had to shoulder their way in to get an unobstructed view of Diddidum and his drum. One of Diddidum's assistants passed him a trumpet, and Diddidum, doubling in brass, played a blaring chorus of "Rock of Ages."

"These 'ere services will naow commence!" Diddidum suddenly shouted, lowering his horn and glaring at the crowd for silence. For the fiery little man not only trumpeted and drummed for the Army, he preached for it as well.

Diddidum resolutely preached for all who would listen, rich or poor, drunk or sober, his big drum turned face up to receive the coins of those moved by his burning eloquence. When he invoked the Lord there was no interminable dry and dusty theology such as the mining crowd had to listen to in their cloistered church across the tracks. In a thrice Diddidum's Savior was miraculously right there before Danny and the boys, " 'ammered to the Cross" before their very eyes.

Licking tongues of verbal hell-fire and burning brimstone glowed and flickered upon the twilit town square. An enchanted Danny stood staring at Diddidum like a sleepwalker. Dancing with excitement, his cowlick bobbing in his eyes, little Diddidum hopped bowlegged about the circle of people, pelting them with words, not merely inviting but challenging sinners and saints alike to step into the magic circle and testify to their conversion.

"Oo'll be the first lam' to com' aout to the Lard!"
he shouted, glaring about him, the cords of his neck
taut and distended. "Oo'll be the Lard's first lam'?"
There was an involuntary "ah" from the crowd as
Daniel Wellington McGinnis, Gideon Bible in one
hand and battered hat in the other, quickly stepped
into the circle. Danny tripped slightly, stepping off
the curb, and performed a nervous little jig as he took
up his stand by the big bass drum.

"Wot 'ave yew to s'y to the Lard?" Diddidum
bridled suspiciously, keeping one birdlike eye on Danny
and the other on the coin-littered bass drum. "Hafter
all these years—wot 'ave yew to s'y to the Lard, Mister Danny?"

Danny's bald head was bowed in contrition. He
threw out his arms and spoke with a quivering eloquence rivaling Diddidum's.

"Oh, Diddidum—I've come back to the fold, I have.
Here I've wasted all them years—fur away from Him
—makin' moonshine, drinkin', gamblin' an' whorin'—"

" 'Ere, damme!" outraged Diddidum broke in,
wheeling on a burly assistant, " 'eave the bloody
booger aout fer sayin' 'oorin'!"

The next morning a grinning small boy bolted from
the "family entrance" of the Chippewa jail with
a shiny new quarter and a package wrapped in soiled
newspaper. He raced up Hematite Avenue, and thence
turned north up First Street to the Chippewa House.
Mrs. Smedburg, the proprietress, was sleepily sorting
keys behind the desk in the dark lobby. The boy
dropped the package on the desk and fled. Mrs. Smedburg shrugged her shoulders and wearily unwrapped
the package. There was a note. "Hm . . . I vunder vat
does it say?" She adjusted her glasses and read.

Dear Mrs. Smedburg—

Thanks for the use of the Gideon bible which I am finely returning. The Book's all right but I don't like some of its deesciples.

I think one of the smartest lines in the hull volyum is by Tim. Tim wrote as follows and it still makes sence:

"Drink no longer water, but use a little wine for thy stummick's sake."

Please be advised that this morning my ulcers is the best they been all Winter.

Yours truly,

A FRIEND

6

LOVE SWEEPS OVER DANNY

Danny and the boys tarried in Chippewa. They tarried for reasons which were not entirely clear to them. It was not strictly the fact of Danny's reconversion, complete as that was. It was more from a sense of relief, of sweet release, as though one had suddenly found himself harboring a renowned magician or distinguished cleric or even a trick billiard shot, and lo! one morning he was gone. One had found his presence exhilarating but a trifle wearing.

The boys and Danny stayed at the Chippewa House on First Street under the watchful eye of Mrs. Smedburg. Danny had arranged for credit. After all, the Chippewa House was one of Hungry Hollow's best customers for firewood. Mrs. Smedburg cheerfully extended the credit, firewood or no firewood. But she was always a little worried when Danny and his chums were guests in her house.

"Dat Dannay an' hiss shums!" She would shake her head. "Dey vere awful yiggers—alvays oop to crazy tricks an' yeneral monkeyshines."

In the meantime Danny's buckskin poke was growing leaner and leaner, notwithstanding he had floated a generous loan from Big Annie. To make matters worse, Buller and he had quarreled. They had not spoken to each other for three days, despite the fact that they were supposed to share the same bed in the bridal suite óf the Chippewa House. Room 205, it was, just beyond the top of the upstairs landing. Danny always insisted upon occupying the bridal suite. For one thing, it possessed the only room-bath in the house. Danny was sensitive about parading the midnight halls in his nightgown and tasseled cap. And contemplation of the dusty pink canopy over the brass bed seemed to do things for him. "I jest likes to lay there an' look up an' dream an' dream," he once confided to Mrs. Smedburg.

The quarrel between Buller and Danny had started over at Charlie's Place. Like many people, Danny could stand almost anything but ridicule. And Buller had insulted him by laughing at him! Outraged Danny had thereupon called Buller "Satch" and "Lard Butt" and some other whimsical names of similar import. He had even challenged Buller to a fight. Buller had nearly pulled up Charlie's mahogany bar by the roots as he gripped it mightily to restrain himself. Buller was sore hurt. But so was Danny. Here he had been talking to Charlie—minding his own business, mind you—and Buller had up and *laughed*!

"How's business, Charlie?" Danny had facetiously asked the proprietor of Charlie's Place as he and the boys came in and shouldered up to the bar. Danny looked the length of the teeming bar. It was a payday at the iron mines.

Charlie considered Danny's question. He drew down his mouth and squeezed out the bar rag. "Oh, dat business she's pretty good. I ain't got no any kick it. You see, I still got dat 'ree 'rinking s'ift!"

"Waddya mean, Charlie—three drinkin' shifts?" Danny inquired, innocently leading with his chin.

Charlie's shrewd eyes twinkled. "Vell, Danny, dere's dat first s'ift—dat's mans who be 'runk an' sick it wit' hanging-overs an' bad s'akes like ever'ting, so he sleep it so's he can go vork vunce more. Hm . . . Den dat numper two s'ift—he's mans who be vork it down mines an' for voods so's he can make more money so's he can come Sarlie's for get 'runk it some more. You see, Danny?" Charlie shrugged and threw down the bar rag. The whole thing so simple.

"Where's the goddam third drinkin' shift?" Danny helplessly asked, ruefully bracing himself.

Charlie grandly waved his arm the length of his noisy, crowded bar. "Oh, dat t'ird s'ift, he's be on da yob right now—getting good an' 'runk it. Hm . . . How's business, you ask it? She's da pretty good me. You like to buy da place, Danny?"

And Buller had laughed and laughed.

Another Saturday night had come along and Danny and the boys were sitting around Mrs. Smedburg's lobby in her creaking chairs—not only dead broke, but with feudin' Danny and Buller still deep in their pout. Gurn S. McIlwain, the traveling man, was telling them his latest story. The ponderous bell in the tower of Braastad's big store was just striking the hour. It was only ten o'clock.

When Gurney had finished Danny rose and stretched and yawned elaborately. "Me, I'm thinkin' I'll go up an' hit the hay—*alone!*" he said to no one in particular, staggering stiff-legged to the stairway, still clutched in the grip of his prodigious yawn. "Good night Gurney, Timmy, Swan, an' Taconite," he enumerated, carefully omitting Buller.

Buller stopped rocking. This was the final insult. And must he sit up in the lobby still another night just to humor this slanderous old goat?

"Timmy," Buller said. "Please ask Mister McGinnis if he expects Mister Beaudin to rock hisself to sleep down here another night. Tell him the other rooms is all full up an' Mister Beaudin's still dead broke—all of which he bloody well knows—an' anyway, who the hell does he think he is?" Timmy was usually made the unwilling interlocutor between Danny and Buller when they quarreled. He shifted restlessly on the old leather sofa and remained silent. Danny paused at the stairway.

"Timmy," Danny shot back, "tell Mister Beaudin that Mister McGinnis'd sooner sleep with a wild hawg than crawl in the hay with him." Danny began to feel sorry for himself. "What's more, tell him that pore sick ol' Danny McGinnis an' his flarin' ulcers wouldn't take in the Queena Sheba tonight—not even if she came poundin' an' sobbin' at his bloody door. Tell him—"

Just then a large and buxom young woman came bouncing down the stairway and brushed past Danny, smiling at him gaily and shaking her blond curls. Danny stared after her, his neck craned forward. "Boy, oh boy—built jest like a thirty-dollar cow!" Danny breathed appreciatively. "Who is she?"

"Looks more like Buller's sister to me," Timmy ventured, ready to bolt.

"Aw, nuts!" tired Buller said, beyond anger, vigorously creaking his chair. "You know I ain't got no sister."

Gurn S. McIlwain spoke up. He was the representative of a hardware and furniture company, and one of Mrs. Smedburg's old customers. He had known Danny and the boys for years. He would try to ease the tension. "Go on up to bed, Danny. Let the help alone. You're old enough to be her grampaw," Gurney said. "Anyway, I'll bet she wouldn't look twice at you even if you was a millionaire." Gurney was one of those curious individuals who would wager anything on anything—any time, any place, anywhere.

"Zat so?" Danny replied testily. "Jest fer that, Gurney, I'll bet you a quart of Ol' Cordwood thet I"—Danny craftily glanced over at Mrs. Smedburg, who stood counting the till at the hotel desk—"thet I kin git her to come in an' make up my bed fer me when she gits back tonight! Is it a bet?"

"Taken," Gurney said. "You're on."

"But who is she?" Danny again inquired, still caught in the rapture of her blond spell. "Boy, oh boy!"

Mrs. Smedburg spoke up quietly from her desk, peering over her glasses. "She vere Hilma, my noo shambermaid, Mester Dannay—an' Ay vant you yiggers to leave her be or Ay vill put you all out!" Mrs. Smedburg slammed shut the door of her iron safe, twirled the shuddering dial, and shuffled to the stairway. "Gude night, yentleman." She turned wearily and plodded up the stairs.

Buller was the first to recover. "Anyway, gentlemen," Buller announced, "bet or no bet, there ain't gonna be no room fer Hilma in the bridal soot. I'm sleepin' there myself tonight—an' what's more, Danny's invitin' me in!"

Danny glared over at Buller. "An' if he ain't too cheap, I'm bettin' Mister Beaudin another quart a Ol' Cordwood I don't invite him in. I'd sooner sleep with a coyote what'd jest tackled a nest of polecats!"

"It's a bet, Mister McGinnis." Buller graciously

nodded his head, always willing to please. Danny's mustaches were bristling as he stomped upstairs to his lonely bed in the bridal suite, muttering to himself.

"And I'll lay you still another quart of Old Cordwood that Old Danny don't ask you in," Gurney McIlwain said to Buller, scenting a vast Cordwoodian weekend.

Buller sat gently creaking his rocking chair, serenely pouting out his lips. "Make it *two* quarts an' I'll take you," he said loftily.

"You're on!" Gurney said. "Two quarts of Old Cordwood that Danny doesn't invite you in the bridal suite—say by midnight. We gotta set a time limit!"

"Sure, sure, by midnight it is," Buller amiably agreed. "Shake!"

So Gurney and Buller shook hands warmly over the pleasant prospect that quite a lot of Old Cordwood would shortly change hands. This manifold discussion and betting over whisky so unnerved Swan and Taconite that they suddenly got up and left for Charlie's Place. "Yust to stan' an' vatch!" Swan wistfully explained.

"Timmy," Buller said softly, looking at the lobby clock, "c'mon take me up to your room fer a spell till Danny invites me in." It was nearing eleven o'clock. Timmy had a cot in Swan and Taconite's room, Room 206, just across the hall from Danny and the bridal suite. "Good night, Gurney," Buller said. "See you in the hall outside Danny's room in exactly half an hour."

"O.K., Buller," Gurney said, gleefully rubbing his hands.

At 11:30 P.M. Gurney McIlwain stealthily tiptoed upstairs and down the deserted corridor past Danny's room. He paused outside Danny's door, Room 205. He smiled and nodded as he heard great snores emanating from the bridal suite. His Old Cordwood was practically in the bag.

"Psst!"

It was Timmy beckoning him inside from his darkened door across from Danny's room. Gurney quickly stepped through the doorway and Timmy closed and locked it. The two stood in the dark. "Sh-h!" Timmy whispered.

"Where's Buller?" Gurney asked.

"I dunno," Timmy whispered. "He up an' went somewheres. Honest, I don't know where he's at, Gurney."

"Can I smoke?" Gurney inquired, nervously finding a cigarette.

"Yes—but stand clear from the door so I kin get these chairs set up for the transom."

"Chairs for the transom! What for?" Gurney asked.

"So's you kin stan' an' see fer yourself whether you win or lose your bloody bet!"

Timmy lowered the squeaking transom carefully as Gurney sat on the bed and finished his cigarette in the dark. Then Gurney joined Timmy on a chair and they both stood staring out at the hotel corridor, deserted and silent except for Danny's great nasal trumpetings from across the hall.

"Boy, is this easy—quarter to twelve and Danny fast asleep," Gurney whispered. "I win both ways! Danny don't get Hilma in—and Buller don't get invited in!"

"Sh-h!" Timmy whispered. "Listen to that!"

Down the carpeted hall, out of the range of their vision, came the sound of soft swishing. Ever so softly the rhythmic swishing sound drew nearer, broken only by Danny's rasping snores.

"My Gawd!" Gurney whispered hoarsely, nearly falling from his chair at the transom.

There, inching along the hall, holding a broom and daintily sweeping every inch of the hall carpet before her, came a great mad bawd of a woman, fantastically mascaraed, rouged, and belipsticked. Clad in an enormous housecoat, she also wore a sort of Mother Hubbard dust cap, from the sides of which protruded a wild thatch of straw blond curls—curls, which to Gurney's practiced eye, looked for all the world like poor Mrs. Smedburg's mattress ticking. After all, he had sold her the mattresses.

"Hmm-m-m," faintly hummed this vast female apparition in a tuneless falsetto, as she swept inevitably along toward Danny's door. At last she drew opposite Room 205. She paused in her sweeping, as though to listen. The snoring continued, but there was a subtle change in its character. A quality of outright strangulation had been added.

"Hmm-m-m," hummed the midnight sweeper, still placidly nodding her blond curls, sweeping, sweeping, sweeping ever onward. She swished slowly past Danny's door, still humming, still sweeping—humming perhaps a little louder, sweeping a trifle more vigorously.

Perspiring Gurney and Timmy, standing on their chairs at the transom, suddenly saw the knob of Danny's door slowly turning. "Swish, swish, swish!" went the broom. Slowly the door opened, an inch, two inches—then Danny's head protruded, drooping mustaches, blinking eyes, tasseled nightcap and all. Still the sweeper swished on and on, girlishly oblivious of her danger.

"*Psst!*" came from the occupant of the bridal suite.

The sweeper paused, startled, and then glanced coyly over her shoulder. Danny reached out a bony hand and beckoned her. She wheeled around toward him, pointing at herself and then at Danny's room in wide-eyed surprise. Could this good fortune really be true? Danny vigorously nodded his head and kept beckoning. But the maiden, so tremulous, so modest, leaned on her broom, cupping the handle against her plump rouged cheek. She cast her eyes down, fluttering her eyelids. She glanced at Danny again, then bit her lip and quickly looked away, exploring the hall carpet with her toe. Again she slowly glanced up, fatally drawn to Danny.

Danny was nodding and gesticulating like a hard-pressed headwaiter. He held the door wide open, frantically waving her in. Suddenly the maid took a few quick dancing steps up to the open doorway. At the threshold she paused uncertainly, poised for sudden flight, like some ponderous Diana. Danny again wildly beckoned her in. Girlishly she lay one flushed ear against both prayerful hands, blinking, and then pointed questioningly at her commodious bosom, then at Danny's canopied bed. To sleep, perchance to dream?

"Sure, sure!" Danny whispered hoarsely. "C'mon in! Hurry afore someone comes along!"

The fear was the father to fact, for at this crucial moment still another buxom blond lass with straw-colored curls came breathlessly running up the stairs. Braastad's clock was booming midnight. The girl stopped short when she spied skinny Danny in his nightshirt and cap. She leaned uncertainly against the wall when she saw this—this creature in her best house-coat and her old dusting cap.

"*Hilma!*" disillusioned Danny croaked at the bewildered girl, at the same time squinting dangerously at the vast sweeper, who had started to melt down the hallway, backwards. Danny commenced to stalk his sweeper, taking a big step when she did, then a series of little steps when she did. One of her curls somehow worked loose and dropped to the floor. Danny stooped and picked it up. Scowling, he resumed the stalk. Gurney and Timmy were nearly falling through the transom, craning their necks to see. Finally the massive sweeper was backed against the far wall, next to the fire extinguisher. There was no further retreat. Danny was stealthily closing in. The nocturnal sweeper raised her broom and closed her eyes, ready to defend her virtue to the bitter end.

"Yentlemen!"

It was the ringing voice of Mrs. Smedburg, who stood at the far end of the hall, holding aloft a lighted candle. She wore a nightcap not unlike Danny's.

"Yentlemen, ef you don't goo to bed at vunce Ay vill call a policemans an' haf you all t'run in yail! At vunce, Ay say! An' you, too, Hilma, you—you foxy street-valker! Pulling vool all over my eyes!"

There was a clattering of chairs against Timmy's door, as though someone were suddenly rioting in 206. Danny picked up the skirts of his nightgown and scampered for his room, closely followed by the sweeper, who dropped his broom, quickly tore off his dust cap and borrowed gown, executed a quick lateral pass to running Hilma in a mist of falling curls, and thence skidded into the bridal suite behind Danny, slamming the door.

Mrs. Smedburg stood blinking at the end of the hall, still indignantly holding up her candle. She waited one full minute. All was silence.

"Gude night, yentlemen!" she said, snuffing out her candle and wearily turning away.

Her only answer came from 205 and from 206 directly across the hall—a quartet, a veritable crescendo, of obedient snores. Peace had descended at last upon the old Chippewa House.

7

BIG ANNIE

There is a legend abroad in the land that there exists no prostitute in America who does not possess a heart of gold, who wouldn't give you the shirt off her back. It is a beautiful legend. Nor breathes one of these romantic toilers, the fable goes, who wasn't at some happier time in her life a fine lady; who couldn't still be found spending her leisure hours reading Proust or perhaps the more obscure Elizabethan poets.

Her professional lot may best be explained, so the legend runs, by ascribing it to the forgivable weakness of an expansive and affectionate heart. She simply can not resist attempting to mother the whole troubled brotherhood of man. That she might be in business to earn what she conceives to be easy money and perchance to avoid the drudgery and boredom of being a waitress or a scullion or a seamstress—this calumny is dismissed as being too churlish and slanderous for sober debate. Or else there is a mortgage to be lifted from the vine-covered home of her arthritic parents and seven little brothers and sisters. Consumptive little brothers and sisters, that is.

Big Annie did not belong to this tribe of fabled whores. Her parents were long since dead and her only close relative was a brother who was residing permanently in a downstate penitentiary. It is true that each Christmas she made an anonymous gift of a hundred or so dollars to the local Salvation Army. Credit must be given where credit is due. But it is equally true that the very same night she would most likely roll a maudlin lumberjack of all his money to make it up. While Big Annie had never read Emerson she was an instinctive believer in the inevitability of the laws of compensation.

Her appetite for poetry and general literature seemed amply nourished by the sentimental effusions of the syndicated newspaper columnists and the magazines devoted to authentic romance. While she was smart by instinct, as a gypsy horse trader is smart, intellectually she presented to the world an armor of invincible ignorance. Her resistance to any idea beyond her ken was absolute; she was superstitious and intolerant, and she drank too much. The most important concerns of her life she usually resolved by consulting tea leaves or the Zodiac. Big Annie was a whore, a good whore, but not a legendary one.

Her establishment embraced the second story of an old frame house on Magnetic Street. She owned the place, which had once stood on a quiet residential street, but which the passage of time had planted in the heart of the Chippewa saloon district. Pilgrims gained entrance to her place by an enclosed wooden stairway she had built on in the rear, the entrance to which was charitably shrouded in darkness. She rented the downstairs to an alcoholic Irish embalmer. Her old friend Danny once chided her over this droll propinquity. She sharply explained that she sought only to avoid annoyance to anyone who might otherwise be disturbed by the nightly revels of her gentlemen guests. She really had her more thoughtful moments.

Big Annie was what is known to the trade as a working madam. Usually she employed three girls to assist her, but the number fluctuated with the seasons and the frequency of the emotional clashes between Big Annie and her girls. For Annie was growing old, a circumstance which she did not relish nor accept with the traditional grace of her legendary sisters. As a consequence, when one of her favorite clients showed a fickle disposition to favor a new girl, Big Annie was apt to swing into jealous action. This usually meant that a local dray would pull up the next morning to speed the offending girl's luggage on its way. And sometimes to remove the wreckage. Sometimes, too, the remaining girls would take their leave out of sympathy for their departed co-worker. Such things are difficult to confirm, of course, but there exists the possibility that the phenomenon of the sympathy strike found its genesis in Big Annie's.

Girls might come and girls might go, but Big Annie always remained—aging, lumpy, henna-haired Annie, with her rubbery, powdered face framed in her flaming mattress-tick hair, which looked as though it had been hurriedly molded by a drunken sculptor. There she reigned, the queen of her second-story flight to romance, sitting amidst her drab, cigarette-burned, overstuffed furniture, holding imaginary conversations with her collection of saucy-skirted Kewpie dolls—mementoes of many a passing carnival—or tastefully rearranging her bowlful of artificial flowers on the radio or gazing at the cheap prints which adorned her walls. Her favorite picture was that authentic chain-store classic, the one depicting the drooping Indian sitting on a drooping horse, both about to be blown away. "It's so—so kinda sadlike," she often sighed. "The poor fella looks all col' an' wet."

"Hello, boys. What's new?" was her invariable greeting to young and old, as she would coyly gather in her dressing gown about her swollen figure, or sit so that she might delicately expose a gaily gartered and lumpy knee. If the place was not busy there would be some small talk and news of local births and deaths. Annie liked to preserve a certain measure of decorum and avoid the appearance of hurry. She cherished the illusion that her visitors were paying a purely social call, drawn solely by her feminine charm and her skill in clever repartee. She had early learned that most men love to talk about their work. Consequently she knew as much about logging and the mining of iron ore as did most of her male callers.

There would be a round of bottled beer, a beverage which Annie quadrupled in price because, as she ingenuously explained, of the risk she took in selling it without a license. Old Danny once pointed out to her that in all the years he had known her she had never once been raided or arrested—"fer peddlin' beer nor nothin' else," he playfully leered—and that considering the money she annually saved on her license fee she should reduce the price of her beer rather than raise it. "Moonshinin' ol' cheapskate!" Big Annie snorted, giving him an affectionate dig in the ribs.

After a sufficient number of trees had crashed to earth and tons of ore had been duly mined, there would be an awkward lull in the conversation. This was the time when Annie's charm and social resource usually reached its fullest flower. If she was tired or out of sorts, or her visitors did not attract her, she would shake her head girlishly and chortle, "Oh! You haven't met our little redheaded Peggy, have you? She just came to visit us from Hurley, an' a swell little pal she is. Shall I call her out? Or would you rather see Eve? Of course you know Eve, you naughty boy. No? Oh, Peggy dear—c'mon out an' meet one of my very partic'lar gen'emen frien's."

No, Big Annie had no truck with foolish legends concerning her profession.

With the exception of Timmy, Danny and the boys were frequent callers at Big Annie's. After one reluctant visit, Timmy had avoided the place. The reason was simple. Romantic Timmy, the idealist, had long ago erected a pedestal upon which stood a shining golden figure called Woman. It appalled him that mere men would dare to worship at this shrine by paying money.

Danny had known Big Annie ever since she had first come to Chippewa as a snake charmer with a traveling carnival. The snakes had crept away but Annie had remained. At the time, Danny was himself a mere fumbling adolescent of fifty. He too had very little traffic with Big Annie and the girls except in the communal revelry of the waiting room. His reasons were less idealistic if perhaps more subtle than Timmy's. They were darkly wrapped up with the ego. The professional tricks and sly bedroom deceits of these ladies chilled him. He was oppressed by the notion that his partner might secretly loathe him.

"Somehow I can't git feelin' to home with a woman what I—I've rented," Danny once confessed to Big Annie. She had clumsily reached over and kissed him on the forehead. "I know," she had muttered in the darkness. "I know—I know." Then she had burst into tears. It was one of the things that had drawn the two together in their curious friendship—their common devotion to the true spirit of the amateur.

No such complex obsession dampened the ardors of Buller and the other boys. When they had a romantic seizure they did something about it, as one took physic for the bellyache. "Boy, oh boy!" Buller would exclaim as they tramped up the creaking backstairs of Big Annie's. "Boy, oh boy!" They entered her domain with all of the determined spirit and gusto with which they attacked a venison steak or a bottle of Old Cordwood.

There was another thing that drew Danny to Big Annie. It was her engaging habit of interrogating her male callers on how they happened to be leading the lives they led. This reversal of traditional bagnio form she conducted in utmost seriousness. "How come you live 'way out in the woods an' don't work nor nothin'?" she had asked Danny during their initial engagement, years before. She had regarded him intently with her big doe eyes. The irony of the situation was not lost on Danny. He had suddenly leapt from her side and bolted to the waiting room. There he insisted on buying drinks for the entire house. "Here's to Annie," he had toasted. "Yep, yep! The only lady I ever knowed what has a sense of humor in the hay!"

Thus it was that Big Annie and Danny were old friends. Each year on Danny's birthday Annie sentimentally baked and cut a huge birthday cake. In times of trouble or doubt they did not hesitate to consult each other. The time Danny was arrested on suspicion of moonshining, Big Annie promptly went his cash bond. She was constantly bailing Buller and the boys out of their endless scrapes. She did it all for Danny— plus nine per cent interest, compounded. Hence it was that in May when one of Big Annie's favorite girls lay at death's door over at the Chippewa Hospital, Danny washed and herded all of the boys in from Hungry Hollow to pay their respects. Even Timmy reluctantly tagged along.

The hospital room was banked with flowers and potted plants and sprays from "Spike" and "Buck" and "Slim" and other of the poor girl's anonymous admirers. Danny and the boys reverently added a huge bouquet of trailing arbutus. Big Annie and her current girls, Pearl and Hazel, stood on one side of the bed and Danny and the boys on the other. The stricken girl lay in an uneasy state of semiconsciousness. Annie was straining at her knotted handkerchief, rivulets of tears coursing down through the powder on her face.

"She—she was the best bedfellow we ever had in the place," Annie sniffled. It was the perfect tribute.

Pearl turned to Hazel with tear-drenched eyes. "See! You gotta nearly up'n die before they'll ever say a good word for you."

The tribute worked. The lady recovered.

On Danny's seventy-fifth birthday Big Annie sent out printed invitations for the gala celebration. It was the finest party she had ever thrown. Only the select were invited and the doors were barred to the mere lovelorn. Little Matti Hunginen and Charlie Jokinen and all the others were there. Even Timmy timidly consented to attend, and wound up serving champagne in the kitchen. "Happy Birthday to you!" reached even the ears of the muttering embalmer laboring below. Buller sat at the kitchen table dandling two of the girls, one on each knee, looking like a beatific and overstuffed ventriloquist. Anointed Swan, the silent lover, stood jealously brooding by the humming refrigerator. Taconite already rested on the linoleum floor, underneath the kitchen sink.

"Where's Danny?" Big Annie suddenly demanded. "We want Danny!"

Clad in a new beaded black dress, with accessories of expensive pearls, and sheepskin slippers to ease her bunions, Annie shuffled into the living room to investigate. Girlishly tilting her head, she peeked through the doorway. There sat old Danny with her newest girl on his lap, Lucinda, a little blonde fresh from a resort in Ashland. Danny was blithely working on a bottle of Old Cordwood. These fancy ladies' wines were not for him.

"I see you're celebratin' your birthday already!" Big Annie laughed, shaking her blazing carrot tresses at Danny.

Danny looked up. "When you're seventy-five, ma'am, you don't celebrate your goddam birthday— you on'y observe it!"

"I'd hate to trust you, you ol' goat," Annie chortled, still gaily shaking her orange curls, turning and flapping back to the kitchen.

"Imagine her insultin' a pore ol' man what wouldn't hurt a bloody fly," Danny muttered darkly. "Anyway, ol' Danny doesn't like flies," he added, giving Lucinda a slow, paternal pat on the buttocks.

Little Lucinda stirred restlessly on his lap. She was beginning vaguely to sense that maybe Big Annie had something there.

"C'mon, Danny," she laughingly teased, leaping to her feet. "Let's go and join the others. What do you think this is—your *birthday*?"

8

THE BURIAL

Little Matti Hunginen was going to town. It was his regular day to deliver milk and eggs to his customers in Chippewa. But that was not all—he had stealthily crept from the side of his snoring wife, Impi, at 3:30 A.M. and worked until daylight currying and rubbing his hay-bloated, dung-coated horses, Fred and Ensio. Matti had scrubbed his face and put on a green necktie and even donned his secondhand burberry overcoat. Such an unwonted burst of industry and display of sartorial elegance filled his dour wife, Impi, with black suspicion.

"Wat you going for do in town, Matti?" she asked in her high-pitched voice as Matti hurriedly put the freshly polished harnesses on Fred and Ensio and hitched them to his long sleigh.

Impi was a vast, besweatered female with great breasts which flowed down her person like sagging bladders of wine. She was rumored to possess a bad temper, which was probably not improved by having to minister to the half-dozen odd little blue-eyed

Hunginens who overran their farm. When she was angry with Matti she always spoke to him in English, swearing at him only in Finnish so that he would surely not miss any of the words. She did this not only because the township schoolteacher had recommended that English be spoken in the home for the sake of the children, but because this alien language seemed to lend an additional iciness to her diatribes. The net result was that she and Matti nearly always conversed in English.

"Wat you going for do in town?" Impi repeated coldly. A purposeful woman, she would not be put off.

"Vy, sell dem milk an' eggs, of course, Impi," Matti answered innocently, drawing back in injured surprise and buttoning his burberry tightly about his throat against the stinging March wind.

Impi stood with her legs apart, her great red hands resting loosely on her broad hips. It was a bad sign. "Wat for you clean horses dat vay an' vash your face an' wear dat bes' coat?" Impi was openly skeptical.

"Oh, dat," Matti said, flushing under her steady scrutiny. "I guess I forget for tell you—Matti's going funeral, too, Impi. You see, I got to put my frien' for box. I be carry man his funeral—what you call dat, palsy bearer? Matti got to get lil dolled up for dat."

"Hm," Impi said. "Who's dat frien' you who's going an' die? Funny you never tell for me. Udder times w'en you come home Sippywa, like ol' vindmill you alvays talk, talk, talk. Who's dis frien' who die so qvick?"

Matti bit his lip. He blinked, wrestling with a recalcitrant memory. "Vell, now ain't dat funny—I forget his names." Matti brushed away a fugitive tear. "But he's my bes' frien'!" he added loyally, clucking the horses into a fast trot.

"Better you be home for you supper," Impi shouted after him. "Sarp on da dot, wit all dat milk an' egg money—or I fix you good, ol' soak man!"

Matti winced under the lash of his wife's voice and clucked the horses to an even faster pace. The sleigh runners sang and squealed over the frosty March snow. Out of sight of the farm, he looked down and lovingly patted the sleeve of his burberry. Next to his team of horses, it was his proudest possession. He had purchased it the year before in Chippewa at a rummage sale conducted by the good ladies of the Methodist church.

"Do you want to sell that there coat?" Timmy had eagerly asked him the first time Matti had appeared at Hungry Hollow with it, the fall before. This was following an unfortunate trip to Chippewa and a bitter quarrel with his wife. Matti had spent all the milk and egg money, and had been obliged to flee to Hungry Hollow for his life. "Where did you get that coat?" Timmy insisted. Matti and Danny and the boys were sitting over their after-breakfast coffee.

"I buy dat coat secking-hand at rummitts sale for pasement of Meddotitts surts in Sippywa," Matti proudly answered. "She's not no any for sale," he added firmly.

Timmy, ordinarily very gentle, was disgruntled and rancorous. He coveted Matti's fine English coat. "Then why in hell don't you get a haircut if you're goin' to sport such a swell coat?" It was not like little Timmy to indulge in such personalities. The coat had become a sudden obsession.

"Hm." Matti grinned, taking up a spoon and thoughtfully agitating his coffee with all the noisy vigor of a Swedish bell ringer. "Matti like vear his hair long dis time of year for vinter driving!"

The laughs had been on Timmy. "An' where did you get those Morse code teeth?" stung Timmy pressed on.

"Wat you mean—Morse cote teets?" Matti had innocently asked.

"Tooth-dash-tooth!" Timmy said, waiting for the laugh on Matti.

"Oh," Matti shot back, "I like dose kind teets— you see, he's new kind air-cooled teets for summer driving!"

"An' why don't you get washed an' cleaned up?" Timmy doggedly pressed on, amidst the leg-slapping guffaws. "You look half froze. Did you sleep outside last night when you was on your drunk in Chippewa? Did you?"

Matti rose from the table and drew himself erect. These insults had gone far enough. He spoke with quiet dignity. "Matti never sleep outside las' night. No, no—Matti sleep boxcar!"

"Lay off, Timmy," Danny said, when he had caught his breath. "You jest can't win."

Little Matti Hunginen was one of those luckless, hag-ridden mortals whom the Goddess of Trouble seemed to have selected for her more imposing experiments. He was continually in the toils of trouble: trouble with his wife, trouble with the Chippewa police, trouble with his milk and egg customers, and sometimes just in plain trouble with trouble. The hot breath of calamity and misfortune dogged his footsteps and fanned his skinny neck like a beagle on the trail of a tired rabbit. But little Matti had the spirit and heart of a lion. When the going got roughest, he held his head high, stuck out the Adam's apple on his wrinkled Tom turkey neck, grinned his Morse code smile—and ordered a double shot of Old Cordwood.

When Matti told Impi he was going to attend a funeral in Chippewa that morning, he told the truth but not the whole truth. That the deceased was his best friend was a slight overstatement. The departed was a prominent local Irishman whom Matti had never laid eyes on, one Shamus John Patrick O'Rourke. Conversely, that Matti was going to be a "carry man" was a slight understatement. He was, in fact, going to drive the hearse. He was head "carry man." He had made it up with the Irish undertaker in charge—Big Annie's alcoholic tenant—in Charlie's Place on his last trip to town, three days before. It seemed that the harried embalmer couldn't rent a team of horses from any of the local liveries because of his droll tendency not to pay. But he could borrow a hearse if Matti would only drive it with his team of horses. Would Matti do it? He'd be well paid—as soon as the services were over.

"Dat's O.K.!" Matti had replied, glad to earn a few extra dollars to invest in Old Cordwood and not have to account for it to Impi as he was obliged to do with every penny of the milk and egg money. "Vat time you like for me to be dere?"

The embalmer and little Matti touched glasses. "When you come to town pick up the hearse and the corpse at my place under Big Annie's, then drive over to St. Xavier's church, prompt at nine o'clock," the embalmer directed.

"Matti'll be dere—Yonny on da dot!" Matti solemnly avowed, tossing down his drink.

On the cold drive into Chippewa for the funeral, Matti kept clucking his horses so that he would arrive in time to imbibe a few drinks at Charlie's Place before the service started. After all, this was his first venture in the solemn business of driving a hearse, and one needed to be fortified for so macabre a task. When he arrived in Chippewa at 8:00 A.M. the horses were steaming from their fast trip. He tied them in the alley in back of Charlie's Place. Charlie was not down yet, but one of his Finnish bartenders was on duty.

"Hello," Matti said. "Gimme big beer an' two double s'ots Ol' Cordvood!" He shivered with mingled cold and anticipation. "S's pretty col' morning dis morning."

"But I guessing not for long," Charlie's bartender cynically remarked, setting up the drinks on the bar.

"Ah!" Matti said, unbuttoning his burberry. "Gimme vun more double s'ots. Please omit beer, please."

"Say!" Charlie's bartender suddenly remembered. "Danny 'Ginnis an' dem crazy Hollow boys vere in las' night for dat big celebrations today. Dey vant you to meet dem at Sippywa House ven you t'rough 'rive dat funerals."

"Wat celebrations?" Matti asked.

"Vy, St. Patrick's Day! Din't you know it vere St. Patrick's Day? Wat for you vearing green neckties den for?"

"Oh," Matti muttered uncertainly, gulping down his drink. "St. Paddy's Day? St. Paddy— Who da hell is dat St. Paddy?"

He hurried out and untied his horses and raced over to the Chippewa House. Mrs. Smedburg stood blinking behind the lobby desk. She shook her head.

"Dannay tole me to tole you he an' da boys vould be vaiting for you at Andy Bjurman's saloon over py the depot," she told anxious Matti.

"Dank you, please." Matti left the hotel and raced his team over to Andy Bjurman's saloon. He dearly loved to be with his good friends from Hungry Hollow. But where could he tie his horses? "Oh, dere's good place!" he exclaimed, spying the L.S. & C. local passenger train, which was drawn up at the depot, the rear platform of the last coach extending halfway across the First Street crossing.

Little Matti hastily tied his perspiring horses, Fred and Ensio, to the rear platform of the passenger train. He'd just leave them there a second while he ran in to explain to the boys that he had to hurry over for the funeral. Yes, he certainly wouldn't want to offend his good pals. "Dere!" He finished tying the horses and hurried happily into the side door of Andy Bjurman's saloon. He peered through the sooty, grimy window of the door. Ah, there they were! He could hear old Danny singing as he opened the door.

"Hello, Matti!" "Well, it's our li'l ol' Matti hisself!" "Do you wanna sell that overcoat!" "Begorra an' hivinly days, if it ain't Matti O'Hunginen wit' the green necktie!" "Have a drink, Matti!" "Have you bin to Iceland wit' a load of snakes, man?"

Yes, these were his loyal, jolly friends from Hungry Hollow—Danny, Buller, and all the boys—who had taken him in and given him refuge and solace so many times when obtuse Impi, his "ol' voman," failed to understand his varying moods. But there was one thing Matti could not fathom, something which sorely perplexed him. Why were Danny and the boys all wearing green: green neckties or shamrocks or sprigs of trailing ground pine? And who was this mysterious St. Paddy? He drew Danny aside and confidentially asked him all about it.

"What!" Danny roared, in the full flush of his two-day siege with Old Cordwood. "You mean you ain't never heard tell of St. Patrick!" Matti hung his head in shame. Danny relented. "Why, Matti," Danny patiently explained. "St. Patrick is the patron saint of Ireland. Every year on March seventeenth—Finns an' everybody's an Irishman fer the day—wearin' o' the green an' celebratin' the gran' an' glorious occasion!"

"Wat for?" Matti asked sheepishly.

"What fer?" Danny repeated, pondering. "What fer? Oh! Why, sure, Mike—because he chased all the goddam snakes out of Ireland!" Danny was incredulous. "You don't mean, Matti, that in the ol' country you ain't got no honest-to-god saints! You dassen't tell me that! Ain't they got no patron saint in Finland? Ain't they, Matti?"

The honor of Finland was at stake. Matti opened the throat of his burberry. He wanted air to make a statement and better to expose his accidentally appropriate green necktie. He threw back his head, his Adam's apple bobbing excitedly. "Oh, yes," he modestly admitted, nodding his head. "Finnish peoples dey got dat big-s'ot saint, too."

"What's he called?" Danny inquired. If there were any more patron saints lurking in the offing to be celebrated, Danny certainly didn't want to miss any of them. "What's his name?"

"He's name is called dat St. Heikki," Matti replied proudly. "But he never s'ase snake." Matti shook his head. "No, never, *never* s'ase snake." Matti was firm on that point.

"What'n hell did he chase?" Danny demanded.

"Hm . . . He s'ase bear. Vun day dat St. Heikki he see bear, he s'ase bear, he kill bear, he eat bear, he eat hair, he eat ears, he eat tail, he eat nass, he eat ever'tings—no salts an' peppers! Dat's to be St. Heikki! He's da bucko!"

"Well I'm a goddam sidehill gouger!" Danny

roared. "Drinks fer the house! Make her snappy, Andy! We gotta hurry over an' watch Matti drive fer Shamus O'Rourke's funeral."

"Vere you attendin' da funeral service, Dannay?" Andy Bjurman respectfully inquired, making conversation as he grabbed up a bottle of Old Cordwood.

Danny glared at poor unsuspecting Andy. Had he forgotten that Shamus O'Rourke and Danny were bitter enemies ever since the deceased, a former saloon-keeper, had tossed Danny from his place of business with the timely aid of two bartenders, some forty-odd years before? Attending his funeral, indeed!

"No, I ain't," Danny replied sharply. "When I hates a man, I hates his corpse! But I'm sure goin' over to make certain Matti hauls the remains away." It was a fine distinction.

Just then a whistle tooted, a bell rang, and the L.S. & C. local coughed and slowly chugged away from the Chippewa depot. Danny glanced at Matti. "My Gawd, Matti, what's the matter! Your face is gone most as green as your bloody necktie!"

Matti's Adam's apple was bobbing like a trip hammer. He staggered to the side door and tragically pointed out the window and down the tracks. Danny and the boys barely caught a last glimpse of Matti's fleeing horses in the wake of the train as the strange procession disappeared around the slow curve by the warehouses just east of the Chippewa Fuel Company. Horrified Matti's words were wrenched from him in dry sobs. "Matti tie horses for train—train go—horses go—now Matti go!" he moaned. He then abruptly turned and charged out the door and down the tracks, his green necktie and the tails of his burberry pointing out straight behind him.

Danny quickly sprang into the breach. "Boys, we

gotta help pore ol' Matti save his horses! We gotta make sure he buries ol' Flannel Mouth O'Rourke this mornin'!" He leapt to the door and held it open, waving the rescue squad on its way. "C'mon, boys! Step lively, now! We gotta help li'l ol' Matti!"

Led by eager Buller, the boys piled pell-mell out of Andy's side door and took up the wild chase to help their friend. Danny then quietly shut the door, stepped nimbly over to the bar, said a brief "Skoal" to Andy, and deftly drained all of the remaining drinks. "Ah!" he said, drying his mustaches and winking at Andy. Then he turned wordlessly and rushed from the place to join the mad cavalcade. He'd personally see to it that old Shamus O'Rourke was buried on schedule.

Danny overtook and passed Buller and the boys just opposite the old gashouse. "Good morning, boys!" he shouted amiably as he sped past them, his legs working like twin pistons. Plunging Buller could only wildly roll the distended whites of his eyes as he lumbered onward, purple from his vast efforts. Danny overhauled Matti just beyond Patridge Creek. "Your coat's unbuttoned, Matti!" he chirped. The two ran a dead heat for fifty paces and then Danny sighted the horses and streaked into the lead.

Since they were tied to it, when the L.S. & C. passenger train slowly drew away from the Chippewa depot, Matti's horses reluctantly deemed it expedient to tag along. The result was not fortunate. This is not to intimate that the L.S. & C. local could outrun Matti's horses. There is no occasion to defame Matti's horses like that. But it was the end of winter, and the pocked roadbed was icy and uneven, and the environment was somewhat strange even for Matti's horses.

Just west of the Goose Lake bend, nearly half a mile outside Chippewa, Matti's Fred horse stumbled over a spur switch and suddenly found himself sitting up in Matti's long sleigh, harness and all, leaving his teammate, Ensio, to carry on alone as best he could. The novelty of the situation suddenly palled on Ensio, a proud animal who was not used to following trains alone. Ensio rebelled, skidding to an abrupt stop. The L.S. & C. was equal to the occasion. The hempen tie rope stretched, strained, and finally parted. As though to celebrate its sudden sense of release, the L.S. & C. tooted and went happily on its way—seeming to gain speed, in fact—none the wiser that it had hauled two "deadheads" for nearly a mile.

As Danny rounded the bend and spied the forlorn team he shouted "Whoa, there!" and let out a final burst of speed. "Steady there, Ensio! Steady boy," Danny spoke soothingly, coming up to the team and patting the perspiring lead horse to comfort him until the others arrived. In a few seconds winded Matti hove into view and tearfully joined him. "Oh, my poor horses—heh, heh, heh—oh, my poor horses—heh, heh, heh—Matti never never going touch nudder drop booze!"

When the boys arrived, Danny directed purple Buller to assist Fred horse down from the sleigh.

"Easy there, Fred! Easy, boy," Buller puffed as he mightily braced himself and eased the squatting horse off his haunches and down onto his quivering legs. "There!" Buller staggered over to the sled and fell into it, lying there heaving and blowing and gasping like a winded whale.

Matti threw both his arms around his horses and drew their heads down against his flapping burberry. "Oh, 'Reddy— Oh, Ensio! Never, never 'gain vill Matti tie you up for godtam choo-choo 'rain!"

Matti's desperate embalmer and the numbed and half-frozen pallbearers were waiting dully at the curb before St. Xavier's church as Matti slithered the sleigh-hearse around the corner of Magnetic Street into Main. He was only an hour and forty-five minutes late. After such a harrowing experience, he and the boys had just had to stop at Andy's and have a few more double shots of Old Cordwood. Danny and the boys had been simply grand. They had hurriedly gotten the body into the hearse from the deserted chapel below Big Annie's. Buller had had to be restrained from doing it all alone.

"Whoa!" Matti shouted, driving up before the church. The perspiration rose from the tired horses like smoke from the L.S. & C. local passenger loco-motive.

"Yep, yep. They was both steamin' like a baker's arm," was the way Danny explained it later over in Charlie's Place.

"Back the hearse into the curb so's we kin git at the body," the harried embalmer hissed at Matti.

"O.K., O.K.," Matti answered placidly. "Hold you horses." Rising to the occasion, he briskly wheeled the horses out on the street, profanely shouting orders at them. "Giddyap, 'Reddy an' Ensio! Whoa, you son-a-bits! Back up, now, li'l bit. Easy! Whoa!" Matti leaned around and brightly inquired, "How's dat, Mister buryman?"

The hearse was backed in at a forty-five degree angle to the curb. "You got 'er in crooked—can't you see! Reef 'em out an' try 'er again!" the embalmer whispered icily through his teeth.

Matti was growing nettled. He tried her again, shouting and sawing at his team, but this time he wound up angled out just as bad on the other side. He sat staring straight ahead, stolidly awaiting developments. "Try her again, you Finlander fathead!" hissed the voice from the rear.

Something snapped inside Matti. After all, he was a United States citizen and a voter and he paid his taxes. Who was this Irisher who worshiped St. Paddy —the patron saint who merely chased snakes? Who was he to be ordering little Matti Hunginen around this way? Matti leaned over the edge of the hearse and leered back at the ecstatic embalmer and the numbed pallbearers. He cleared his throat. Enough of this buffoonery.

"Take da son-a-bits oudt!" he ordered gutturally.

9

D. McGINNIS: GUIDE

During the long winter nights of Danny's conversion the boys had pondered various ways to make enough money out at the Hollow so that they might avoid going into Chippewa quite so often. It had gradually become impressed upon their collective consciousness that Trouble was all that seemed to follow in the wake of their visits to the bright lights.

It did not seem to matter how many of the boys went to town. If but one of them made the trek it was usually just a question of time before the others had to follow him in to bail him out—or perhaps to discover that he was already nestling down in the county jail at Iron Bay. And when they all went in, that generally meant a riotous two or three days, with the boys finally straggling back to camp with advanced cases of the trembles. And worst of all, Danny's buckskin poke usually emerged from these pilgrimages as flat as the belly of a cub bear in the spring.

The solution, the great vision, came one windy March evening. Danny was engaged in bottling home-brew and Buller was darning some yawning woolen socks. Swan and Taconite had retired early, while Timmy was seated at the oilcloth table, poring over a dog-eared copy of the *American Sportsman*. Timmy looked over at busy Danny, who was starting to siphon a new crock of beer, his cheeks sunken like those of a victim of pellagra.

"I see by an ad here, Dan," Timmy said, "where some fellas down in Wisconsin git eight bucks a day for boardin' an' guidin' *bass* fishermen!" He shook his head over the wonder of it all. "Jest imagine," he snorted, "payin' that dough to fish them bloody scrubs! An' here we got a river outside our door jest jumpin' an' crawlin' with beautiful rainbow." Timmy wet his finger and prepared to turn the page.

Danny still had the siphon hose in his mouth, his cheeks bulging and pouched with new beer. He shook his head at Timmy, *no no*, waving his free hand like a frantic brakeman. "Pah!" he said, pulling the hose from his mouth and swallowing the bitter new beer. Buller held his darning needle poised in mid air.

"Look!" Danny exclaimed, "lemme see that there ad!" The old man's eyes were dancing with excitement. His voice grew hoarse. "Look, Timmy, boys—if them fellas down in Wisconsin kin git paid fer lettin' them city dudes ketch those grubby tourist fish—why in hell can't we do the same bloody thing with our own beautiful rainbows down in the river."

Inspired Danny and Timmy worked far into the night on their roseate plans to make Hungry Hollow a mecca for tired city dwellers. They would run the first ad in a Chicago newspaper. Every small town in America has its "big town," and Chicago was Chippewa's. Anyway, Timmy had a cousin that had married a girl whose brother was a pressman on one of the big Chicago sheets.

It was easy. When the first batch of tourists arrived, Timmy and the boys would go and stay at Matti's farm. It was deemed fitting that Danny should act as official host and guide at the debut. Then with the money they made on their first venture they could build a nice new cabin to house future tourists, perhaps on the birch ridge behind the camp. After that they could all pitch in and entertain.

"How much'll we charge 'em?" Timmy asked, knitting his brows and biting his pencil over the ad he was composing.

Danny pursed his lips and blinked his eyes. "Hm," he said. "Well, of course they're gonna have to pay a hull lot more fare gittin' 'way up here. Le's see— Maybe we ought to charge 'em half price, say four bucks a head for food an' lodgin'."

"Four bucks it is," Timmy said, filling in this item and proudly presenting the finished ad to Danny with a secretarial flourish. Danny adjusted his ten-cent-store glasses and cleared his throat and read the ad aloud to Timmy by the lamplight.

NOTICE

I got rainbow trout up here at Hungry Hollow as big as sleigh dogs. You capture 'em and I'll cook 'em. $4 per day per head for food and lodging. Expert guide free. Write me c/o Charlie's Place, Chippewa, Michigan.

Resp.

D. McGinnis, prop.

Danny blinked at Timmy with shining eyes. "Boy," he breathed rapturously, "that there's so purty that—

that I'm all kinda swole up inside." Danny blissfully closed his eyes and shook his head. "Timmy, you're a genius!"

It was early in May and the haunting, delicate scent of the trailing arbutus hung in the clear spring air. Old Danny walked into Chippewa to meet the first contingent of city visitors. Matti Hunginen had brought the magic letter out from Charlie's the week before. One of Makela the Finn's logging trucks picked up Danny near the bridge over Barnhardt Creek, so he got into town just at the dusk of the beautiful May evening. This gave him several additional hours to celebrate undisturbed before the party of Chicago fishermen he was to guide would arrive on the L. S. & C. to spend the week end. Timmy's ad had worked like a dream.

Following the instructions in the letter from Dr. George, one of the city anglers, old Dan did not go to Charlie's Place or any of his usual haunts. Instead he went to await their arrival in the rarified atmosphere of the new Cliff Dwellers Inn. This red-brick colonial hotel—conceived by an architect from Boston, transplanted elms and all—looked rather incongruous in the afterglow, pitched on a glacial side hill of the mining town of Chippewa. It was the favorite haunt of the mining officials and their wives.

Dan's letter didn't say that he had to wait in the hotel bar, but it neglected to state that he shouldn't, either. And Danny always had a fine instinct for the best place to wait. Entering the bar he was momentarily bemused by the colorful Welsh and Old English hunting and drinking scenes which adorned the walls. The resourceful Boston architect was not going to let any indigenous scenes of logging and iron-mining corrupt his faery brain child. "Well, I'm damned if one of 'em ain't pinchin' her butt," Danny muttered, staring at a heckled barmaid painted on the wall. "I wouldn't mind it meself!"

He discovered the glittering new un-Welshian neon and chromium bar, where he eased his packsack under an unemployed pinball machine. Eyebrows and weedy mustache bobbing in synchronized anticipation, Danny loudly ordered a double shot of pile run whisky. There was a pause in the bar's occupation, known as the drinking hour. "I sed I wanted a double shot of pile run!" Danny repeated, his mustaches bristling dangerously.

The chipper young bartender, just fresh from Duluth, superciliously eyed Dan's aromatic red plaid hunting jumper and his "high water" stag pants and muddy rubber boots. "What do you prefer for a mix, sir?" He asked, disdainfully wrinkling his nose. He was sure it was not arbutus he was smelling. Danny stared at him. "Whaddya want for a wash?" the bartender repeated, wearily sinking to the argot of the proletariat.

"Gin!" Danny shot back, whereupon the cocktail-hour stragglers giggled and roared and carelessly flung down their dry Martinis. Spring was in the air.

At midnight old Danny betook himself and his packsack outside for a little fresh air. And, oh yes, to meet his Chicago fishermen. In the meantime he had achieved that state of gentle glow sometimes known as drunk to advanced students of semantics. But Danny did not get to meet the train. The unmet Chicago fishermen arrived at the hotel just in time to discover their official guide all tangled up in the hotel's new terraced rock garden, from which the wiry little Cornish gardener was vainly trying to dislodge him.

" 'Ere, damme, man, you're a-tramplin' all hover my

crocus 'n' tulip beds, you are! Come aout of there!"
Cooky the gardener shrilled.

"Is zat so, me lad? An' me preferrin' peonies—
whersh the bloody peonies?" Danny answered, charging like a bewildered gnu through a trellis designed
for sweet peas, thence over the steep edge of the rock
garden, thence to the sidewalk below, where he and
his packsack lay with a dignity befitting their years—
quite sodden and quite still.

"Oo, oo, oo— 'e 'urted my flawers, 'e did," wailed
old Cooky, doing a skinny dance of anger at midnight
in the spring.

The next morning the little old Ford and trailer
rented from Burke's livery stable rumbled their thun-
der over the loose planking of the bridge at Barnhardt
Creek, noisily puffing and dragging the four Chicago
fishermen and old Dan up to Hungry Hollow—together with the mountain of city fishing tackle on the
trailer behind. Old Dan sat wedged in the back seat,
quietly sipping his stained mustache, occasionally gingerly feeling his side, tapping the armor of Dr.
George's adhesive tape around his three freshly cracked
ribs.

"How do you feel now, Dan?" asked Raymond, the
driver, one of the Chicago fishermen, as they were
passing Matti Hunginen's farm. Lo! Matti and Buller
and Taconite were perched on the wooden entrance
gate, grinning broadly. "Mornin', gentlemen," Danny
said, bowing and saluting.

"I said, how are you feeling?" Raymond repeated as
they drove on.

Dan removed his hat and massaged his bald head
thoughtfully. The question deserved sober deliberation.
His little gray eyes twinkled. He sat up, suddenly all
pert and bright. "Me, I feel like another drink."

"What, before noon?" Raymond said, aghast.

At the top of the long muddy pull out of the Barnhardt valley, before the winding two-rut road began
its long descent into the drainage area of the Big
Dead River, worried Raymond stopped the car. He
looked at his watch. It was still forenoon.

"What's the use? Give him a drink, Doc," Raymond
said with a little sigh.

Dr. George sighed too, and passed back a quart of
city whisky. "Skoal!" Dan said, expertly flipping up
his mustache with one hand and raising the bottle with
the other. He played a long solo on the bottle—"ah"—
and ran his tongue over his mustache, then quickly
pulled out each end of his mustache with his free hand,
rubbing the hand on his jumper sleeve. Danny was
nothing if not neat.

"You boys havin' a snort too?" he said, conscience-
stricken at last. He made as though to surrender the
bottle. All of them hastily shook their heads *no*.

"Dan," Raymond said wearily, like a teacher to a
slow but lovable pupil, "we came north over four hundred miles to get some of those big rainbow trout you
mentioned in that intriguing ad of yours. We're in
training for that. Fishing before drinking, see?"

"Sure, sure—sure thing," Danny agreed. "Jes'
thought you might, lads. Mind if I have a wee drop
more?"

"And it would be kind of nice, Dan, being our guide
and all," Carl, the big fellow, added wistfully, "if you'd
stay sober long enough—just long enough to kind of
point out the river to us."

But Danny's bald head had sagged to his chest in
noisy lip-puttering slumber as the Ford threaded its
way down through the endless spruce and jack pine
cuttings of Makela the Finn. Gradually the descent
became steeper, the fishermen passed the last of the

cuttings, and in the distance loomed the silent, glacier-scarred mountains of the Mulligan Range, their sentinel Norway pines tall and still in the glittering May sunshine.

Danny woke up for another drink as they clattered over the rushing black waters of Mulligan Creek, just above where it joined the Big Dead. "In less'n five minutes we'll be there, lads," he said quietly, going back to sleep.

The little Ford snorted up the steep sand hill out of the Mulligan valley. There was a brief glimpse of the gleaming rocky waters of the Big Dead. A mile north stretched the broad plateau before Hungry Hollow, the stumps of the once mighty white pine rising out of the sweet fern and huckleberry bushes like gravestones in an abandoned graveyard. At the beginning of the Silver Lake hardwood the little car ground to a shuddering stop. The city dwellers had arrived at Hungry Hollow.

"Moo!" Bessie called from her woodshed.

"Here we are, lads," Dan said, suddenly awake, leaping nimbly from the car, taking a quick dogtrot around the car to limber up his bones including his three cracked ribs.

Crafty Dan tried to beguile the fishermen into a card game—with benefit of bottle. "You got all week end to fish," he told them. "Way too bright right now." He squinted professionally at the sun. But with a fanatical gleam in their eyes the zealous fishermen at once began tearing at mounds of waders and aluminum rod cases. Would their guide kindly show them the trail to the river? *They* were going fishing.

After a quick lunch, during which the city fishermen got into their uniforms and argued whether or not to start fishing dry or wet fly, it was decided to start wet from the pool below the camp and work down river. First there was the endless business of dressing their tapered fly lines. Dan was able to spear three secret drinks during these mighty preparations.

At length they were ready to leave the camp to walk down to the pool. Raymond asked Dan if he was going to fish. Flushed Danny was sitting on the saw-buck, taking in the proceedings, industriously plucking a hair from his nose.

"Sure, sure lads. I'll fish a bit after you get started. 'Member, I'm the guide—payin' gents first."

"But where's your rod—your waders and all?" Carl asked.

Danny walked over to the side of the camp and took down a battered fly rod, all set up, which was resting on two rusty nails in the logs under the eaves. Each joint was a mass of adhesive tape, like Danny's ribs, the cracked old line already threaded. On the business end was tied a scant two feet of frayed gut leader, all spiraled and curled like a pig's tail or a tired bedspring. On the end of this chunk of leader was tied a sort of super-fly that was faintly reminiscent of an old red feather duster, the mighty hook itself protruding from the surrounding underbrush like half of a rusty ice tong.

"Won this in a raffle durin' the Fireman's tournament in Chippewa six—no seventeen years ago—fly 'n' all," Dan said, proudly fondling his little pet.

The Chicago fishermen looked at each other and then charitably averted their eyes. What had they gotten into? Led by Old Danny, their expert guide, who fished without waders or landing net, they trudged down the trail to the Big Dead pool.

"That's it," Dan said, elaborately pointing out the

pool. "That there's where you start." The guide was beginning to feel his responsibilities.

A faint hint of morning mist still lingered over the pool, which churned restlessly in the shadows, hissing and boiling like some giant witch's cauldron. The four fishermen looked like a quartet of deep-sea divers as they slid and clambered down to the pool, clad in their manifold waders, jackets, bibs, landing nets, dangling scissors, gadgets, and goggles, all the while delicately holding their glistening fly rods like four fairy godfathers at a convention of wand wavers. "A hull damn sports goods store on the march," Danny muttered to himself, shaking his head. He sat on a rock above them, in the warm sun, leisurely gnawing on a chew of plug, scratching his head, occasionally tenderly feeling his ribs.

Raymond was the first to complete the elaborate ritual of selecting and tying a fly on his long tapered leader. He made a few false casts, feeding out line, and finally placed a graceful thistle cast into the very heart of the pool. There was a silvery flash, the line drew taut for an instant, then suddenly went limp.

"Whoopee!" shouted Raymond. "Cleaned out on my first cast! *Whoopee!*"

"Hm," Danny said to himself, squinting one eye. "Guess they're on the prod."

He sat quietly spitting tobacco juice at a migrating beetle as the Chicago fishermen got under way. Two of them took fair brook trout on their first few casts. But as Dan watched them fish out of the pool and around the first bend and out of sight, no more big rainbow struck.

"Too much equipment, too much hurry," he observed sorrowfully to the pool as the fishermen moved out of sight. He rose, sighted, spat and washed out a colony

of ants. Shifting his cud he reached in his jumper and
fished out a quart of purloined Chicago whisky and
played another long solo to the sun. He hid the bottle
under a young spruce, then leisurely took himself and
his rod down to the pool. He sat on the bank and
watched the water, working his cud. He soaked the
leader in the water at his feet, slowly feeding out his
cracked fly line.

There were no fish rising. Over his shoulder Danny
sighted the sun. It was about to disappear behind a
fleecy cloud. He reached into his jumper and pulled
out a slice of Swan's freshly baked bread. Breaking off
a small piece, he tossed it into the pool. There was a
quick, silvery flash. "Hm." Dan casually flipped his
bedspring fly into the pool at this spot. *"Clap!"* like an
explosion, and he was on to a beauty. He dropped his
rod, calmly pulled in the threshing fish hand over hand,
unhooked him, and dropped him into the game bag of
his jumper. Again he cast his bread upon the waters.
And again not in vain. He had three rainbow, all over
two pounds, before the sun came from behind the cloud.

"Guess I'll have me a little drink and meander downstream," Danny said. "Guess the big ones ain't here
today. Yep, yep! Guess I'll have me another bloody
drink—mebbe two."

Meanwhile the city fishermen worked downstream,
fishing with the easy precision and grace of finished ex-
perts. They'd waited all winter for this moment. The
firm graveled bottom, rarely over waist-deep, made
ideal wading. The air sang and whined with the whish
of their long, beautiful casts. Not a single pocket or
riffle did they miss. Once the short fat one, Hank, got
a boiling rise from a big one but missed the strike.
They took several more decent brook trout and quite
a few youngsters, all of which they carefully returned

to the water. For they were after the big rainbow. But the big rainbow were not after them.

A half mile or so below the pool they had a smoke and held a council. Hank and big Carl decided to shore-walk downstream a mile and work back, fishing dry. Raymond and Dr. George continued to work carefully down the broad river, fishing every possible place that could hide a trout, continually changing flies, now tying on a monkeytail creation of Dr. George's, then perhaps a little polar bear number of Hank's. Finally they rounded a broad bend where they could see the other two working up toward them. Still the big rainbow continued to ignore their best offerings.

The four met again on a little gravel-bar island in midstream, under the shade of a great leaning spruce which stood swaying precariously on the undercut east bank. They were all a little downcast.

Carl said, "If it weren't for those two big rises we had, I'd say there weren't any rainbow in this damn river. Looks like we came on a wild-goose chase. I suppose our guzzling old guide is safely in bed by now."

"Maybe we had better fish upstream and try the pool again," Raymond ventured, remembering his first big strike.

Dr. George thought old Dan might be able to show them a woods short cut to farther downstream. "If he's still sober enough to walk, that is. I wonder what the old goat is up to now—"

The answer came abruptly. "Hallo-o-o," they heard, and all of them wheeled and looked upstream. Danny was rounding the far bend, in the middle of the river, leaping through the water as though he had sat on a porcupine, his old fly rod bent double before him like a graduation hoop. He was being towed, hauled, and tugged by the grandfather of all rainbows, the dorsal fin and snout of which, with its feather-duster fly, occasionally showed above water about twenty feet ahead of Dan, like a spaniel retrieving a waterfowl.

Down, down came this threshing, splashing apparition toward the transfixed Chicago fishermen, standing about drugged and open-mouthed on their gravel bar. Danny, his skinny shanks working like pistons, looked as though he were tied to a runaway bloodhound. "Loo'gout—loo' gout!" he shouted, but the fishermen were helpless. "I knowed it—I knowed he was in here. *Loo'gout—here I come!*" he shrilled.

Dan's leader broke—*spung*—just as the huge fish, in the blind fury of his run, charged up onto the gravel bar clear out of the water and lay at the Chicago fishermen's feet, puffing like the winner of a fat man's race.

"Grab 'im!" Danny cackled in cold horror, but the enchanted fishermen were beyond all movement. The giant fish made a mighty flop just as shouting old Danny dove through the air, making a superb flying tackle and landing on top of Granpaw—"whoosh!" The two of them lay there, both very wet and both very still.

It took three drinks from Dr. George's first-aid flask to bring old Dan around. "Who hit me?" Danny said, slowly sitting up. The game bag of his jumper had come open, scattering rainbow trout everywhere. He clutched his side—the other side. "Oo—oo—gimme another swaller of that there. I can't breathe without'n I have another swaller."

Dr. George carefully fed old Dan another drink and tenderly felt his side. He spoke softly. "I guess, Danny—I guess maybe you cracked three or four more ribs on the other side."

Danny sat up on the gravel bar, blinking, gulping, looking at all the fish lying around him. But mostly he looked at his big fish, which lay glistening in the light like a big wet silver fox—stone dead. Then he looked up at the four Chicago fishermen. He smiled at them, and slowly winked.

"It kinda looks, lads, like pretty soon the ol' man is gonna run out a ribs. Yep, yep! It kinda looks like mebbe we'd ought to go back to camp and kinda celebrate like. I'll fry up the bloody fish. What do you say, lads?"

The four wan fishermen looked at each other and nodded. Without a word they gently gathered up Danny and his rainbow trout—including Granpaw—and slowly splashed upstream in the dappled sunlight. Old Danny, full of visions of the big time ahead, managed to sing a quavering little song. It was one of his favorite ditties.

> *"Oh when I'm dead 'n' in my grave,*
> *No more whisky will I crave,*
> *On my tombstone let this be wrote*
> *'Ten thousand quarts run down his throat!' "*

The Chicago fishermen woke up the next morning throbbing of pulse and coated of tongue, blindly groping for the water pail. But aching Danny soon had them relaxed and smiling with a round of Highland Flings. The Highland Fling was simplicity itself. Danny carefully explained it to the fishermen: All one needed was a "tripler" of Hungry Hollow moonshine, a dash of lemon juice, a little sugar, and some boiling hot water. "You dassen't put too much water!" he warned, expertly flipping over a batch of buckwheat cakes on the smoky griddle. "Yep, yep. Never too much water."

After breakfast he presented his guests with some

of Timmy's big bucktail flies ("big flies fer big fish")
and lectured them for ten minutes on the need for cau-
tion and stillness in stalking the big ones. "Easy does
it, lads." Walking like an aging Junker general in
his corset of adhesive tape, Danny led them down to
the pool where he initiated them into the mysteries of
the trick with the bread. "Git ready, now, one of you,"
he said, tossing out a morsel of bread. It did not fail.
There was the boil, the cast, the strike—and grinning
Doctor George was snug on to a tail-standing beauty.

"Good luck, boys," Danny said, leaving them there
still fighting the fish. "Think I'll stick aroun' camp an'
curry Bessie today. Mebbe take a snooze, too." He
smiled a trifle wanly. "You see, about all I got left to
break is the bones in my goddam head. Yep, yep . . ."

The Chicago fishermen had a good day. Their creels
were bulging with lovely rainbows. None of them was
as big as Granpaw, of course. That night they were ex-
ultant. There just had to be another celebration. The
next morning they were up and clamoring for their
Highland Flings. And so it went.

They overstayed their leave two days, and when
they left they proudly presented Danny with a brand
new fly rod and tapered line. They also insisted on paying double for their keep. In addition, they made glowing plans to return in November for the deer-hunting
season. They were completely captivated with Hungry
Hollow.

"Good-by, Danny," they called, waving from the
little Ford as they started away. "Take care of yourself, old man. See you in the fall."

"Yep, yep," Danny said from the camp doorway,
briefly saluting them with two bent fingers.

Buller and the boys rushed into camp a few hours
later to conduct the audit. Muttering Danny was seated

at the oilcloth table, absorbed, scratching his head, still counting out the money into neat little piles, "Four gents fer five days at eight bucks a head makes—le's see—a hunnert an' sixty dollars. Yep, yep. It comes out exac' ag'in. Well I'm a goddam bowlegged tadpole! Jest stayin' to home an' gittin' drunk—an' mind, gittin' bloody well paid for it." Danny looked up. "Oh, hello, boys. Look, Buller, fetch a quart of Chicago hooch hid in one of Timmy's hip boots there hangin' on the wall. We gotta celebrate. My Gawd, we made a fortune! We're rich, *we're rich!*"

10

AND THEN THE BALLOON
WENT UP

Chubby Miller's All-American Menagerie and Circus
came to Chippewa in July. Despite its grandiose name,
the circus was a modest one, consisting largely of
Chubby Miller himself, several assorted Mrs. Chubby
Millers, three despondent clowns, two camels, a drop-
sical elephant, a zebra, and one tired lion. There was
also a patriotic trained seal that, in consideration of a
sufficient quantity of herring, could be persuaded to flip
around reluctantly and toot "America" on a series of
brass horns. But by all odds the circus' main attraction
—"stupendous, thrilling, death-defying"—was Little
Eva, "The Queen of the Skies," who, clad only in
pink tights, would ascend in a balloon over Chippewa
Thursday evening promptly at 7:00 P.M., weather permitting—"thence to be whisked whither the fugitive
winds listeth," the *Hematite Weekly* and the bill-
boards poetically announced.

The advent of circuses and carnivals to Chippewa

was generally greeted with dismay by the officials of the Chippewa Ore Company. They knew from long experience that a paperweight could scarcely be manufactured from the iron ore that was mined in Chippewa when a circus or carnival came to town. The miners simply wouldn't work. However, the mining officials didn't feel quite so bad over Chubby's circus because it was billed to remain for but a one-day stand—a Thursday. Yes, they righteously concluded, an occasional day off for the miners was really a good thing— especially when the Chippewa Ore Company didn't have to pay for it.

Of course Danny and the boys had to attend the circus. But Danny was firm on one point. This time they were going to try a noble experiment: they were going into Chippewa and see the circus all right, but on this trip they were going to avoid religiously all saloons and groggeries, view the circus and balloon ascension like dignified gentlemen, and return promptly to Hungry Hollow that same night, strictly sober and with money left in Danny's buckskin wallet. Yes, Thursday was far too early to commence any week end, and much too hard on the battered wallet. But they just had to see beautiful Little Eva go up in the balloon.

It was not that Danny and the people of Chippewa hadn't seen a balloon ascension before. They had, in fact, seen many. But all previous balloon risings had been made by hairy, grinning, cocky, muscle-bound males, curiously revolting fellows whose early and permanent disappearance skyward or elsewhere one could contemplate without a pang.

Not counting the swarm of small boys, there must have been nearly two thousand people milling around the main tent when Danny and the boys arrived in town late that afternoon. Most of them were iron miners.

Being without man power, every mine in town had sensibly shut down for the day. The bulk of the crowd was gathered around the balloon itself, which was held to the ground by ropes attached to sandbags, the huge bag itself being only partially filled with air. A couple of disconsolate circus attendants were throwing wood on the fire that made the hot air to fill the balloon. The vast bag swayed and rocked and bellied in the stiff west wind like a huge sausage, tugging and straining at the sandbags which held it to the ground.

Danny and Buller and the boys worked their way into the crowd until they gained the edge of the platform upon which stood Chubby Miller and Little Eva herself, complete with pink tights. Chubby Miller was a rotund, slack-bellied little man, cut from the same pattern as W. C. Fields, even to the nasal, froggy voice and minute blue veins which channeled his bulbous nose. Eva was a curvacious blonde of indeterminate age who possessed fluttering eyelashes and the bluest, widest, most innocent eyes Danny had ever seen. He was immediately prostrated with adoration.

"Ain't she purty as an angel?" he breathed in Buller's ear. Buller nodded and moistened his pursed lips. His thoughts were not precisely celestial. "She'd make a dog break his chain," Buller whispered back.

Chubby was glibly exhorting the crowd. He consulted a large gold watch. "In just one hour, ladies and gentlemen, Little Eva here will leave the earth an' rise heavenward! Yessir, folks! Clingin' only to that fragile trapeze attached to the wicker basket of the balloon there, the little lady will soar amongst the clouds over your fair city, doin' amazin' tricks of acrobatics, even to hangin' by her shapely knees!" The men in the crowd studied Eva's shapely knees intently. Chubby turned to the circus touts who were firing the balloon. "How's the balloon comin', boys? Is she fillin' up so's Little Eva can take off before dark?" The two attendants shrugged noncommittally and one of them threw another slab of wood on the small fire.

In the meantime a small army of concessionaires swarmed upon the milling holiday crowd, doing a land-office business selling toy balloons, bamboo canes, feather ticklers, paper reptiles that uncoiled abruptly when you blew them, not to mention bags of confetti, trick hats, and assorted false noses rivaling even Chubby's. But the most popular item was autographed photographs of Little Eva clad in an extensive state of deshabille—a real bargain at "only a quarter of a silver dollar!" Danny contented himself with buying four, evidently bent upon viewing Little Eva from every point of the compass. Then there were hot dogs and hamburgers, of course, and vats full of pink lemonade, dripping ice-cream cones, popcorn, and a frothy-appearing pink confection that looked more like sea foam than candy and tasted like neither.

Promptly at 7:00 P. M. Chubby turned to Eva. "Little Eva," he declared, fixing her with a fat finger, "are you ready an' willin' to ascend into the ether waves over the fair city of Chippewa tonight?"

"I am," Little Eva replied in a small, piping voice.

"An', whereas, to wit, considerin' the hazardous nature of your enterprise, an' for other valuable consideration, do you agree to waive, release, and replevin the Walter C. Miller shows, its heirs and assigns, from any and all torts an' other liability in the sad event of your death or great bodily harm?" Chubby legalistically demanded.

"I do," Eva bravely replied, tremulously fluttering her eyelashes.

"Then prepare yourself to go aloft—and may the

Lord be with you!" Chubby grimly declared. Little
Eva was on her own.

Chubby briskly left the platform and held a whispered consultation with the balloon attendants. He
looked up at the sky and then studied the balloon. Before the watchful eyes of the crowd he took a tent
stake and judiciously poked the flabby sides of the half-
filled balloon. Chubby shook his head. He returned to
the platform and put his forefinger in his mouth and
then expertly held his finger up to the wind, like a Boy
Scout leader confirming the imminent approach of a
tornado. He again gravely shook his head and cleared
his throat.

"Ladies and gentlemen!" Chubby announced. "We
have bad news for you. We greatly regret that Little
Eva will be unable to take off tonight. Due to as how
the balloon is only half full of air an' won't be ready
before nightfall, we've reluctantly had to cancel the
great ascension." Chubby paused. There was a menac-
ing rumble of male voices. Chubby went on anxiously.
"What's more, men, they's a bad wind comin' from the
west, as you can plainly see, an' they tell me it's only
twelve-fifteen miles east of here to Lake Superior."
Chubby paused and then issued his challenge. "If
there's a single man in this here crowd what wants to
risk our Little Eva goin' to her watery grave tonight
in the dark an' icy waters of Lake Superior, let him
speak up now or forever hold his peace!" Eva blinked
her blue eyes through tremulous, downcast lashes. To
a man the crowd roared, "No, no, no!" Little Eva
must be spared.

Chubby then delivered the clincher. "However, since
Little Eva can't take off tonight, an' we realize the
keen disappointment that is yours, we've decided, at
great expense, to hold the entire show over for another

day. Little Eva will take off tomorrow night prompt at seven, rain or shine, wind or calm!" Chubby held up his hand to silence the approving cheer of the crowd. He lowered his voice and gave the assembled menfolk an amiable leer. "An' since Li'l Eva can't take off tonight in her balloon—ah—we've made special arrangements for her to—er—take off this an' take off that"—Chubby daintily plucked at his own clothing —"in a special stag performance immediately followin' the main show. Yessir, it's for men only! The attendants will now pass among you with tickets for Eva's special midnight performance. Just think, men, for only one silver dollar you can witness Little Eva here personally show you things what you never saw before! An' they tell me it's a-plenty. It's educational and inspirational! It's astronomical and anatomical! A hilook! Who'll be the first lucky gent to help little Eva here take off?"

"I'll take five tickets!" eager Danny spoke up, nervously fingering his buckskin poke.

What wonders Danny and the hundreds of other men saw at Little Eva's midnight show they later spoke not of. At any rate, Danny was so transported by the exhibition that he took the boys to Charlie's for a closing round of drinks. All resolutions were overboard. Then they went over to Big Annie's to pay a social call. Danny held the center of the kitchen floor, recounting to Annie the wondrous beauty and bravery of Little Eva, the Queen of the Skies. Big Annie listened to Danny's raptures in grave silence. When he had finished she snorted and tossed her head and led him into the pantry and closed the door.

"Lissen, Danny, I hates to see an ol' friend of mine make a complete fool of hisself," she whispered. "Last night I promised Chubby I wouldn't tell, but I'll tell

jest you in strick confidence—the plain truth is your
Little Eva there ain't never been higher in the air
than the observation platform at Niagara Falls."
Annie pondered. "Le's see, was it on her second or
third honeymoon? Hm . . . Yes, I guess it was her
third. Before she went with Chubby she was jest a leg-
show girl at the same carnival I used to travel with.
Of course she's considerable younger'n me. She jest
joined up with Chubby's show last month. 'Queen of
the Skies' my foot! Hangin' by her knees from a
balloon! The only place that baby-faced blonde could
hang by her knees from is the head of a walnut bed!"

Disillusioned, Danny leaned against the pantry wall
as Big Annie went on. "As fer that Chubby Miller
there, he's jest an ex-carnie himself, a cheap shill what
picked up this one-horse circus of his, balloon an' all,
in a crap game down in Florida las' winter. I heard
the whole story from a friend in the business. His
show's nothing but a clip carnival disguised as a circus.
He comes to town for one day an' stays on as long as
the crowd lasts. That ol' balloon bag of his is jest a
gag, a sucker's come-on to draw a crowd to work on.
It's never been higher offen the ground than this here
pantry ceiling since he won it las' winter like I told
you."

"But she's so purty—Little Eva, I mean, not the
goddam balloon. She—she's jest like an angel," Danny
murmured fatuously when Annie had concluded her
amazing revelation. "Can't you fix it up fer to intro-
duce her to me?"

"O.K., then," Annie snorted in disgust. "Have it
your own way. Like the fella said, there's no fool like
an ol' fool. But don't forget I warned you. Daniel,
you'll get into a basket of trouble with that dame sure's
you're a foot high!"

Again no ore was mined in Chippewa the next day. The circus was still in town. Friday was a still, windless day and that evening an even larger throng pressed around the balloon to watch the belated ascension of Eva. Around 6:00 P.M. Chubby Miller went into his act, consulted his gold watch, had Eva publicly absolve the Walter C. Miller shows from all liability, consulted the sleepy circus touts, judiciously poked the sides of the flabby balloon, held up his moistened finger to test the wind. He even added a barometer to the act. "Hm . . ." In the meantime the gleeful concessionaires busily ladled out their colorful gimcracks.

There was a bad moment when Chubby finally declared that the balloon would not go up; that the show would have to be held over for still another day. No, it wasn't the wind tonight, it was simply a lack of hot air. He was awfully afraid they'd sprung a leak in their balloon. He'd have his special imported balloon seamstress go over the bag tomorrow with a fine-tooth comb. And, oh yes, Little Eva would give a midnight performance for men only. "A hi-look!"

When Chubby finished his announcement there was an involuntary surge toward the platform and the balloon by the miners in the crowd. Here they'd lost two days' wages in the mines and still the bloody balloon hadn't gone up. One shouting miner waggishly suggested that Chubby simply talk into the balloon if it needed hot air. The tense situation was saved when the circus band suddenly appeared on the scene and struck up a tune. Little Eva went into a sinuous dance and held the thralled miners at bay. That night her midnight show was jammed.

Danny met Little Eva and Chubby later that night at an informal reception down at Big Annie's. To insure privacy Annie graciously barred the doors against the "riff and the raff," as she called them. Her graciousness was short-lived, however. She glowered jealously as she watched Danny extend himself to amuse Little Eva. Danny was in fine fettle. He sang songs to Eva, he told her droll stories, and he even did a lumberjack dance to the accompaniment of Annie's gramophone. Eva laughed gaily and fluttered her eyelashes. "Yep, yep, yep," Danny said, and launched into another story. When Chubby hilariously suggested that Danny join the show and travel with them, Annie excused herself and crept to her lonely bed and wept. Danny finally taxied Eva and Chubby back to the show grounds in Rocco Pantalone's old Cadillac. It was dawn.

The third day, Saturday, was another beautiful day, with just a slight east wind—perfect for ballooning— and the crowd gathered early. Especially the miners. They began appearing singly and in pairs as early as three o'clock. Chubby grew sore perplexed as he nervously peered out from the flaps of his office tent. Who were all these men soberly toting old railroad ties, empty wooden dynamite boxes, lengths of hematite-stained cedar lagging? What were they up to? The Lord save us, there came a man carrying an old wooden baby crib! What in the world were these yokels planning to do with all that wood? What in the world, indeed!

For some odd reason Chubby came to the platform at 6:00 P.M. flanked by a half-dozen odd circus roustabouts. The roustabouts proceeded to lean around nonchalantly on unemployed tent stakes, looking bored. Little Eva blinked her blue eyes even more tremulously as she surveyed the sea of grim male faces in front of her.

There were no smiles when Chubby went into his

familiar act. There was a stony silence when, accompanied by his six roustabouts, he retired from the platform to confer with the balloon attendants. He spent an unaccountably long time jabbing and poking at the flabby balloon and whispering to the attendants. In fact, he looked as though he were contemplating a sudden trip of his own. Finally he returned to the platform followed closely by his bodyguards. It was a pale and wan Chubby that finally faced the throng. He did not have to hold up his hand for silence as he gulped and wet his lips and launched into his familiar cancellation speech. It was one which the miners had now learned by heart.

"Unfortunately, ladies and gentlemen—" he began. Alas, he did not get any farther. A dozen miners leapt up on the platform, led by big Tom Trebilcock of the Cambria mine. The miners advanced slowly upon Chubby, carrying strange walking sticks consisting of assorted drill cores, coupling bolts, pick handles, and the like. After one appraising look the roustabouts silently melted from the platform. Chubby and Little Eva were left alone to face the delegation of determined miners.

Tom Trebilcock was the first to speak. "Mister Miller," he respectfully demanded, "didn't your circus play last week in Calumet, up on the copper range?"

"Wa-wa—what's it to you?" Chubby blustered. "Git offen this platform—I'll call an officer. Yass, we showed in Calumet."

"An' did Little Eva an' her balloon go up over Calumet?" the big miner pressed on.

"Er-ah—of course they did," Chubby sputtered. "I—I— Why, I'll call an officer—"

At this juncture a strange miner vaulted up on the platform. Tom Trebilcock turned to the newcomer.

"Tell the boys, Jack," Tom said. "Tell 'em what really happened up'n the copper country."

The newcomer faced the silent crowd. "Boys," he began quietly, "I'm Jack Beaufort, a copper miner from the Quincy Mine up at Calumet. Boys, as true as I'm standin' here"—Jack pointed at the sagging balloon—"that bloody balloon there never rose an inch offen the ground in Calumet! It happened there exactly same as it's happened here. We all lost three shifts at the mine—an' no balloon never went up. Boys," Jack concluded, "I'm afeared this hull bloomin' balloon business is a bloody fake!"

There was an angry rumble from the crowd as Tom Trebilcock turned to Little Eva. "I'm sorry, ma'am," he said, "but will you go git in the balloon nice an' quiet—or must we carry you there?"

Little Eva glanced at horrified Chubby and Chubby stared wildly back at Eva. Finally she courageously bowed her blond head and murmured, "I'll go." There was a prolonged cheer from the crowd, which neither heard nor heeded Chubby's wild "No, no!" as he rushed over to save Eva. The crowd howled and roared its approval when several miners roughly seized chattering Chubby and tied him to the bars of the near-by lion's cage. The lion frowned, wrinkled up his nose ("like a polecat eatin' bumblebees," Buller later declared), and retreated to the rear of his cage. Chubby's misery was complete.

Little Eva clung quietly to the ropes of her wicker basket. She maintained the calm of Joan of Arc at the stake as a hundred-odd miners descended upon the balloon with their firewood, shouldering aside the frightened attendants. Soon there was a wildly leaping fire under the swelling balloon. The crowd cheered and sang "There'll Be a Hot Time in the Old Town

Tonight!" Lo! the balloon was fattening prodigiously before their very eyes. In a few minutes a thousand willing hands were needed to hold the swollen bag to earth. Gleaming hunting knives appeared in the hands of other miners. Finally the last sandbag was cut from the straining balloon. All was in readiness.

Big Tom Trebilcock held up his hand to give the signal.

"Are you ready, Little Eva?" he inquired respectfully.

"Y-y-yes," Eva replied faintly.

"*Wait!*" someone shouted.

There was an amazed "ah" from the crowd as an old man suddenly darted from the throng, raced up to the wicker basket and, standing on tiptoe, threw his arms about Little Eva, vainly straining to lift her from the basket. Eva threw her arms wildly about her would-be savior, clinging to him like one who was drowning. "Danny, Danny," she shrilled, clutching him to her even more tightly.

"Git back, ol' man!" Tom Trebilcock grimly shouted at Danny. "I'll give you three!"

"Better start countin', mister!" Danny chirped blissfully.

"One!" Tom announced, as Danny started to clamber into the wicker basket.

"*Two!*" Tom called, as Danny got one leg over the edge of the basket.

"THREE!" Tom shouted, bringing down his arm. With a great whish and rush the straining balloon shot up into the air, the basket swaying precariously. The crowd cheered; Chubby squealed; the lion roared. Up, up soared the balloon. Soon it was a mere dot in the sky. When last seen, Danny's dangling leg was just disappearing over the edge of the wicker basket. Some witnesses later declared they saw the fluttering of a red bandanna handkerchief as the balloon majestically sailed westward and disappeared into the sunset.

Three days later the state constabulary discovered Danny and Eva dwelling in blissful contentment at Maki's tourist cabins at Nestoria.

"What was it like?" the young reporter from the *Hematite Weekly* asked Danny, pushing his way through the cheering crowd that gathered to greet the balloonists upon their triumphal return to Chippewa. "What was it like?" the reporter repeated, holding his pencil importantly poised. The welcoming throng fell silent, awaiting Danny's verdict. Danny shot an adoring look at Little Eva.

"Hm . . . Well now, young feller, jest tell the folks it was plain heaven," he declared. "Yep, yep! In fack, it's the closest I've ever been to heaven in my hull life —an' I'm damn sure it's the closest I'll ever git to there when I'm dead. Yep, yep. You kin also tell 'em I sorta kinda offered Miss Eva my han' in marriage —but it looks like they's still a coupla husbands standin' 'tween me an' Eva an' the altar. So I guess Danny'll stay single yet for a while. Yep, yep! *Say, is anybody here got a drink?*"

11

THE SIDEHILL GOUGER

The next visitors at Hungry Hollow arrived unheralded. They simply drove up in front of the camp one August afternoon in a little blue roadster bearing Illinois license plates. Danny was alone in camp. He moved to the door and looked out. The visitors were a bespectacled young man and a girl. The two sat in the car looking around uncertainly. Bessie strode up from the river and sniffed the hot radiator. It was not good eating. "Moo!" she bawled. The young couple clutched at each other and stared at Bessie.

"C'mon out," Danny called out. "Ol' Bess won't hurt you."

Somewhat dubiously the young woman alighted from the car and hurried up the trail toward Danny. She was clad in a pull-over sweater and jodhpurs. She had a colorful scarf tied about her head peasant fashion. Her eyes were wide and brown and she had deep dimples. She smiled sweetly at Danny.

"You lost, little girl?" Danny asked.

"No-o, I don't think so," she replied, smiling. "My

husband and I are looking for Mr. McGinnis' home at Hungry Hollow. The proprietor of Charlie's Place in Chippewa drew us this crude road map. He was so droll about it. This *should* be it. Are you Mr. McGinnis?"

"Your *husband*!" Danny exclaimed incredulously. "Why, I thought— Yes, I'm Danny McGinnis."

"I'm Carol Andrews of Evanston." She smiled. "You see, Bruce—my husband—and I are on our honeymoon. We came to stay with you for a week, if we may. We saw your ad in one of the Chicago papers this spring and we saved it—it was so very droll."

"Drool?" Danny said, bridling.

"No, no," the young bride laughed. "Droll—amusing, clever."

Danny could readily see that this discerning young lady had a head on her shoulders. That was the kind of people to have around—folks that knew a real droll when they saw him. He walked around the front of the camp and proudly pointed at the trim new log cabin which stood on the birch ridge. "That there's our new tourist camp, ma'am. Me an' the boys jest finished it las' week. We'd be mighty glad to have you stay with us, ma'am."

"Oh, you don't live alone?" Carol said, widening her expressive dark eyes.

"No, ma'am. There's Buller an' Timmy an' Swan an' Taconite lives here with me," Danny said.

"How utterly droll! Snow White and the five Dwarfs. Brucie will be terribly fascinated," Carol said. "You know, he's working on his master's."

"Workin' on his master's what, ma'am?" Danny respectfully inquired.

Carol laughed her trilling little-girl laugh. "Of course, how silly of me! Brucie's working on his master's degree in biology. You see, we both attend school at Evanston. Brucie's in graduate school, of course. He's majoring in vertebrate ecology."

"Oh," Danny said. He pondered this intelligence for a moment. "Well, mebbe you better tell the Major to fetch up your suitcases."

"Lambie dear," Carol called down to her husband, who still sat stolidly staring at Bessie. "You'd better bring our things up. This is going to be simply priceless, darling. I feel it in my bones."

Brucie dubiously disengaged his lanky six-feet-some-odd from the little roadster and stood blinking at Bessie through his horn-rim glasses.

"Moo!" Bessie bawled, arching her head, as Brucie hurriedly clambered back into the car.

"Lambie," Danny muttered, leading the way up the ridge to Hungry Hollow's virgin tourist cabin.

Carol came tripping down to the main camp the next morning, bright and early. Danny, frying the breakfast bacon, introduced the other boys. "Pleased to meetcha, ma'am" ran around the room. Smiling Swan had got up at daybreak and carefully shaved and anointed himself, putting on his best blue serge suit. His scented blond hair was parted and smacked down like a movie villain's.

"Mr. McGinnis," Carol began uncertainly, "I don't like to complain, b-but there's a live mouse swimming around in our water pail." She paused, her dark eyes wide and pleading.

"Yep, ain't it queer how the little devils like the water pail?" Danny amiably agreed.

"Should we throw the p-pail of water out, Mr. McGinnis?" Carol said.

"No. Jest throw the mouse out," Danny said, expertly turning the bacon.

"*Oh!* I simply couldn't do that!" Carol shrilled.

"Then let the Major do it," Danny said.

"B-but Brucie's still asleep. He read so late last night."

"*Read!*" Danny exclaimed, horrified. It was abundantly plain from his expression what he thought of the future security of a nation whose young majors stooped to reading a goddam book on their honeymoons. "Timmy," Danny said, "you go on up an' tend to the Major's mouse."

Carol and gentle little Timmy got along famously after that. He immediately became her favorite dwarf. After breakfast, whistling Timmy got his canoe down from the rafters of Bessie's woodshed and carried it down to the pool.

"Vat vere you oop to, Tammy?" Swan inquired suspiciously when Timmy returned to the camp.

"Oh," Timmy replied casually, "me an' Carol's going upstream in the canoe."

"Vat for you goin' oopstream?" Swan went on doggedly. Timmy walked over and regarded the envious Swan scornfully. "To spawn, of course, you bloody lunkhead," bristling Timmy answered with a fine and withering sarcasm.

"Awright, awright!" Buller said, pushing between them and spinning both of them back a dozen feet. "How the hell you 'spect we kin keep any tourists if you bloody mopes is gonna start fightin' over 'em?"

Carol appeared in the doorway. "I'm all ready, Timmy," she called sweetly. "Brucie's sitting up now—reading in bed."

As Carol and Timmy went down the river trail, Swan began mussing his hair until he looked like one of the desperate "before" ads of the tonic preparations. Irate and disheveled, the spurned swain slipped off his blue serge suit and wearily grabbed up his old clothes. "Com' now, Taconite," Swan said. "Ve vil! goo an' cut some vood. Dat vere our speed aroun' dis hare ladies' sammanary!"

"Lambie," Danny muttered dolefully, staring out the open door.

While Carol and Timmy were out canoeing, lanky Brucie so far bestirred himself as actually to get out of bed, dress, and saunter languidly down to the main camp. He was obliged to stoop under the camp doorway as he entered. Danny and Buller were playing cribbage with the aid of the last bottle of Chicago whisky, which stood open on the table before them.

"—and a pair are six," Buller counted, pegging his hand.

"Pardon me," Brucie said, in measured accents. He peered at them through his horn-rim glasses, his pale eyes staring and magnified through the thick lenses.

"Oh," Danny said, looking up. "If it ain't the Major hisself. Did you finely git tired of readin'? Here, have a snort—it might be good fer what ails you." Danny pushed the bottle along the oilcloth cover. "Seven-year-ol' stuff. Made it myself, las' night. Have a snort!"

"Snort?" Brucie repeated, savoring the word. "What's a 'snort'?" His scientific curiosity was aroused. He looked almost eager.

Danny and Buller glanced at each other. "Hm," Danny said. "A snort—le's see—a snort's three fingers of the hair of the dog what chased the cat what clawed the rat what played Ta-ra-ra-boom-dee-ay." It was Danny's turn to be precise. "Do you want a slug of whisky, mister, or do you not want a slug of whisky?"

"Oh," Brucie said, smiling faintly. "No. No thanks. What I came to ask you about is where Mrs. Andrews and I might go to observe some of the wild life of the north woods. It just occurred to me that this is our second day here and we haven't seen any indigenous fauna."

"Did you say 'seen' or 'had'?" Danny asked.

Brucie almost broke into a grin. "Bully," he said. "Very good, indeed." Then his thin face grew serious again. "We'd really like to absorb more of your local atmosphere. Best of all, we'd like to see some wild animals if we could." He turned to leave. "I'd greatly appreciate it if you would arrange it." It was not strictly a request. Brucie strode to the door. "Pardon the intrusion, gentlemen," he said, ducking out under the doorway.

"Run down the river, Buller, an' turn on the wild animals," Danny whispered. Danny and Buller had themselves two rapid snorts. "Do we really have to put up with that there spook fer a hull week?" Buller mused aloud. Their interest in the cribbage game had palled. "An' here's Timmy an' Swan at swords' points over the little lady," Danny said. "Not that I blame 'em," he added wistfully. They sat lost in thought. *"Moo!"* came the bawling of Bessie, outside, as she spied Brucie striding back to his cabin. "Hm . . ." Danny said thoughtfully. He had himself another snort. Suddenly he slapped his leg. Buller looked at him inquiringly.

"Mister Beaudin," Danny said, enunciating carefully, "pardon the introosion, sir, but could you manage to meet me behin' Bessie's domicile tonight at midnight? It just occurred to me, sir, that if our Lambie Pie won't stir from his shack long enough to see any atmospheric north woods animals, p'raps we'd better arrange to fetch 'em up to him. Payin' guests, you know. It's jest a droll idea what come to me kinda sudden-like, is all."

Buller gravely nodded his head. "Mister McGinnis,"

he said, "the idlest passin' whim of our guests is a bloody command, sir. Mister Beaudin allows he would be deelighted to join Mister McGinnis tonight behin' Bessie's woodshed." Buller smiled and fluttered his eyelids girlishly. "Goddam deelighted," he added. He glanced toward the open door. "Sh-h! Here comes Timmy an' the girl back from their spawnin' tour!"

At midnight Danny arose and stealthily shook Buller awake. The two dressed quickly and quietly stole from their snoring comrades. Outside the moon sailed high from out behind a jagged cliff of cloud. Danny and Buller hurried over to Bessie's barn through the dewy grass and ferns.

"You take an' lead Bessie," Danny commanded Buller in a sharp whisper, "an' I'll fetch the rest of the equipment." In a few seconds a strange procession filed up the moonlit trail to the tourist camp: Buller half pulling and half dragging sleepy Bessie, who placidly continued to chew her cud; then Danny padding along carrying a saw, a piece of cedar board, an auger, and—of all things—a cake of livestock salt.

Arriving at the darkened tourist camp the three carefully made their way behind the camp and out of the path of the moonlight. Danny held up a warning finger for silence. No sounds came from the tourist camp. All was hushed save the chirping of the crickets and the shrill piping of the frogs down by the river. From far away came the plaintive call of a whippoorwill.

Danny nodded his head and quickly hung the cake of salt from a nail on the side of the camp. Bessie spotted the salt and immediately made for it, eagerly running her rasping tongue over the block of salt. Soon the wet sounds of vast salivary gulpings and lappings and swallowings filled the summer air. Danny thrust the cedar board and the saw at Buller and, as Buller noisily sawed the board, Danny took the auger and drilled a series of holes in the logs of the camp.

Even Bessie was astounded over this strange nocturnal behavior. She paused in her salty feast to stare at the two. Still perplexed, she opened her mouth to give vent to a questioning moo. Buller quickly clamped both of his hands over Bessie's mouth just as Danny lunged over and bunted her in the belly with his knee. The result was not like any sound ever emitted by a cow: a vast intestinal rumbling ending in an abruptly strangled belch. Then all was silence.

Danny and Buller and Bessie waited in the shadows behind the camp until the moon disappeared behind a cloud. Then the two men rushed Bessie down to her barn and secured her in her stall and put their tools away. Danny gave her the rest of the cake of salt for her reward. "Moo," she softly lowed. Danny and Buller then ran back up the trail toward the tourist camp, Danny brandishing a pitchfork and Buller a shovel. They ran behind the camp, flailing the ground with their weapons, shouting in a curiously restrained way, "Scat, you insane divil!" "Git away from this here now camp!" "Loo' gout, Buller—the monster's makin' fer to charge you!"

Gradually their voices grew fainter as Danny and Buller valiantly forced their imaginary adversary deeper into the midnight forest. Nothing stirred in the tourist camp. Peace descended at last upon Hungry Hollow.

It was but little past daybreak the next morning when the white-faced bride of Hungry Hollow came running down to the main camp. She was wearing a sort of kimono, which flew out behind her as she ran. Danny intercepted her at Bessie's woodshed. *"Psst!"* Spying Danny, she ran into his arms, nearly sobbing. "Oh, Mr. McGinnis—" she began. *"Sh-h!"* Danny whispered, a warning finger over his lips. "Don't tell me! I know what you heard las' night! Thank goodness me an' Buller heard it too. Though it most scared us clean out of our nightshirts, we went out an' drove him off. But don't tell the other boys about it," Danny warned darkly. "If they knowed them awful things was back ag'in they'd up an' desert us sure an' leave us here to protec' ourselfs alone."

"What awful things?" Carol whispered hoarsely.

"Sh-h," Danny whispered. "You wait till the other boys is gone, after breakfast, an' then Buller an' me'll tell you all about it." Danny the comforter patted Carol's shoulder. She managed to smile up at him wanly. "If it weren't for the perfectly horrible sounds the—the thing made, I-I'd have sworn that in the darkness it looked just like Bessie the cow," she whispered.

Danny blinked his eyes and swallowed. He was equal to the occasion. "That's exactly what I thought the first one I run across! The reason they look somethin' like a cow's because they's most as big as one. But Bessie's been locked up the hull night, thank goodness. See the latch on her door? Now you run back to your great big Lambie an' he'll console you."

Carol's eyes flashed darkly. "Lambie my foot," she said. Then she was nearly in tears over her disloyal thoughts. "B-Brucie hasn't stirred from under the b-bedclothes all n-night! O-o-o— I wish my m-mother were here."

After breakfast Taconite and smoldering Swan left for their beloved wood-cutting. Danny craftily dispatched willing Timmy down to the river to catch a few fresh trout for Carol. Grabbing his fly rod, Timmy went blithely whistling on his way. He'd scale a mountain for little Carol. The coast was clear. Danny and Buller met breathless Carol at the camp door.

"What was it! *What was it!*" Carol exclaimed. "I've just got to know. Brucie's gone frantically through all his books and he simply can't make it out. Especially that grating, sawing noise."

Danny looked at Buller significantly. "See, we weren't a minute too soon las' night," he said in an awed voice. "The critter'd already started his awful drillin'." He turned to Carol. "Sit down, ma'am," he said gravely. "This is goin' to be hard to take. Jest try to ca'm yourself while we explain about this here thing."

"W-what thing?" Carol whispered.

Danny took a deep breath. "The plain fack of the matter, ma'am, is one of them terrible sidehill gougers is back ag'in." Danny shook his head. "Buller an' me'll have to set up tonight an lay fer him with flares an' the ol' .44. That's if we kin keep awake after all the ruction las' night." Danny stifled a yawn. "They usually allus come back to the very same place the nex' night when they're driven off that way. Awful stubborn critters, they are." Danny wagged his head dolefully. "Yep, yep. The sidehill gougers is back ag'in!"

"S-sidehill gougers!" Carol said, her eyes dilating. "What're they?"

"You mean you ain't never heard tell of the sidehill gouger?" incredulous Danny demanded.

"No-o," Carol confessed in a small voice.

Danny wanted to be perfectly fair. "Well it's true they's only natives of the Upper Peninsula. An' I guess they ain't many folks is ever really laid eyes on 'em," he conceded. "You see, ma'am, they perform most of their diviltry late at night. Gen'rally at the stroke of midnight they come groanin' an' moanin' out of their lairs in the hills—"

"Hills!" Carol exclaimed.

"Yes, ma'am," Danny went on quietly. "You see, the full-grown sidehill gouger's most as big as a bear, 'cept he's terrible nearsighted an' he can't climb worth a tinker's— Well, he's awful pore at climbin'. Seems like the critters is all got high blood pressure—an' climbin' makes 'em dizzy. Anyway, when one of 'em comes on to a hill or a stump or anythin' in his way, he jest nacherly bores an' drills his way plumb through it. An' the more he drills the madder he gits!" Danny shook his head. "It's an awful sight to view the slashin' an' rootin' left in the wake of a real mad sidehill gouger." Danny blinked his gray eyes reflectively, sadly recollecting past ruination. "It's horrible an' torrible, ma'am."

"You—you mean they'll go right through any obstruction—even a log cabin?" Carol whispered.

"Log cabins!" Danny exclaimed. "They's 'specially fond of cabins, ma'am. I mind the time one of 'em drilled clean through Billy Grill's bunk up to his camp on the Connor's Creek. You couldn't find a piece left as big as a toothpick. Lucky fer Billy he weren't in it. Many's the time we've had to drive 'em off, right here, with pitchforks an' cant hooks. Ain't that right, Buller?"

"You bet," Buller solemnly avowed. "Sometimes even with hot coals, ma'am. 'Member that time, Dan, I had to take an'—"

"Yep, yep." Danny was not going to yield the floor to Buller's hot coals. "It was awful bad here fer a spell. They ain't been near so ornery of late years," he ran on. "We thought mebbe they'd all finely drilled their way clear through to the other side of the Mulligan Mountains." Danny sorrowfully shook his head again. "But it looks like we're in fer it ag'in."

"But how do they *do* it?" Carol said. "It seems incredible."

It was a fair question. "That we don't rightly know, ma'am," he went on. Danny was as perplexed as Carol. "To tell you the truth we ain't never really kilt one nor even seen one of 'em close up in daylight. You see, travelin' only by night that way, they's even harder to assassinate than the five-footed swamp grizzle—"

"*Swamp grizzles!*" Carol echoed in dismay. "What are they!" Buller was suddenly seized with a choking spell and hurried from the camp.

"The five-footed swamp grizzle?" Danny repeated slowly, his eyes widening. He ran his tongue over his lips. "Hm . . . Well, never you mind about them right now, ma'am. We slew the sole survivor of them devils jest last fall. But gittin' back to the sidehill gouger an' as how he does his drillin'—we know from his tracks he's got terrible big powerful webbed feet with claws on 'em like a spring-tooth harrow. That time when Buller thrun the hot coals he got a pretty good squint at one. It was an awful sight. Pore Buller had nightmares fer weeks."

"What did it look like?" Carol breathed, morbidly fascinated.

"Well, I kin only tell you what I heard tell from Buller. But Buller swore up an' down later that the critter's big drippin' snout looked jest like a post-hole digger, but sorta rigged out with long sharp rotatin' teeth. An' he claims the slaverin' critter's head had openin's in the sides, jest like big gills. I s'pose them gills is to let the gravel an' stuff out of when he's got a big job a drillin' to do. Of course that's jest my own personal guess, mind."

A long shadow filled the camp doorway. "Oh, Brucie!" Carol cried, running over and wildly throwing her arms about her husband. "I've just found out what was making those awful sounds last night. O-oh —we're lucky to be alive!"

Brucie slowly blinked his eyes. "Let's be both objective and coherent, dear," he said in his precise voice. "Now, tell me about it—dispassionately and lucidly."

"No, no, I c-can't, Lambie," Carol wailed, clutching him more tightly. "A-ask Mr. McGinnis what it is—he's practically seen one. They—they only come out at m-midnight." Brucie turned and regarded old Dan owlishly. But Danny had suddenly grown very weary of the sidehill gouger. "Sorry, folks, I gotta go down an' git some fresh water," he said, grabbing up the pails and clanging them out of the camp and down the river trail.

Buller was sitting outside on the sawbuck chewing a straw. "Hello, Mister McGinnis," he said in a boy-soprano voice. "Would you kindly tell me where I could find a real live five-footed swamp grizzle? I'm a new Eagle Scout an' I—"

"You go high-dive to hell, you swollen ol' rum pot," Danny snorted, banging the pails together. Down at the Big Dead spring he stood staring sightlessly at the churning pool.

"Lambie!" he snorted. "If I hear that jest once more—not twice—I-I'll drill clean through the Mulligan Mountains myself!"

Came the mystic hour of midnight, when sidehill gougers are wont to roam. Peace reigned over Hungry Hollow. Not a soul heard the little blue roadster as it rapidly slithered away. The next morning Timmy was the first to notice that the car was gone. Bereft, he raced up to the deserted tourist cabin. In a few minutes he was back at the main camp, shaken and tight-lipped. Danny was clattering the stove lids, preparing to gargle his morning Highland Fling. Timmy handed him a penciled note to which some paper money was pinned.

"What's up, Timmy?" Danny innocently demanded. "You look as though you lost your best girl."

"I guess I d-did," Timmy said sadly. "They've gone!"

"*Gone!*" Danny said, elaborately surprised. "My Gawd, what fer?"

"Read the note," Timmy said listlessly.

"You read it," Danny answered testily. "You know I ain't never in no shape to read nothin' till I swaller my mornin' tonic!" Timmy, his voice halting and strained, read Danny the hurriedly scrawled note.

> "*Dear Boys,*   11 :55 P.M.
>   *Brucie's so restless and nervous tonight over his approaching thesis that we simply have to leave at once. I'm terribly sorry we can't wait till morning to say good-by. We're leaving an extra day's money. I really had a lovely time. I'll never forget how sweet Timmy was to row me up the river.*
>
>   *Love,*
>   CAROL
>   P. S. *to Mr. McGinnis: Perhaps when you finally exterminate them we can visit you again.*
>   C.A."

Danny took the news bravely, "Why they *are* up an' gone!" he said, taking a big swallow of his Highland Fling. "Now if that ain't gratitood! Here they didn't stop to say good-by. They didn't give no reasons why." Danny finally broke raucously into the song. " 'They jest walked right in and turned aroun', an' walked right out ag'in!' Yep, yep . . . May Lambie Pie lan' in heaven three days before the devil knows he's dead. What's the matter, Timmy?"

Timmy was glaring suspiciously at old Dan. "What's she mean there that part about exterminatin' somethin'? Whadda you bin up to now, you ol' goat!"

Danny choked over his drink. "Hm . . . Bloody drink's too hot. Why-ah—didn't I tell you? Brucie was complainin' jest the other day to me an' Buller about there bein' bugs in the new camp. *Bugs,* mind you! I was never so mortified since Mrs. Smedburg caught me in bed that time with her new chambermaid. Yep, yep. That's gratitood fer you."

"Bunk!" Timmy snorted. "How could there be varmints in a camp what ain't never been lived in before?"

"That's jest what I tole him," Danny eagerly agreed. "I kinda hated to hint maybe he fetched 'em here hisself. You know, in his schoolin' he works with all kinds of snails an' bugs. Yep, yep. Thinks I mebbe this tourist idea ain't what it's cracked up to be. You never know what kine of folks you're gonna git holt of. Imagine bein' insulted right in your own house by a fella by the name of Lambie!" Danny scowled at the thought.

Timmy stood squinting uncertainly at Dan, dubiously stroking his chin. "If I thought you engineered this here thing on purpose, you bald-headed fox, I'd pack all my stuff an' up an' quit. I really would."

"Why, Timmy," Danny said mournfully, cut to the

quick. "How could you even think such a thing about a pore sick ol' man who's more dead'n alive with his flarin' ulcers?" Danny moaned, clutching at his stomach, his voice nearly breaking. "It's—why it's horrible an' torrible!"

12

THE CHASE

Little Matti Hunginen celebrated his fifty-fourth birthday that Labor Day. He launched the celebration at dawn by doggedly disposing of a quart of Old Cordwood out in the cow barn while he was doing the morning milking. His wife, Impi, studied his dreamy blue eyes intently as he staggered into the kitchen sagging under the weight of the frothy pails of warm milk. Matti tried to disarm suspicion. "Hello, Missus," he brightly greeted her, smiling engagingly at his frowning wife. "Guess whose birt'day it is today." Impi restlessly sniffed the air like a pointer at a field trial. She possessed an allergy to the aroma of alcohol which amounted to a form of dementia. Her frown grew more ominous. She was getting the scent.

"Viskey dog!" she shrilled, violently brandishing the nearest offensive weapon, which happened to be the butter mallet. She gave chase to Matti, who promptly dropped his pails of milk and turned and fled. Matti instinctively wheeled at his entrance gate and headed north for Hungry Hollow, some seven miles away. He arrived there breathless less than two hours later.

"Safe me! Safe me!" he cried as he reeled into the camp. The boys were still sitting over their breakfast coffee. Panting Matti insisted that he had run all the way, and that Impi was still plunging after him the last time he had dared to look over his shoulder, away back at the Barnhardt bridge. Danny waited until Matti had caught his breath. Then he gave him a tumblerful of Hungry Hollow moonshine. So abject was Matti's terror that it seemed the only thing to do. In ten minutes the little man's courage had so far returned that the boys had to restrain him manually from running back to his farm and soliciting Impi to engage in mortal combat.

Matti puffed and strained to get away from Buller, who held him by the simple expedient of sitting on him. "Matti—heh-heh—never let ol' voman scare for him! I—heh-heh-heh—I fix dat big fat crabby!"

"Taker 'er easy, Matti," Buller counseled soothingly. "Don't do nothin' rash. Don't fergit them seven —eight wet-pants kids of yours. What would they do without their lovin' maw? Pore little runny-nose orphints." Buller was about to blubber over his own eloquence. But Matti did not answer. He had suddenly subsided into that dreamless kind slumber in which he had indulged exactly fifty-four years before.

That evening at dusk Danny and the boys smuggled Matti into Chippewa in the Model A. Fearing a sudden flank attack, as they passed Matti's farm they first hid Matti by laying him across the floor of the back seat like a sack of oats, and placing their feet on him. Sure enough, Impi was lurking in the shadows near the farm gate, still keeping the lonely vigil with her butter mallet. She ran out to stop them. "Step on 'er, Timmy," Danny ordered under his breath.

"You see my ol' man?" Impi shouted, brandishing her mallet, trying to head off the car.

Resourceful Danny quickly threw out a blanket to the wolf pack. "He's pickin' huckleberries up on the Mulligan plains!" he shouted back, prodding Timmy to even greater bursts of speed. Shouting Impi did not pause in her sweeping end run. It was touch and go for fifty yards, but Timmy knew his Model A, and Impi had already put in a full day of sprinting. She gradually fell behind, using her remaining energy in hurling vast guttural Finnish oaths at these marital defilers from Hungry Hollow.

At last the boys saw the lights of Chippewa. To show his gratitude for his deliverance Matti invited Danny and the boys to be his birthday guests that night at the Labor Day celebration in the Finnish Labor Temple in Chippewa. This one-story sheet-metal temple of toil stood on Pearl Street and was built and run by an organization composed largely of Finnish miners. But the board of directors did not bar farmers, and Matti was a member in good standing, paying his dues in milk and eggs pilfered from watchful Impi. Tonight the temple was to be dedicated more to the dance than to labor. Taisto Saastamoinen, Chippewa's one-man band, was to provide the music.

Timmy parked the Model A in the alley at the rear of Charlie's Place. Naturally they all had to stop in at Charlie's and lubricate themselves for the big dance. So enjoyable was this preliminary process that it was nearly eleven o'clock when they paraded down Pearl Street, proudly led by their host, little Matti Hunginen. At the ticket window they were not given the usual tickets, but were each handed a piece of yellow silk ribbon and a common pin.

"What's this fer?" Danny asked the man at the window, dubiously fingering his yellow ribbon.

"Dat's you dicket! It's new wrinkles dis place. You lose dat yellow ribbon, ve t'row you out!" Danny hastily pinned his ribbon to his wool jumper.

The dusty hall was crowded with perspiring dancing couples. Taisto Saastamoinen, the one-man band, was giving out with his all, playing a spirited Finnish polka. The floor shuddered with the dancers' exertions, and overhead the faded pink paper streamers rustled and billowed from the accompanying tremors. Swan Kellstrom, his nostrils twitching dangerously, immediately swung into the dance with a pretty blond Finnish girl. Taconite sat by the entrance door and morosely contemplated his calloused hands. He had forgotten his buckskin mitts. Timmy didn't dance, but he was already deep in heartfelt conversation with another comely lass. Buller was coaxing one of Mrs. Smedburg's buxom chambermaids to dance with him. The reluctant maid was shaking her head. Buller was drunk, she said. Look, he just staggered again.

"Aw, c'mon, Lempi," Buller coaxed. "I ain't drunk. I'm jest tired. You must remember—I only got one pair a legs, an' they's really holdin' up two men. C'mon, Lempi!" Shrugging, Lempi surrendered to such sweet reasonableness. New tremblors suddenly seized the dance floor as she and Buller got under way.

Lucky Matti Hunginen met a Finnish miner friend with a full pint bottle, and they immediately repaired to the basement for an important labor conference in the men's toilets. Old Danny was irresistibly drawn to big Taisto Saastamoinen, the one-man band, who sat at the far end of the hall threshing around amidst his various instruments. Fascinated, Danny walked the length of the dance floor and sat gazing raptly at this musical genius.

Perspiring Taisto looked like a madman sitting in the window of a pawnshop. He was literally hemmed in by his music. His right foot played his big bass drum while the other foot was held poised, free to tinkle some little bells or suddenly crash a cymbal or roll a snare drum, whichever fugitive impulse might seize him. Big Taisto was playing the accordion during the polka, but a fiddle and two saxophones hung near at hand. To his left stood an electric guitar. Taisto's face was partially hidden by a harmonica and a kazoo, which were rigidly attached to a metal frame. He leaned over and blared the kazoo as Danny watched, open-mouthed. The music suddenly stopped. Taisto rolled the snare drum and then crashed the cymbals. He stood up and glared at the dancers.

"Latees an' yentlemans!" he announced. "Dis here is da intermissi'n. Vee vill now ha'f few vords from you 'resident, Mester Turri Leppanen." Big Taisto wanted silence. "S'ut up, now, few minoot!" he warned.

President Turri Leppanen walked resolutely to the center of the floor, and, wheeling mechanically around the hall, delivered his brief peroration. It seemed that some menfolks had entered the dance hall that night, as they had in the recent past, without paying their way. But he and the board of directors had found a cure for all that. What they needed was a little co-operation.

"Latees an' yentlemens! Because many kind crook-man an' seap-skate like for 'neak in dis dance place free, me an' poard 'rectors deecide tonight to give it each ones what pay dat fares one yellow ribbons!" Turri glared darkly at a knot of whispering women.

"Now latees an' kits—to help me an' dat poard 'rec-tors"—he wagged his finger at them—"don't you give it no dance to no any mans 'cept he have it dat yellow ribbons! Yellow ribbons also 'title everybody for da free lunches in pasement during dis intermissi'n. Yes-sirree! Ve now serving coffee an' da two kinds cake— socklate cake an' apples pie! Dank you, please!"

Enchanted Danny would not leave Taisto Saasta-moinen's side even for the free lunch, whether with two kinds of cake or not. Big Taisto, sensing that at last he had a truly appreciative auditor, pretended to rehearse, soulfully extending himself in marvelous feats which were more akin to tricks of sleight-of-hand than a musical performance. The exhibition left both of them breathless.

"I go have coffee now," Taisto said, carefully un-winding himself from the maze of instruments.

"A goddam genius," Danny muttered, shaking his head in wonder. "He throws hisself aroun' like a dyin' hog!" But it was all a trifle cloying. Danny searched the room to find the other boys. He was getting power-fully thirsty, and he wondered how he could lure Buller and the boys away from the dance.

The milling crowd slowly filed up from the base-ment. There still remained two long hours of dancing. Danny stifled a yawn. Perspiring Taisto, refreshed by his coffee, again settled himself firmly among his ingenious trapezes and dangling instruments. The dance must go on— Or must it? Danny chose that moment to make a little practical suggestion to Taisto. Danny was always generous with helpful hints to others. He sought only to promote efficiency in an im-perfect world—and perhaps to speed the end of the dance.

"Say, mister," he said thoughtfully, addressing Taisto. "Since you was gone I was just settin' here thinkin'."

"Vat's dat?" Taisto beamed modestly, expectantly awaiting a glowing compliment to his musical virtuosity.

"I was jest thinkin'—thinks I if you took an hitched a broom to your rear end, you could even sweep the goddam floor!"

Because of the tangle of musical instruments, Danny gained a thirty-foot start on Taisto. The chase led up Pearl Street to Main, up Main to Charlie's Place, through crowded Charlie's Place and out the back door, thence east on Hematite Avenue, thence over to Magnetic Street and into the darkened rear of Big Annie's, up the clattering wooden stairs, through the smoky waiting room—not to mention two occupied bedrooms—thence into the kitchen. There sat Buller and Matti and all the boys, calmly having a quiet midnight drink with Big Annie.

"What's all the big rush, Danny?" Buller inquired. "You seem kinda outa breath."

"Naw," panting Danny retorted. "It was jest kinda stuffy over in that there hall. I-I jest thought I'd up'n take some air. *Whew!*"

Just then big Taisto burst wildly into the kitchen. He spotted Danny and slowly advanced. Catlike, Buller sprang from his chair and got between the two men. He raised his arms before him, yawning elaborately. He was so very tired.

"Hello, mister," he said softly, looking at Taisto. "Was you lookin' fer somethin'?"

Taisto stood regarding Buller closely. The appraisal was not encouraging. Taisto dropped his eyes and fumbled to find a cigarette. "Yes, I look it for match."

"What kin' of match, partner?" Buller was eager to please.

"Vy—I mean—yust vun match for dat paper see-gar," Taisto hastily clarified.

"Here," Buller said, magically presenting a lighted match. "Have a light."

"Dank you, please," watchful Taisto said.

"It's nothin' at all, pal," Buller said, smiling. "Good night," he added softly.

"Good night," Taisto said, backing out of the kitchen door.

Buller turned to Danny. "Some day, ol' man, they's goin' to pin thet there mustache aroun' your bloody ears."

Danny bristled indignantly. "Gwan! What'd you go buttin' in fer? I coulda cleaned up thet big moosical tramp with one han' tied behin' my back—an' a goddam broom handle stuck"—Danny paused and glanced thoughtfully at Big Annie—"stuck in my free han'! Yep, yep."

"You bet!" little Matti Hunginen chimed in loyally, rolling his inflamed eyes up at his hero. "An' if dat Danny he can't for do it, li'l Matti he fix dat big Finlander son-a-bits all by his lonely! Yes-sirree!" To illustrate his point Matti executed a wild imaginary haymaker, the terminal arc of which miraculously found the point of his own jaw. With a little sigh, he spun on his toe and, for the second time that crowded day, gently subsided into dreamless slumber, this time on Big Annie's linoleum floor. Matti's birthday celebration was officially ended.

Lucky Matti didn't realize his good fortune. The kitchen door again burst open. There stood Impi, still holding the butter mallet. Buller got behind Danny.

"Hm," Impi said, advancing ominously.

13

STATION D-E-E-R!

The stricken summer waned into colorful northern autumn like a beautiful woman flushed and waxen with the fevers of approaching death. Snowless November came, a month of raw and cold, leaving the naked earth a frozen, lumpy tundra. No one had stayed in the new tourist cabin at Hungry Hollow since the young honeymooners had fled before the groaning sidehill gougers. Accordingly, Danny and the boys were overjoyed when a letter finally arrived at Charlie's Place announcing that the Chicago fishermen were coming north for the deer-hunting season. Danny rubbed his hands gleefully.

"Boy, will that ever be bootiful! Drinkin' all that fine Chicago whisky ag'in—an' gittin' paid fer it! See! It'll be our money fer Christmas!"

The Chicago hunters arrived at the Hollow on the eve of deer season in a stinging cold drizzle. At dusk a heavy fog rolled up from the river. This time Danny did not go to town to meet his guests at the Cliff

Dwellers Inn. For some unstated reason, Dr. George had directed that he await them at camp.

"There they be!" Danny shouted, as he heard the hunters' rented Ford and trailer rattling down off the Mulligan ridge. Hatless, he bolted out into the dark and rain. Its headlights a dull coppery glow, the little Ford emerged from a fog bank like a big fish coming out of a lake.

"Danny!" the hunters shouted.

They were very glad to see old Danny. "How's the old goat!" "Did you break any more ribs, Dan!" Danny introduced them to Buller and the boys, and then led them up the ridge to the new camp, where he had a roaring fire going in the new wood stove that Timmy had made out of an old metal oil barrel. The rain slanted against the camp windows. Danny proudly showed the hunters about the camp and then waited around expectantly as they began lovingly unpacking their high-powered rifles and other duffel. But where was their whisky? Danny craned and peeked. He cleared his throat nervously. Dr. George looked up at him.

"Was there something else, Danny?"

The old man shook his head vigorously. "Nope, nope! I mean—that is, not exackly." Danny was floundering. "I was jest wonderin', it bein' so col' an' all— I was jest wonderin' if you fellas wanted me to mix you up a roun' of nice hot drinks, is all?"

Dr. George looked at his companions and smiled. He had won his private bet. He turned to Danny. "I'm afraid not, Danny, old man. Thanks just the same. You see, we make it a practice never to bring spirits into a deer-hunting camp. Firearms and whisky don't mix. So it's no drinking in our deer camp! It's a standing rule of ours. Sorry, old man."

"Oh," Danny said. "Oh," he repeated dully, blinking uncertainly. "Well, good night," he finally said, quietly opening the camp door and stepping out into the chilly night. "Standin' rule," Danny whispered to himself in the pelting rain.

The prospect of a whiskyless deer hunt was the first bad omen. "Imagine them goddam Chicago millionaires comin' 'way up here without a bloody drop to drink!" Danny lamented to Buller and the boys that night when they were alone. "If I hed all their money, every mornin' I'd up an' take a bath in the bloody fluid. Jest fer divilment. Yep, yep! What's they holdin' back fer?" Mystified, Danny shook his head. "The way I looks at it, we's all goin' through this goddam worl' fer the first an' last time! An' no one's ever yet got out of it alive." Thus Danny stated his philosophy in a nutshell. An instinctive hedonist, he mournfully shook his head. "Yep, yep. It's horrible an' torrible!"

Retribution for such niggardliness was swift. It rained for three days. After the third sodden day of hunting the Chicago Nimrods had not so much as seen a deer. They were desolate. After supper that night Dr. George summoned Danny and Timmy up to their camp for a council. What was the trouble? Weren't there any deer left in the country? "You haven't shot *all* of them, have you Dan?"

Danny spat thoughtfully at the glowing oil-barrel stove. "Nope. I left a few fer seed." He paused. "In fack, they's more deer in these parts than whisky," he slyly added. "What we need is trackin' snow. The rain is keepin' 'em in the bloody swamps. Thinks I they's feelin' too goddam blue even to move. Yep, yep . . ."

Timmy spoke up. "I agree with Dan," he said quietly. "With this damp, foggy weather the deer are all swamping up. They only seem to be movin' out at night to drink an' make love. I was down by the Mulligan swamp today an' by all the signs they made goin' down to the river an' back last night, it looks like as though they was cattle stampedin' a corral."

"Yep, yep," Danny said. "It's too bad it ain't legal to use a dog fer deer-huntin'! A good houn' dog'd drive that bloody Mulligan swamp—an' you'd all git your deer."

The hunters stared skeptically at each other. They didn't know quite what to believe. Dr. George tried to explain their situation to old Dan. Here they had waited and planned all summer for this deer hunt, and they hadn't even seen a single flag. They were busy men and their time was short. He was awfully sorry, but it looked like they'd have to move on if they couldn't get some shooting at Hungry Hollow.

"We'll give her one more day," Dr. George concluded. "If things don't happen tomorrow, Dan, I'm afraid we'll have to push on to a likelier spot."

Danny glanced at Timmy and shrugged eloquently. "Here they don't fetch no goddam whisky—an' now they's gonna up an cheat us outa all the money we was figgerin' on makin' fer our Christmas celebration," his attitude plainly told Timmy.

"Good night, boys," he said glumly, sadly turning away. He and Timmy walked silently down the ridge to the main camp in the driving rain. Buller and the other boys were already in bed. Danny turned in listlessly without taking his nightly toddy. Even his mustaches had wilted into a damp and disconsolate droop. Timmy lay in bed in the dark, unblinking, pondering far into the night. What to do to get some deer for the city hunters? How to hold them at Hungry Hollow so as to swell the Christmas fund? Timmy tossed and turned. Danny's words kept coming back to him. "A good houn' dog'd drive that Mulligan swamp—an' you'd all git your deer!" But that wasn't legal. What to do, what to do?

The next morning the dawn came like an endless twilight, accompanied by a thin, biting drizzle and a fog so thick that a man looked like a stump at twenty paces. Led by dogged Danny, who had determined to guide the hunters to their deer personally, the Chicago sportsmen left to hunt the tangled north shore of Silver Lake. Danny clutched the heavy old .44 nervously. He'd swell the Christmas fund even if he had to assassinate fifty deer to do it.

The hunters had no sooner disappeared than there was a great flurry of activity in camp. Buller and Taconite and Swan were getting ready to flee to Chippewa in the Model A. Since the hunters had arrived, whiskyless, Danny had petulantly refused to dole out even his moonshine. Buller couldn't stand it any longer. He was going in to Charlie's Place. He wanted to be near the fountainhead of Old Cordwood.

Timmy wrestled himself into an enormous packsack. "Timmy, are you goin' to town with us too?" surprised Buller inquired. Timmy was the undrinkingest man at Hungry Hollow. What had gotten into him? "Was you goin' in?" Buller repeated.

"Nope," Timmy answered mysteriously. "Jest leave me off at the Mulligan swamp."

"What you got in that bloody heavy packsack?" Buller asked.

"None of your bloody heavy business," Timmy replied courteously.

"O.K.," Buller pouted. "I on'y hope it's a hemp rope —an' that you fin' a fifty-foot Norway pine to drape yourself from!"

Danny and his party were wet and cold and hungry when they returned from the day's hunt. The rain was turning into a cold sleet. The drooping points of Danny's mustaches nearly met. They had not seen a solitary deer. To make things worse, there were no lights in camp. The door was locked, the fires were out. Danny found Buller's farewell note on the oil-cloth table.

"Gone to town," he said, crumpling the note and shaking his fist with it. "Jest like rats desertin' a sinkin' ship!" He regarded the four shivering Chicagoans cynically. These were the fine laddie-bucks that had a standing rule against drinking in a deer camp.

"Fer Gawd's sake, men, let's have a snort!" he finally said. "Mebbe ha'f a dozen of 'em! After all, it's your las' night in camp! Don't hold back! 'Tain't a snake—it won't bite you!"

Danny perked up at the very thought of a drink—even if it had to be his own moonshine. In a half hour he had the fires roaring and had crammed a half-dozen Highland Flings into himself and the wearily willing hunters. He even managed to sing a chorus of "Steve O'Donnell's Wake."

Just as they were sitting down to supper the camp door swung open. There stood Timmy in the open doorway. He was wet and shivering and covered with mud from head to foot.

Danny put down his knife. "My Gawd, Timmy, where you bin at!" he demanded. "You look like you was out swimmin' in a fi'e dollar suit!"

Timmy came in and closed the door and stood in the light, silent and shivering, still dripping water.

"Where in hell you bin at?" Danny repeated.

"I—I bin down to the Mul-Mulligan s-swamp l-lookin' fer them there d-damn d-deer," Timmy chattered.

"Did you see any, man?" Danny demanded, hope rising in his breast.

"N-no, but I heard lots of 'em. I-I w-went into the

s-swamp an' I guess I fell in a great b-big h-hole,"
Timmy answered plaintively.

Danny's disgust was boundless. "Imagine a sober
lunatic drivin' a goddam swamp all by his lonesome,"
he remarked scathingly. Timmy's teeth were chattering
like castanets. Danny finally relented. What was the
use? "Here Timmy, I'll fix you a Highland Fling
before you up'n die. Hell's fire! We might's so well
all have another one! Yep, yep."

The supper grew cold. Danny and Timmy and the
Chicago hunters mixed and drank Highland Flings
before, during, and after supper, and far on into the
night.

The next morning broke clear and cold, with six
inches of beautiful tracking snow. Quaking Danny and
Timmy helped the wan guests out of bed to the breakfast table, and then again to pack their car and trailer
to take their departure. The decision had been made.

Everyone was glum but Timmy. No one had seen
him purloin a quart of Danny's moonshine during the
festivities of the night before. He had been up and
at it since dawn. In addition he had consumed three
generous Highland Flings with the others before
breakfast. Timmy kept chattering away at a great rate.

"Leave your rifles out ready, boys. Me an' Danny'll
ride down as far as the Mulligan swamp with you.
That's the place fer deer. You'll git 'em down there!
You jest wait an' see!"

"Give him another drink, Danny, and shut him up,"
Dr. George finally said.

"Keep your rifles ready," Timmy chirped as he
downed his fourth Highland Fling.

"An' your bloody powder dry," Danny added sar-
castically.

Coming down along the ridge road, overlooking the

Mulligan Plateau, the light new snow was crisscrossed with the fresh tracks of deer. Danny suddenly spotted three deer a half mile away, but before the little car could be stopped their flags were up and they had drifted wraithlike down into the big Mulligan swamp.

"It won't be long," Timmy said. "It won't be long before—"

"Before we'll throw you out," Danny growled.

The little car dropped off the Mulligan Plateau and rattled down the sand hill and alongside the big Mulligan swamp. Timmy grabbed Dr. George's arm.

"Stop the car!" he shouted.

Dr. George slammed on the brakes. He and Danny and the others stared at Timmy. Gentle Timmy was a changed man, a rugged, purposeful leader. He wrenched open the car door and leapt out.

"Take your rifles an' follow me—an' shut up!" he whispered.

Bewildered, Danny and the hunters mechanically obeyed the electrified Timmy. Taking big strides, Timmy led the party toward the Mulligan swamp. The ground was a maze of fresh deer tracks leading up from the Big Dead into the abrupt wall of the tangled cedar swamp.

Timmy led Danny and the hunters to a huge old hollow white pine stump about fifty paces from the swamp. He stopped and held up his hand. His cheeks were glowing, his brown eyes flashing.

"Doc!" he whispered. "You an' two of your party go to the north side of the swamp. Spot your men along the edge an' then you come back where you kin give me the signal when they's ready!"

"Yes, sir," Doc whispered meekly.

"Danny, you an' one of the hunters stay here with me. I'll be way too busy fer any shootin.'"

Danny stood and stared at Timmy. Was he starting to take fits? It couldn't only be the whisky. Danny shook his head sorrowfully.

"An' lissen, Doc," Timmy barked on, "wave your rifle at me when everyone is in his place! Now git goin'—an' shut up!"

When the others had left, Timmy turned and winked triumphantly at Danny and Ray, the remaining hunter. "I'll show you fellas how to hunt deer!" he whispered hoarsely.

Dr. George was waiting at his station on a rise of ground several hundred yards from Timmy and the white pine stump. Timmy crouched over his stump, keeping one eye on the mystified doctor.

Then Dr. George raised his rifle and waved it at Timmy. All was ready.

Things happened rapidly after that. First Timmy ducked headfirst down into the hollow stump as though he were escaping a bullet. Mystified, Danny saw him quickly cup something into his hands and raise it to his mouth. "Does he have a goddam bottle cached there?" Danny whispered wildly. But no— Suddenly from out of the swamp came a weird conglomeration of sound. Dogs barked, bayed, and howled—big dogs, little dogs; soprano dogs, baritone dogs; hairless dogs and shaggy dogs. Cats squealed and spat! Men shouted and swore and sang snatches of ribald song. Horses whinnied and cows mooed amidst the dreadful cacophony.

And then they came!

First came the rabbits and partridge and then the terrified deer, big deer and little deer—bucks, does, yearlings, fawns—running in every direction, whisking past Timmy's stump toward the river, like animals fleeing before a forest fire. A pair of undulating red

foxes slunk by. A great white arctic owl flapped noise-
lessly overhead. A young bear broke from the swamp,
blinked a moment, and wildly tore back.

"Mother Machree!" Danny shouted, side-stepping
a charging doe, gazing raptly at Timmy. "Oh, my
Gawd!" he exclaimed, his eyes bugging out. For little
Timmy was standing up and shouting into a microphone—howling, dancing, barking, braying!

"Shoot, you damn fools! *Shoot!*" came from Timmy
and the swamp at the same time. "Woof! Psst!
Meow! *Shoot, you bloody mopes!*"

Danny and Ray stood looking at Timmy with their
mouths hanging open. Dr. George and the other hunters ran up to him breathlessly.

"Are—are you all right, Timmy?" Dr. George
puffed.

Timmy stood glaring at Danny and the hunters,
still clutching his microphone. *"Am I all right!"* the
swamp boomed. "Here I damn near ketch my death
of cold yesterday, wirin' this goddam swamp fer you
guys—an' you asks me if I'm all right! Fer Gawd's
sake, why didn't you nail 'em?"

"But we can't do that, Timmy," Dr. George said
soothingly, like a worried psychiatrist to a truant
patient squatting on the sill of his open office window.
"We can't do that, old boy."

" 'Tain't illegal, is it?" the swamp demanded.

"No—no, but it just isn't cricket, Timmy," Dr.
George said dazedly. "I-I never heard of such a thing."

Timmy shook his head dully. "You fellows can go
plumb to—"

"Look out, Timmy!" Danny shouted, just as a hold-
out, a big old gray-haired buck with a magnificent rack
of antlers, ran between him and Timmy, snapping
Timmy's microphone wire—*spung!*—and blowing

mightily as he leapt over the hunters' trailer and bounced down to the river bottom, his tall flag wagging a final fond farewell.

"It's Ol' Rockin' Chair hisself!" Danny shouted after the fabulous deer. "I ain't set eyes on him in three-four years!"

Timmy seemed to wilt as though the broken wire had suddenly snapped his spirit. Still holding his microphone, he fished in his jumper pocket and brought out the remains of a quart of Danny's moonshine. He sheepishly handed it to Danny.

"I'm sorry, men," he said listlessly. "I guess I didn't understan'. You see, I jest wanted you to stay on with us to help our Christmas fund—an' to help you git your deer."

"We're staying, Timmy," Dr. George said warmly. "Of that you can be sure! But first we're going into town and get a big supply of this—this Old Firewood!"

"Ol' Cordwood!" Danny briskly corrected.

"Old Cordwood, then," the doctor said.

"Skoal," Danny said in a grave voice like a benediction, reverently tilting the bottle.

14

THE RAID

Danny had been making moonshine and beer at Hungry Hollow long before an obscure politician called Volstead had leapt to a dreary sort of fame by vainly dreaming that he could impose sobriety on a restless nation by legislative fiat. The only noticeable effect Prohibition had ever had on the Hollow was to place a greater strain on the resources of Danny's battered still, and perhaps to make Danny more careful. "They's more smellers and snoopers runnin' aroun' the woods these days than they's mosquitoes in our goddam swamp," he had indignantly snorted.

Yes, in those days a man had to be mighty careful. Wild raids and abrupt arrests had been the order of the day. There was the occasion before Repeal when Danny had been arrested on suspicion—the time he was transporting a new copper coil out to Hungry Hollow for his overworked moonshine still. The "smellers and snoopers" had lain in wait in the darkness and had gleefully pounced upon Danny and his copper coil.

They had unceremoniously flung him into jail down at Iron Bay, right in among all the other moonshiners. There they had held him for three restless days and nights until loyal Big Annie had put on her finery and ridden down to Iron Bay on the L. S. & C. and posted his cash bail—all in wrinkled one dollar-bills. Crafty old Crocker, the Chippewa lawyer, had finally got the charges dismissed and the copper coil returned.

"I s'pose you met some purty tough birds down there when you was in jail?" Buller had politely inquired when Danny returned to Hungry Hollow with his copper coil.

"Nope," emancipated Danny promptly replied. "Not so tough. But I sure got some goddam swell new recipes fer makin' moon, though! Yep, yep."

Even after Repeal Danny and the boys still called his moonshine "cookin' whisky," not only to distinguish it from Old Cordwood but also to avoid the possible inadvertent public use of the dreaded word "moonshine." For Repeal had not legalized the manufacture of moonshine whisky. Permitting his moonshine to be called "cookin' whisky" was not to say that Danny was not intensely proud of his prowess as a distiller. He claimed to be among the Peninsula's best. After all, when he was a boy hadn't he nailed whisky crates for three weeks in a Canadian distillery?

So proud, in fact, was Danny of his own brand of moonshine that he even stacked it up against Old Cordwood itself. Only the fall before he and Charlie Jokinen had gotten into a heated argument over the relative merits of the two brands. Charlie was aghast at Danny's violent slurs on Old Cordwood. The argument flared fitfully for days and weeks. At length he and Danny finally sat down in the back room of Charlie's, with an open quart of each brand before them—

Danny's moonshine and Charlie's Old Cordwood—
looking for all the world like two self-sacrificing in-
vestigators crouching over their retorts, freely offering
themselves up as human guinea pigs for the deathless
cause of science. The bout was on.

"I'm tellin' you," Danny said when it again came his
turn, carefully measuring out still another drink of
his cooking whisky, "they ain't no finer goddam moon
made this side of hell! My secret is easy. I makes it
fer love, not fer profit. An' it's pure, too, jest like
mother's milk."

"Mudder's milk my feets!" Charlie retorted skeptically. "Notting but 'wamp water, mosquitoes, an'
li'l c'icken corn!"

"O.K., then!" Danny said heatedly, with corded
neck, cut to the quick. "Fetch me a goddam pencil an'
paper an' a little bottle, an' we'll see about that. We're
goin' to settle this thing up scientific—once an' fer
all!"

Mystified, Charlie went out front and got the pencil
and paper and little bottle and placed them on the green
poker table beside Danny. "Wat crazy bizness you
being up to now, Danny?"

"Never you mind," Danny said, carefully filling the
bottle with his moonshine. "Lemme alone. I gotta write
a letter to smart folks what knows good cookin'
whisky when they sees it!"

Charlie shrugged amiably and went out front, leaving Danny ah-ing and grunting and biting his tongue
over his letter to the head of the chemistry laboratory
of the University of Michigan at Ann Arbor. He'd
show 'em.

Laboring over his letter, Danny sorely missed the
services of his social secretary, little Timmy. And besides, so exhausting were the rigors of his recent re-

search, Danny was gently drunk. His letter wandered. Ah, yes—while he was about it he might just as well let the tail go with the hide and tell the good professor about Bessie, the cow, and her epic spree on his powerful moonshine mash. That would show 'im. And would he kindly please test the accompanying sample and send Danny the results by return mail in care of Charlie's Place?

The reply did not come for several weeks. Danny was sure that the delay was due solely to the delight and thralldom inevitably sweeping over scientific circles in Ann Arbor. But one day the letter arrived. The envelope read:

"Daniel Wellington McGinnis, Esq.

% Charlie's Place

Chippewa, Michigan"

Charlie importantly handed the letter to Danny when next he came to town. Danny got out his ten-cent-store glasses and sat in Charlie's back room. He read the address over aloud for several minutes and then, at Charlie's insistence, finally opened the letter. Ahem! The report was brief and to the point.

"Dear Mr. McGinnis:
We received your recent specimen, and we regret to inform you that in our opinion your cow is suffering from sugar diabetes."

Charlie leaned over the table on his hands and regarded Danny intently with his faded blue eyes. "Wat does it say?" he asked.

Danny peered over the tops of his glasses at Charlie. "Hm," he said quietly. "Imagine the pore taxpayers forkin' over money to support the likes of them!"

"Wat does it say?" Charlie insisted.

"Oh, that," Danny said, crumpling the letter in his fist. "It said on the letter that—that they was awful sorry, but a public institootion like them ain't allowed fer to make scientific tests on illegal producks. Yep, yep. I mighta known. Say, Charlie, bring me a double shot of Ol' Cordwood! Have one yourself."

When Prohibition was finally repealed and Andrew Volstead had retired to Minnesota to contemplate the majestic results of his handiwork, Danny had blithely continued to make his moonshine and home-brew. It was true that he didn't have to make quite so much any more, since the supply could now be supplemented by regular Saturday night baths of Old Cordwood and real brewery beer. But Chippewa was seventeen miles away; real whisky cost money; and a man never knew when he might get bitten by a snake or drilled by a marauding sidehill gouger.

Everything had gone along fine until that bright March afternoon, the spring after Timmy had wired the Mulligan swamp for sound. Late that fateful afternoon lean Billy Grill, the hermit trapper, had perspiringly burst into camp, snowshoes and all, and had haltingly announced to Danny that the police were perhaps even then on their way out to raid Hungry Hollow.

Hungry Hollow was going to be raided!

"Sit down and rest yourself, Billy," were Danny's calm words after hearing the astounding news. "Take it easy, man—you're all blown an' winded. Now take a five an' tell me the hull story from the beginnin', nice and quiet-like."

While Billy was mopping his pounding temples and pantingly getting his wind, Danny proceeded to deliver himself of an extemporaneous indictment of any government that continued to dispatch hordes of spies and stool pigeons over the countryside like a swarm of locusts, there to prey upon innocent and God-fearing citizens like himself. "It's gittin' so bad, Billy, that a good citizen an' taxpayer can't blow his bloody nose nor even sneak a visit to a one-room outhouse 'thout some bloody snoopers is spyin' on him an' tryin' to cast him into prison!" he concluded.

"That's right!" Billy rejoined feelingly, remembering his frequent unhappy brushes with the local gamewardens. "You sure said a mouthful there, Danny. I mind the time—"

"Hm," Danny quietly broke in. "I see you got your wind back. Now tell me all about this here now raid."

"I tell you, Danny, I heared it with my own ears," Billy said, standing up in his excitement. "This forenoon while I was standin' in the public can down in the city jail in Chippewa. Right through the bloody ventilator I heared the chief of police tellin' two members of the state constabulary jest where your place was at!"

"Hm . . . When is they aimin' to conduck this here raid?" Danny asked.

"I couldn't make out exackly fer certain," Billy replied. "You see, jest then the goddam outfit up an' flushed. It works automatic. But as near as I could figger out, they was plannin' to surprise you tonight. They seemed to know that Buller an' the other boys was all in town."

"Did you happen to run into Buller an' the boys?" Danny asked hopefully. He disliked having to face this ordeal all alone. After all, it was their home too.

"Nope," Billy answered. "I looked see in Charlie's an' a few more places—they allus seemed jest two rounds of drinks ahead of me—so then I figgered since as how someone had to stay sober, an' I was comin' north myself to trap beaver an' they was no time to lose, I'd jest up an' come right along. So I made the hull trip afoot in less'n four hours."

"Billy!" Danny stood and grasped the trapper's hand. "Billy, I know there's some folks what don't like you. As a matter of plain fack, I never thought a hull lot of you myself. You allus kinda reminded me of a cross between a snake an' a starved wolf. But I guess even them divils has their good spells." He went on pumping Billy's hand, continuing to win him with flattery. "I'm mighty thankful for your warnin', Billy. You may look like a goddam wolf to some folks, but now I know you gotta heart a gold. Yep, yep. Here! Set down an' have a drink!"

"Thanks, Dan," Billy said, swallowing the lump in his throat, deeply touched.

Danny got out his keys and went to the tall wooden cupboard and unlocked it, throwing open the double doors. There stood the neat rows of bejugged and bebottled Hungry Hollow moonshine and home-brew. Danny shrugged philosophically. "If the goddam stuff's gotta be thrun out, Billy, we might jest so well sample it good afore the awful deed is done."

After a preliminary round of drinks Danny and Billy spent a perspiring hour packing the bottles and jugs down to the frozen Big Dead pool. Danny planned to cut a hole in the ice and sink the entire works in the pool. After each heavy load they naturally had to pause and uncork a moonshine container and take a generous swig, along with some home-brew for a wash. The March sun was a sunken glow in the southwest when they were through.

"Shay, Danny—howsh about your still?" Billy suddenly remembered.

Danny squinted at him keenly. "Never you min' about the bloody still, Billy boy. That there's miles away, snug as a bug in a rug, hid safe in the Mulligan Mountains. Neither you nor this here Sherlock Holmes could fin' ol' Danny's still." As he spoke, his battered copper still nestled in the little swamp less than a hundred yards away. But since it had snowed hard two days before, indeed the devil himself could hardly have discovered it.

"Well then, kin I give you a han' makin' the hole in the goddam icesh?" Billy might have been a wolf, but he was a willing one. "An' I'll help you throw the stuff in."

"No, no," Danny said. He looked up at the sky. "I'll do it later. The damn stuff's outa my house now. An' it's near to dark. If you're gonna make your camp up on Connor's Creek tonight you better high-tail, Billy. You better not be here when the law arrives." Danny sniffed. "I'll face 'er all alone—as usual. Here —take this last jug along with you. An' let's have jest one more snort afore you go."

"I doan min' if I do," Billy said. "Thanksh, Danny. Hersh bumps!"

"Drink hearty, Billy," Danny said. "You're a real pal. Skoal!"

Danny accompanied the wavering Billy from the camp to the top of the Mulligan ridge. He had to help him adjust his snowshoe harness. "Good-by, Billy," he called as he stood watching the lone trapper weaving uncertainly along the ridge in the fading light, slowly swinging his jug, finally reeling from sight into the dense Silver Lake hardwood.

"Yep, yep," Danny said, squinting one eye after Billy and biting his lip. "That there fella ain't no cross between a snake an' a wolf. They's another critter in there. He's part fox, too. Mebbe he's figgered out this raid business jest to git himself a free skinful. But if he's foolin' ol' Danny about this here goddam raid, I'll trap him alive an' mount him by han' an' hang him in plain sight over the goddam bar in Charlie's Place!"

Whereupon Danny hurried down the ridge, locked the darkened camp from the outside, and then scampered over to Bessie's woodshed and locked that too, from the outside. He then crept nimbly through Bessie's window, carefully closing the window from the inside. He stretched and yawned. He had put in a hard afternoon. "Yep, yep . . ." He would take a little snooze alongside of Bessie before he inaugurated his private scorched earth policy. He pulled down some fresh clover hay and nestled against warm Bessie, who lay placidly chewing her cud.

"Moo," Bessie lowed contentedly.

"Yep, yep," whispered Danny. "Let the goddam raiders come, Bess."

It was midnight. The lonely March moon bathed the rigid, gleaming snow-shield of the iron earth in blue. Over the Silver Lake forest the smoky, eerie shafts of the northern lights wavered and raced, shifting and melting across the brilliant northern sky in great dripping organ pipes of silent melody—dancing and leaping far and away and beyond the loneliness of the snow-clad valleys and hills. The darkened windows of the camp at Hungry Hollow gleamed in the changing light. No smoke rose from the chimney. The night was still.

Down at the frozen Big Dead pool, lighted only by the sky, Danny was stealthily chipping at the ice which covered the river. Occasionally he paused and cupped his ear, as though to listen. Then he resumed his chipping. All around him, like silent, watchful penguins, stood an assortment of gleaming bottles and jugs. Danny kept chipping away at the ice. At length he reached the open water. He glanced quickly up the river trail. Then he began hurriedly dropping an endless variety of loaded jugs and bottles and decanters and crocks and jars down through the hole in the ice. The only sound was an answering, ascending gurgle from the water.

Old Danny came to the last bottle, a full quart of moonshine. He held it poised over the hole, as though debating. Far down the lonely river a hunting owl hooted its ghostly "hoo, hoo." Danny quickly uncorked the bottle and tilted it to his lips. "Hoo, hoo," went the distant owl. "Ah!" went Danny. He replaced the cork, tamped it with his fist, held the bottle poised over the hole, hesitated for a wistful instant, and then plunged it to the bottom as though he were spearing a fish.

"Pah! Let the tail go with the hide. Take that, you divils!" Danny straightened up. He spat a stream of Peerless juice into the hole. Then he hurriedly gathered the loose chipped ice into the opening, shoveled some fresh snow over the ice, and gently tamped the wintry shrine below which lay every last drop of the moonshine and home-brew of Hungry Hollow.

Reeling uncertainly, Danny plodded wearily up the trail to the deserted camp. He had had a full day. He lighted the kerosene lamp in the chilly camp and watched the film of creeping mist slowly disappear from the lamp chimney. He glanced at the ticking alarm clock. "Twenty minutes past midnight," he said, clattering the stove lids. A man could always have a warm cup of tea. There had been no fire in the camp since perspiring Billy Grill, the hermit trapper, had snow-shoed by late that afternoon and warned Danny of the impending raid.

Two days passed. Danny was growing lonely. Here he had kept the vigil for two whole days, waiting vainly for the raiders to descend upon Hungry Hollow. His thirst was assuming Death Valley proportions. He began seeing mirages, conjuring up roseate visions of his cupboard shelves sagging with their imaginary burden of beer and moonshine. He combed the premises to find a drink but, alas! Inspector Buller Beaudin had thoroughly gone before.

On the second night Danny was sore tempted to snowshoe into Chippewa. But he restrained himself. After all, he was a man of property. One had to meet one's responsibilities, even if the other boys were still in Chippewa, heedlessly roistering and obliviously wading up to their hips in Old Cordwood. He pondered visiting Billy Grill up on Connor's Creek. "Nope, nope! If I laid eyes on thet lyin' snake right now, we's sure to tangle fer keeps. I'll git him later." That night a lonely Danny crept into the woodshed and slept with Bessie. Dolefully, he had just about concluded that a man's best friend was his cow.

On the morning of the third day Danny found and drank a bottle of Swan's hair tonic. "Harrump!" he went, his eyes growing glazed and enlarged with wonder. He lay back on his bunk, waiting patiently either for the release of death or for the hair to grow in his throat. Instead he was seized with an irresistible impulse toward song. Raising his voice in a quavering falsetto, he burst into "Steve O'Donnell's Wake." He hadn't sung it in years.

"Steve O'Donnell was a gintleman, that everybody said;
He was liked by all the rich and all the poor.
And they all felt so sorry when they heard that Steve
    was dead,
They tied a knot of crepe upon his door.

They sent for the barber to cut the spindles from his
    throat,
Then they cut his hair à la pompadour;
Red necktie and buttonhole bouquet was in his coat,
And a bunch of shamrock in his hand he bore.

O meself and Annie Fieldie helped to lay the rascal out,
There were lots of flowers sent for friendship's sake.
'O Steve me boy, why did you die?' the weeping widow
    cried—
And we all got drunk at Steve O'Donnell's wake!

CHORUS:

O there were fighters, and biters, bums and dynamiters,
Ale, wine and whisky; there was cake.
There were men of high position, there were Irish
    politicians—
And we *all got floored* at Ste-e-eve O'Donnell's
    wa-a-a-ke!"

Danny sat up in bed. "Aw, hell!" he snorted in disgust. It was no use. No man could sing on mere hair tonic. Only fools and sly barbers ever tried to. Danny was in bad shape. He couldn't sing, he couldn't eat, he couldn't sleep. A man might just as well crouch under Chief Booze-in-the-Face and try to fish in the horse trough at the public fountain in Chippewa.

"Fishin'? Fishin'?" Danny repeated, slowly savoring the word in different keys. *"Why, a course!"* he shouted, leaping from his bunk. He ran to the wall and got down Timmy's metal duck hook. Then he raced outside and got his trusty fly rod from its nails on the camp logs, where it rested winter and summer. He hurriedly tied the hook of the duck strap to the end of his fly line and ran pell-mell down the trail to the Big Dead pool.

Danny knelt and eagerly clawed the snow and ice from the hole where he had plunged all of Hungry Hollow's alcohol to its watery grave. Singing "Steve O'Donnell's Wake" with new gusto, he lowered the duck strap and fly line into the hole and squatted on his haunches, fishing as he had never fished before.

"I don't give a rattlin' goddam if the hull worl' ketches me," he muttered to himself.

Absorbed, Danny fished all morning, oblivious of hunger. He could hear the dull glassy clink as the metal duck hook fumbled and scraped across the sunken treasure. Around two-thirty he got a real bite and he eagerly raised his catch to the top. "My Gawd! It's a gallon jug a moon!" But Danny had to back up to raise his hooped and straining fly rod. The jug hit the side of the hole and suddenly fell off the hook, merrily gurgling back to join its sleeping comrades.

Bereft, Danny leapt in the air as though he had lost the biggest fish in America. The entire Big Dead valley rang and echoed with the agony of his lament. Shaken, he discarded the rod, and kneeling, fished avidly with only the line. Dusk settled imperceptibly over Hungry Hollow. Danny fished on and on, oblivious.

The waning March moon lighted his task as he finally caught on to another bottle. Slowly, lovingly, he raised his catch to the surface. His lips moved in prayerful whispers. The moment the neck broke surface he dropped everything and clutched at it with both hands. *"I gotcha!"* He held the dripping bottle up in the moonlight. A strangled moan came from Danny. It was merely a bottle of home-brew.

"Danny don't want no beer! Danny wants *whisky!*" he cried in anguish, wrathfully plunging the bottle back in the gaping hole. Still on his aching knees, he bowed his head over the hole, a broken old man.

Danny automatically lowered his line and for the thousandth time that day heard the hook clink aimlessly and glassily across the sunken treasure. Then, miracle of miracles, the line suddenly tightened! Danny tensed and rapidly drew up his catch. In a thrice he was clutching to his bosom a glistening and dripping gallon jug of moonshine whisky. He knelt in the moonlight and dazedly shook his head in wordless thanksgiving.

Just then there was a salty, frozen crunching on the snow behind him. He wheeled around, still on his knees. "Oh, my Gawd!" he whispered. Slowly advancing were two uniformed members of the state constabulary. They were wearing snowshoes, and walked curiously bowlegged. They seemed to be in great distress. They stopped at the edge of the snow-covered bank above Danny. The blue moonlight gleamed on their police badges.

"What you doin', old man?" one of them wearily asked.

"Fishin'," Danny wearily replied.

"Are you old Danny McGinnis of Hungry Hollow?" the other trooper asked.

"Yep, yep. This is me an' this is it." Danny gulped. "Though neither of us is a hull lot to brag about."

"What you got there in your arms?" one of the troopers asked. The inquisition was on.

"Who, me? Oh, that! Why of all things—I'm damned if it ain't a gallon of whisky!" Danny replied weakly.

"Whisky!" the two troopers breathed. There seemed a note more of wistfulness than official triumph in their voices.

The subtle intonation was not lost on Danny. He quickly rose to his feet and held the jug up to the moonlight, sighting it carefully. "Yep, yep. A full gallon of the rarest ol' whisky in Michigan—if not in the hull bloody worl'." He paused and blinked, sparring for words, and then warmed to his theme, talking rapidly and glibly, like a desperate barker trying to hold a reluctant crowd at a side show. "Would you young fellas believe it—this here whisky's been planted in this pool here for goin' on nigh half a century—so long ago that you young fellers was nothin' but a twinkle in your paw's eye. It was ol' Angus Ferguson, the King of the White Pine, what put it there—did you ever hear tell of him? Yep, yep. Poor ol' Angus." Danny shook his head. "He done it one night when he was half snaky. He was an awful Angus when he was drinkin'—an' stubborn, too. Right here is where he thrun it—I saw it with my own eyes. I tried to stop him, but he done it so quick-like. I kept sayin' to him, pleadin'-like, 'Don't, Angus. Don't, Angus! Lissen to reason, Angus! Now Angus, please refrain!' says I. But it was no use. No use a-tall. He thrun it in—the hull full gallon."

"Listen here—" one of the troopers began ominously.

Danny was not to be stopped. He shrugged and shook his head sadly and the torrent went on. "Man and boy I've spent years out here fishin' fer this goddam jug. It weren't on'y fer the whisky, but sorta the sentiment, too. But now in a way I'm kinda sorry I finely landed it. Sounds sorta crazy, don't it? Still an' all you know how a fella kinda gets attached to doin' a certain sumpin. I guess we's all creatures of habit—

the high an' the low. Now ain't it a funny thing you young fellas should jest happen along? I was gittin' powerful lonesome, too. Kinda seems like Fate musta sent you. Yep, yep, that's it. But, like I says, I'm goin' to miss fishin' fer this jug. There ain't much else fer an ol' fella to do these days 'way up here in the frozen woods. *Brr!* It sure do git cold! Specially at night when you ain't got no place to stay. Yep, yep. I'm sure goin' to miss fishin' fer this here jug, that I am. Mebbe like as not I'll fill 'er up agin an' drop 'er back in. Mebbe forty-fifty years from now one of you lucky young fellas kin come back up here an' ketch it."

"But, look here, Mr. McGinnis, why didn't you dive in for it years ago?" one of the troopers began. "Why didn't—"

"Yep," Danny ran on, "a pore ol' fella who's had rheumatism so bad for over forty years he can scarce take a bath is sure goin' to miss settin' here for a quiet evenin's fish." He patted the jug and resolutely squared his shoulders. One must be brave. What was done was done. "But now's I got it I mights so well drink it. That's what whisky's made fer, as the fella said. Um . . . I can just taste it now. Tain't every day a man kin lay holt of a jug of forty-fifty-year-old whisky— 'specially out fishin'."

The shivering troopers no longer tried to question or stop Danny. They just stood there in silence, miserable and dejected in the moonlight, waiting for the flood of words to stop. "Yep, yep," Danny ran on, clambering stiffly up the bank, grimly hugging his jug. "I think I'll go up to the shack an' light me a fire an' put on a big pot of Mulligan stew. Le's see, now— rabbit, venison, beaver, muskrat, turnips, a little barley, potatoes, a dash of garlic, a coupla onions . . . Yum, yum! Makes me hungry as a bear jest to think of it!

But first I'll boil a kettle of water fer hot drinks. I allus said there's nothin' like a good slug a scaldin' whisky to warm a man's innards." He paused and cocked his head sideways. "You fellas figurin' to stay long in these parts?"

"L-l-look!" broke in one of the weary troopers, his teeth chattering like castanets. "All we want is to get off these damn torturing snowshoes, find a warm place and a hot meal and a bed—and then get to hell out of this Godforsaken country. C-c-can you fix us up?"

Danny blinked his eyes and sipped his mustache. Then very casually, "Hm . . . When was you figurin' to leave?"

"At d-daybreak," the trooper answered.

"Alone?" Danny innocently inquired.

"Absolutely," both troopers answered in spirited unison.

"Hm," Danny said. "My, my! Now that's too bad. Jest when I was figgerin' that at last I had some company. But I guess that's the way a the worl'—here today an' gone tomorrow—an' at daybreak, too." He shrugged. "Well, I'll tell you what—you young fellas take an' fill up this hole in the ice. Step lively now, an' be sure to tamp it an' seal it over real nice an' careful so's my lovely trout won't up an' ketch their death a cold. They's awful delicate critters. Would you believe it—many's the time I've seen full-grown trout what was caught in a draft up an' contrack double pneumonia an' come roarin' to the top, hackin' an' spittin' an' coughin'—then jest lay there on their sides, rollin' their eyes at me, sadlike, an' dyin' like flies. Yep, yep, I mind the time—"

"Please, Mr. McGinnis," one of the disconsolate troopers plaintively began.

"Now, me," Danny went on heedlessly, "I'll go up

an' start a roarin' fire an' figure out as if I kin fin' room
to bed you boys down." He paused. "Hm—come to
think of it mebbe I could even take an' fix up a few
extra hot drinks." He craned his neck forward, squinting. "Or mebbe you bus driver fellas ain't allowed to
drink spirits." Danny squinted harder. "Or is it cab
drivers?" He paused. "Or mebbe I hadn't ought to of
mentioned it."

One of the chilled young troopers turned desperately
to the other. "Corporal, d-d-do you d-declare us off
d-duty?"

"Absolutely," the shivering corporal replied, grateful for the inspiration. "It is a s-s-so ordered." The
two troopers quickly removed their officer's badges and
pocketed them. They turned to Danny. There was an
imploring look in their eyes.

"Please, can we stay?" they pleaded.

Danny stroked his chin thoughtfully with one hand
and slowly swung the gurgling jug with the other. He
blinked reflectively, carefully weighing the situation.
"Hm," he said. Then he nodded curtly. "Yep, yep," he
said.

The raiders were in.

15

THE BOURBON BONANZA

Wink Vivian conducted the Chippewa dray line. He drove a team of unruly roan geldings called Cub and Dick. This Cub horse was particularly wicked, possessing a Roman nose, permanently flattened ears, sharp yellow teeth, and a knockout punch in all four legs. There was only one man besides Wink who could properly handle his team. That was Buller Beaudin. For when Cub horse kicked at Buller, Buller swiftly kicked him back; when Cub bit Buller, Buller promptly returned the compliment. In this way the two had established a strained sort of rapport based upon mutual respect and fear.

Whenever Wink was laid up his dray business languished until Buller could be coaxed and teased into town to relieve him. Thus it was that when Wink broke his collarbone early in June, Buller reluctantly found himself flailing the wild horses about the streets of Chippewa, imposing discipline with a dray stake, morosely hauling everything from pianos to pincushions.

Buller had an unnatural penchant for carrying pianos. He always said a piano was something a man could really get his hands on. But the new dwarfed spinet type filled him with disgust. Nothing short of a full-sized piano ever challenged Buller to flex his biceps willingly. He accordingly contrived to lure at least one small boy onto the dray to deliver loaded trunks and kegs of nails and other paltry things. This saved Buller many weary steps. By judiciously permitting the youngsters to drive Cub and Dick a few blocks, he somehow managed to get himself through the day with a minimum of toil.

Dr. Martin's son, Buddy, was a particularly avid customer of Buller's. Buller had met thirteen-year-old Buddy a few weeks before while delivering a spinet piano, of all things, to his parents' home. Buddy's mother had asked Buller to let the boy ride on the dray with him. Gallant Buller had let Buddy drive Cub and Dick back downtown. Since then Buller found smiling Buddy awaiting him at the freight depot every morning, teasing to be allowed to drive the horses.

One Monday morning Buller was greatly relieved to find Buddy there eagerly waiting to help him. This particular morning Buller was dubious about his ability to deliver even a small crate of powder puffs. He had had a particularly rocky week end. In addition to his epic hangover, he was flat broke and so was helpless to put out the fire. He accordingly let Buddy drive the horses all morning, while he sat dangling his fat legs off the side of the dray, intermittently holding his head and moaning. Buddy was in a small boy's heaven.

After lunch Buller's plight grew worse. His huge body was one vast pulse. Little Buddy was touched to see his hero in such travail. "What's the matter, Mister

Buller—are you sick?" he finally piped up. Buller turned his weary, inflamed eyes on the boy. "Lissen, Bud—I'd sell this hull bloody dray fer the price of one drink of whisky."

"Is *that* all," Buddy said, breaking into a relieved smile. "Then we'll drive straight up to my house right away. My daddy's got ever so many bottles of whisky in our basement."

"Wah—what's that!" Buller said. "What's that you jest said?"

"Daddy keeps it locked in a closet in the basement— but I know where he hides the key," Buddy ran on.

Buller became full of craft and low cunning. He held his head in his plump hands, rocking in elaborate symptoms of anguish. He peeked up at Buddy. "O-ooh! My pore head! Buddy, are you sure your folks ain't to home?"

"Oh, no, Mister Buller, Mama's at a card party this afternoon—and Daddy's out on his calls."

"Make 'em run, Bud, make 'em run!" Buller burst out. "Giddap, Cub, Dick! O-ooh, my pore head!"

Buller's eyes gleamed like shoe buttons as Buddy threw open the wooden closet door and proudly exposed the rows of glistening bottles. Buller took a short step forward and extravagantly folded his plump hands together in front of him in a prayerful attitude, like a husky church tenor about to burst into song during the offertory. He moistened his dry lips, which involuntarily drew up into a wet rosebud pout. The damp basement grew hushed. Buller gulped and puffed out his cheeks. No words came.

"There it is, Mister Buller," Buddy said. "Help yourself. Take any kind you want."

Buller slowly turned and regarded Buddy as though

he were a stranger. "Wa-what's that?" he mumbled. "What'd you say?"

"Help yourself," Buddy repeated.

Buller incredulously poked a fat finger at his own bosom and then at the closet.

"Who? You mean me?"

"Sure, sure," Buddy said. "But let's hurry before Mama comes home."

This electrified Buller, who lurched toward the cupboard only to trample into a lawn mower, the blades of which spun crazily. Ignoring the clatter and din, he reached toward the bottles. He paused. Then he tenderly ran his hand over the nearest bottle. It was a bonded Bourbon. He quickly withdrew his hand and put two fingers to his lips, gnawing them with indecision. He plucked tentatively at another bottle and again quickly withdrew his hand. Sore puzzled, he shook his head and glanced quickly at Buddy. Worried Buddy grabbed the nearest bottle and thrust it into Buller's hands. Lo! it was Old Cordwood! Buller cradled the bottle in his arms as though it were a baby, gently fondling and caressing it, his breath coming in great and mighty heaves.

"Drink it!" Buddy ordered. Dr. Martin's son had made his first prescription.

Before they left, Buller had sluiced down one bottle of Old Cordwood and had still another snuggling under his coat. "Take another one," said Buddy in the grand manner. "Mama's often said she wished Daddy'd get rid of the awful stuff."

Smiling in droopy-eyed unconcern, Buller let the boy proudly drive the horses back to the freight depot. Just as Buddy was leaving to run home he turned to Buller. "Would you like to come back after supper and get some more of Daddy's whisky, Mister Buller? I think Mama and Daddy are going to the second show."

"Who—me? Wh-why—are you sure they're goin' out?" Buller said, his eyes alight with visions of what he had just left.

"No-o," fertile-minded Buddy said, "but I'll tell you what. When they go out I'll leave a light on in the front room. That's our signal. When you see the parlor light you'll know the coast is clear. Better make it five minutes after nine—just to be on the safe side."

"Five after nine it is," Buller said, solemnly shaking Buddy's hand.

"There's just one more thing, Mister Buller," Buddy added, having a boyish angle of his own. "For curing your illness this way kin I drive Cub and Dick all day tomorrow? Kin I?"

Precocious was the word for Buddy.

"Buddy," Buller said airily, carelessly throwing out a fat hand. "Buddy, fer what you done today you kin drive these nags the hull bloody week!"

"Five after nine, then," Buddy sang out, leaping from the dray.

"On the dot—*hic!*" Buller said, clucking Cub and Dick toward the barn.

So strange are the devices of fortune, that Buller ran into little Matti Hunginen during supper hour at the Chippewa House. Taking Matti aside, he excitedly told him of the bonanza he had struck. "You c'mon along tonight, Matti, to help me carry the goddam swag. Here, have a drink." Buller casually produced a quart of Old Cordwood. After a few generous samples, Matti would have agreed to assist in the abduction of a live tiger. He nodded his head vigorously, a man of great decision. "Yes-sirree! Matti doan care. Matti's all time villing to help a frien'!"

Promptly at 9:05 Buller and Matti stood on Dr. Martin's corner. "See!" Buller whispered hoarsely.

"The bloody coast is clear. The light's on in the parlor
—jest like Buddy and me planned it. C'mon, Matti!
Boy, oh boy!"

The two men walked boldly up on Dr. Martin's
front porch and rang the bell. They could hear the
tortured strains of halting piano music. "See," Buller
whispered, "that's Buddy in there practicin' on the
new piano, jest killin' time waitin' fer us." After an
interval the porch light switched on. Matti and Buller
stood blinking uncertainly. The front door opened.
There stood Mrs. Martin. The blurts of piano music
ceased abruptly. Buller swept off his cap and elbowed
Matti to remove his. Since the Martins had changed
their plans about attending the movies, they had naturally left the light on in the living room.

"Good evening, gentlemen—oh, it's Mr. Beaudin,"
Mrs. Martin said graciously. "Won't you come in?"

Buller glanced at Matti and Matti glanced at Buller.

"Won't you come in?" Mrs. Martin repeated.

"No'm," Buller managed to mumble, twisting his
cap in his hands.

"Isn't there something I can do for you?" Mrs.
Martin said. "Doctor is out on a sick call."

"Missus Martin," Buller began in grievous desperation. His world was reeling. He gulped and rolled
his eyes like a dying water buffalo. "Look, Missus
Martin—" Buller finally blurted, *"kin Buddy come
out an' play?"*

16

UNDER THE SPREADING BANYAN TREE

The bats flitted and circled in oiled flight over the town square, feeding greedily on the swarming moths and mosquitoes attracted there by the glare of Doc Halliday's medicine show. The banjo-shaped gasoline flares guttered and spat fitfully in the chill summer night's breeze, noisily devouring those swirling insects which had not fallen prey to the bats. Far above the heads of the knot of townspeople the hunting night-hawks wheeled and screeched and endlessly soared.

Danny and the boys had gradually worked in near the edge of the platform, their eyes unblinking as they drank in the magic of the medicine show. Doc Halliday's colored Dixieland Ragtime Band blared out the final chorus of "Alexander's Ragtime Band" from their vapor-steaming horns and twanging banjo—eye-rolling, shivering, devoutly wishing they were back in Dixie. Their music finished, they crowded in gangling haste to the comparative warmth of the changing tent.

Doc Halliday, privately nettled, but beaming at his retreating assistants, winked broadly at his audience, nodding at its answering chuckle. After the last musician had left he pushed back his sombrero, removed his cigar, and strode to the front of the platform. Hooking his thumb through his colored vest, he rocked thoughtfully on his booted heels, gazing with sightless eyes over the heads of the waiting people. The crowd grew silent. His was now the misty eye of the healer. Fun was fun, see—but there was the *word*, there was the *message*. There was *Banyan*!

Danny and the boys eagerly absorbed every gesture, every pause of the great Herr Doktor. Here was the persuasive, successful leader of men; the actor, the master of timing, subtle nuance, modulation, mood. With visible effort the great man withdrew from his tinctured dream, trumpeted into a large silk handkerchief, and began to speak.

"Lay-dees and gentlemen!

"Before we move on to the next act, which follows immediately, we wish to tell our many friends in Chippewa how glad we are to be back again in Michigan's Northern Peninsula; how much we look forward each year to visiting your invigorating clime, to breathing once again your clean pine-scented Lake Superior air—that air which spells the greatest of God's gifts" —he closed his eyes—"abundant *health!*"

Smiling benevolently, he surveyed the group of boys down in front of him. He put on his Uncle Hal voice, generous, bluff, hearty. "I wonder if one of you fine young boys would help me out tonight. Looks like the members of my band's got to thaw out between acts." The crowd rumbled its appreciation of this vast, gold-toothed good humor. It made him one of them, a sturdy, hardy Northerner. His roving eyes lit on Buddy Martin's eager, small face.

"Here, you—give me your hand, young man. Tonight you're going to intern under ol' Doc Halliday." He reached down and grabbed Buddy's helplessly upraised arm and lifted him—"ups-a-daisy"—onto the platform. Buddy stood blinking down at his giggling, envious comrades, his face surging with color.

Doc Halliday reached out his big palm to Buddy. "My name's Doc Halliday, pardner. Put her there. What's yours?"

"Buddy Martin, sir."

"How old are you?"

"Thirteen, sir," Buddy answered.

"Don't 'sir' me, Bud. Now suppose we get to work. Would you reach in that there carton, please, and fetch me a bottle of my life-giving medicine—Banyan?"

"Yes, sir," Buddy said, scrambling to the carton, glad to hide in action the delightful terror of his embarrassment. He rummaged in the carton and drew out a tall bottle of inky black fluid and handed it to Doc Halliday. Doc lay the bottle in the palm of one big hand and patted it with the other. Lovingly, he patted it. He looked out over the spellbound audience. Buddy stood there, spindly in his corduroy knee-pants and red knitted pull-over sweater, drinking in the words of the great man along with the pungent, delicious aroma of raw gasoline from the lamps.

"Good friends of Chippewa, due to the scarcity of the rare and exotic ingredients which go into Banyan, we are, alas! not able to offer you as much of our health-giving medicine this year as we have in the past." Doc Halliday again favored the crowd with his broad gold-carat smile. "And so we regret that we must restrict each lucky person to one bottle of Banyan. One only—

our supply is limited. But the quality is even better than ever. And the price remains the same—one dollar per bottle. Yessir, ladies and gentlemen—Banyan is still only one silver dollar per bottle, just ten silver dimes."

His voice boomed on rapidly now, in a kind of a chant, on sure and steady ground.

"Folks, do you ever wake up in the morning with spots before your eyes, a pain in the small of your back, and a strong and highly offensive u-rine? *Then take Banyan!* Here is the medicine that rids you of your aches and pains, releases the internal juices, tunes up the system, unclogs the human pipes and valves— in a word, Banyan. Banyan! *Banyan!* Made from the roots of that ancient tree which flowers only in the Holy Land."

The wretched, shivering Dixieland band, hearing its cue, again lined up under the flapping canopy of moths. The voice of medicine rolled glibly on, gathering speed.

"Banyan, that age-old remedy blessed by the wise men of yore—*Banyan*, just one silver dollar, ten silver dimes. Banyan cures or our money's yours. Who's the first lucky person? Here! Thank you, sir. Take her away, Dixieland. Who's the next? Right—and four are five. Another carton, Buddy boy! Banyan, Banyan! A-hi look! Step right up, ladies and gentlemen! Ring the cane, the cane you ring, the cane you carry away! Get Banyan, that soothing elixir of life. Columbus took a chance—why not you? *Banyan, Banyan . . .*"

"Da da da, da da da, da da da," tooted the Dixieland band.

Danny was fidgeting nervously with the drawstring of his buckskin purse. When the band subsided he caught the great doctor's eye. "Look, mister, is that there stuff any good fer a bum stummick? My ulcer's been flarin' somethin' awful today."

Oddly enough, peptic ulcers were right down Doc Halliday's alley. "Listen, friend," he boomed genially, "did you ever hear tell of one of them ancient Egyptians or old Biblical fellows that ever had the bellyache? Did you?"

"No-o," Danny was obliged to agree. "I don't mind that I ever did."

"Of course not. And why?" Doc's question was purely rhetorical. "Because every mother's son of 'em was raised, mind you, on Banyan. They drank gallons of it—that's why!" Doc triumphantly concluded. Danny fumbled in his buckskin purse.

"I'll take a bottle, then," he said, handing up a wrinkled dollar bill and receiving a bottle of precious Banyan from the hot hands of the great healer.

Danny could scarcely wait for the medicine show to end, so anxious was he to get at his bottle of magical Banyan. After the Dixieland band had tootled its last tune and the gasoline flares had been extinguished by the great doctor himself, Buller and the rest of the boys insisted upon repairing to Charlie's Place. They'd still take Old Cordwood. But Danny shook his head and resolutely scurried down the side streets to the Chippewa House, hugging his bottle of Banyan to him like a Notre Dame quarterback making a sweeping end run against Army.

Danny hurriedly got the key to Room 205—the bridal suite—from the sleepy night clerk, and in a thrice he had locked himself in his room, donned his nightshirt and sleeping cap, and was owlishly regarding himself in the rippled dresser mirror. He held the open bottle of Banyan in his hand.

"Here's bumps, Mister McGinnis," Danny toasted himself, tilting the bottle to his lips. What was good enough for the Pharaohs of Egypt was good enough for Daniel Wellington McGinnis. Gurgle, gurgle, gurgle went the Banyan. *"Pah!"* went Danny when the bottle was finally drained, wrinkling his nose in distaste.

Danny stood looking at himself in the mirror. His lips began to twitch. See, the ancient elixir was already doing its work. Danny's hands began to moisten. He gingerly placed the empty Banyan bottle on the dresser. Presently he began making a series of involuntary gulps, yawning and gasping and chumping his jaws like an undersized ostrich that had but recently swallowed an oversized orange. Then his cheeks began to blow out and in, rhythmically, convulsively, like those of an enchanted musician playing an invisible tuba. Danny stood helplessly regarding his remarkable symptoms. "It's releasin' the internal juices," he whispered hoarsely, wildly quoting the great Herr Doktor. "It's jest uncloggin' the pipes an' valves."

When Buller and the boys finally weaved their way over to the Chippewa House and up the carpeted stairs, a strange apparition greeted their eyes. A sleepwalker was groping his way down the hall and into the men's washroom, arms and fingers extended, walking rigid and stiff-legged, like a robot—or possibly even like the animated mummy of an Egyptian Pharaoh.

"It's the ol' man hisself," Buller whispered in awe. "It's ol' Danny staggerin' aroun' like a poisoned pup. I'll bet the ol' tightwad's gone an' floored every last drop of his Banyan."

Late the next afternoon there was a knock on the door of Doc Halliday's room in the Chippewa House. The doctor went to the door and found a wan and shaken Danny, yellowed and jaundiced from his bout with Banyan. Danny glimpsed an uncorked bottle on the bureau which, strangely enough, resembled Old Cordwood much more than it did Banyan.

"What can I do for you, chum?" Doc demanded, eager to return to his bureau.

"I want my money back——" Danny began plaintively.

"The face is familiar but I don't seem to remember the walrus mustache," Doc said wearily, with a fine note of sarcasm.

"The goddam vile stuff near kilt me," Danny went on doggedly. "I want my money back—like what you promised."

All of Doc's urbanity seemed to have deserted him since the evening before. The Pharaohs of Egypt had been insulted. The fair name of Banyan had been sullied. He was not amused. "Listen, Billy Whiskers," he said, "go 'way. Go peddle your rutabagas!" Danny found himself staring at the closed door. He heard the lock click. He backed away from the door and lowered his head for the charge. Just then another spasm of pain caught him. "O-ooh," he moaned, clutching his stomach and helplessly clenching his fist at the closed door. "If you hadn't of went an' poisoned me I-I'd jar your uppers loose an' swap 'em for your lowers. 'Billy Whiskers,' is it! We'll bloody well see about that!"

That night a large Banyan-bent crowd gathered at the feet of the great Doc Halliday. Doc was in glowing good humor. It was a warm evening and the grinning Dixieland band was doing right well with "St. Louis Blues." Next would come a soft-shoe dance, then another selection by the band. Then would be released the magic flood of Banyan.

A block away Danny entered Jabber Gleason's shooting gallery. Except for the disconsolate proprietor, the place was deserted. All of Jabber's customers were over being bedazzled by Banyan. Danny had a cold, fanatical look in his eye.

"Lissen, Jab," he said rapidly, "I want to borry my favorite .22 rifle and three shells—make 'em shorts—jest for ten minutes. C'mon, Jab, I gotta hurry."

Danny was one of Jabber's good customers and best shots, but Jabber didn't like the feverish look in his eye. "Look, Danny," he said, "you know you're welcome to the whole bloody joint, but what you aimin' to shoot? You—you look kind of sick an' wildlike tonight, Dan. I—"

"I am sick," Danny said quietly. "But I'm aimin' to save some of those other bloody damn fools from gettin' sick like me." He became full of guile. "An' I'll have this rats' nest of yours chuck full of cash customers in no time a-tall. Wait'n see. All I want is to shoot down a goddam tree."

"A tree?" Jabber echoed.

"Yep! A banyan tree. Ever hear tell of one? No, I figgered not. Here, man, han' me the bloody gun before it's too late!"

Danny grabbed the .22 and the three shells from a reluctant and fearful Jabber. He quickly broke down the rifle and tucked it under his jacket. "See you in ten minutes, Jab," he called over his shoulder. Jabber glumly stroked his chin and pondered the punishment which would be the lot of an accessory before the fact to first degree murder.

Back at the medicine show Doc Halliday was loudly extolling the manifold virtues of Banyan. He held the first bottle of the evening in his hands. So intent was the crowd on the glowing words of this traveling

Hippocrates that no one noticed a bald head quickly peek over the parapet of the roof of the city hall directly across from the town square. The two spitting gasoline flares lighted up the target nicely.

"—it's made from that ancient tree which flowers only in the Holy Land," Doc boomed on. "Banyan cures or our money's yours. Who's the first—Wah— what's that!"

"*Ping!*"

Something had sharply struck the round gasoline drum of one of the flares. Lo! it was punctured!

"*Spang!*" went the gasoline tank on the remaining flare.

Raw gasoline alternately sprayed, spurted, and dribbled from both flares, down on the platform, up in the air, and out at the hastily retreating crowd.

"Come back! Come back!" Doc Halliday wildly implored the waning crowd, leaning over the edge of his gasoline-soaked platform. "Look!" he beseeched, waving a bottle of Banyan. "We're gonna have a sale on Banyan tonight—fifty cents fer one bottle, three fer a dollar!" Doc continued to shout his startling bargain as he held a bottle of Banyan aloft for the crowd to see.

"*Plink!*"

The inky juice of the root of the ancient banyan tree ran down Doc's upraised arm. He stood quizzically studying the jagged pattern of the broken bottle in his hand just as the gasoline flares sputtered, flared up, and then died away into utter darkness. "Billy Whiskers," Doc whispered, grinning ruefully to himself in the dark.

Danny deftly edged his way through the crowd which thronged Jabber Gleason's shooting gallery. He handed grinning Jabber a long package wrapped in newspaper.

"T'is a fine rainbow trout fer your Friday dinner tomorrow," Danny shouted above the spat of the rifles. "I jest caught him!" He turned to leave.

"Don't you want to stay an' try your aim at a flock of clay pipes?" Jabber shouted back, tendering Danny a loaded rifle.

"No thanks, Jabber." Danny dolefully drew in his cheeks and winked at Jabber. "I'm jest a sick ol' man —an' anyway my eyes ain't what they used to be. If it's all the same, I'll jest step right over to Charlie's Place and git my medicine. An' it ain't Banyan. Good night, Jabber."

"Good night, Dan. Thanks for the fish."

17

DANIEL IN THE
LIONS' DEN

Chippewa was planning a home-coming celebration for
the Fourth of July, the occasion being the seventy-fifth
anniversary of the incorporation of the town. The
Chippewa common council had generously appropri-
ated money for the celebration. The *Hematite Weekly*
carried banner headlines on the event. "GALA
PARADE! 3 BANDS 3! LAVISH FLOATS!
PRIZES! COME ONE, COME ALL! DON'T
MISS IT!"

The residents of Chippewa were helpless slaves to
that gentle and harmless form of exhibitionism known
as a parade. Bearded psychiatrists might have spun
fine theories to prove that this innocent form of
ostentation sprang from nothing but a thwarted love
of pageantry and display; that the dwellers in this
rugged area, where it was said there were nine months
winter and three months bad sleighing, simply couldn't
resist a periodic expression of communal glee, espe-

(199)

cially during the fleeting and golden months of summer.

In any event, this was to be the finest parade Chippewa had ever seen. Every iron mine, business house, school, church, and fraternal lodge in town agreed to be represented by a float depicting some event of world or local significance. The floats could represent any event, serious or humorous, current or historical. This afforded a broad scope for the imagination. The town's merchants gladly contributed prizes: Tim Hughes, a barrel of flour for the best historical float; M. A. Kahn, a natty new blue serge suit for the best mining float; J. J. Leffler, three hams for the most humorous float; Fred Braastad, a live pig for the best float depicting a religious theme.

The Sons of St. Hubert had their eyes glued on the live pig. The Sons was a fraternal lodge composed largely of Cornish miners. Its float committee publicly announced its entry simply as "The Mystery Float." This naturally caused the townspeople to speculate for days on the probable nature of the offering by the Sons of St. Hubert. Not a soul outside of the Sons knew that the chairman of the Lodge's float committee had paid a secret visit to Danny McGinnis out at Hungry Hollow. There in the dead of night he had engaged old Danny and his wolf pelt to play the part of Daniel in the Lions' Den. It was abundantly evident that Fred Braastad's live pig was not long for this world.

"You mean your lodge wants *me* to wear this here wolf skin an' play the part of Daniel in the Lion's Den?" Danny again asked Jan Tregembo, dubiously rubbing his bald head.

" 'Zackly, partner, 'zackly," Jan answered pertly.

"All I gotta do is stand in the goddam float an'

ride down Main Street—an' say nothin'?" Danny queried.

" 'Zackly," Jan agreed.

"An' all alone, you say?" asked Danny, fearful that he might have to share the spotlight.

Jan swallowed hard before answering. "Yew'll be the only bloody 'uman in the float," he said.

"Hm . . . Where you aim to git the lions?" Danny asked.

"Naow don't worry your 'ead 'bout that, partner— we'll tend to the bloody lions," Jan answered airily.

"How much you aim to pay me fer bein' this here Daniel?"

"Thirty dollars and fifty cents. Five dollars of wot will be for your chum Buller tew 'aul the float with. 'Ee'll drive Wink Vivian's dray 'orses, Cub an' Dick. Mister Vivian's the 'onorable 'ead of our lodge, yew knaow."

"What's the extra fifty cents fer?" Danny asked.

"For the white tennis slippers," Jan promptly answered.

"Tennis slippers! Why in hell tennis slippers?"

"Well, we 'ave figgered aout everything, we 'ave," Jan modestly admitted. "We figgered yew'd need to 'ave something on your bloody feet in there with all them lions. Something fitting also for Daniel to 'ave on 'is feet on such a sacred hoccasion. So we fixed on tennis slippers. Yew can buy of 'em to size fer 'bout fifty cents at Will Trathen's variety store. Reason they ain't donated is because Will Trathen don't 'appen to be a lodge brother, yew knaow. Wot say, partner?"

Delighted Danny still pretended to be dubious of the proposal. He thoughtfully combed out his mustaches with his fingers. "Hm," he said.

Jan played his final trump.

"In haddition tew the money we shall pay yew, w'en our float wins the prize—as it most certainly shall—yew shall 'ave that, tew. It's a live pig, yew knaow, for the best religious float. The Sons of St. 'Ubert ain't ones to 'old back, they ain't. Wot say, partner?"

Danny looked Jan squarely in the eye. "I ain't been much of a hand lately at this here religion business," he said. "But fer you boys I'll bloody well do it—lions an' all." Danny put out his hand. "Put her there, partner."

"Pretty," Jan said, clasping Danny's hand.

Standing in the wavering lamplight, they had a drink of Old Cordwood to seal the bargain. Danny walked down to the car with Jan.

"Where'll I show up to the mornin' of the Fourth?" he asked.

"In the back 'arness room of 'Odgkin's livery stable. Knock three times on the door—it's very secret, yew knaow. Don't heven tell your chums 'ere. Mum's the bloody word, partner," Jan said, throwing his old Maxwell into gear and rattling away into the night.

Old Danny stood looking down at the midnight blackness of the river. "Daniel in the Lions' Den," he mused aloud. "Twenty-five dollars, a bran' new pair of tennis shoes—an' a live pig!" He slapped his leg and chuckled to himself. "I wisht my dear ol' mother could be here to see it."

The Fourth of July was a beautiful, cloudless day. That morning shortly after nine o'clock the colorful floats began gathering in the big vacant lot next to St. Xavier's church on South Main Street. The members of the local parade committee ran up and down in perspiring, straw-hatted hysteria. The Sons of St.

Hubert's mystery float rumbled out of Hodgkin's livery stable driven by Buller Beaudin. For the occasion Buller was wearing a tall, fur hussar's hat and a red necktie. A large canvas tarpaulin completely covered the mystery float, beside which walked Jan Tregembo and four other watchful Sons of St. Hubert. Even Buller did not know precisely what he was hauling. He maneuvered the horses deftly through the milling sea of floats and contrived to get at the end of the entire parade.

The Mayor was finally helped up on his horse at the head of the parade. All was in readiness. The warning whistle blew. Sousa and Pryor were joined in mortal combat, the three brass bands starting to play as many different selections simultaneously. The solemn Sons of St. Hubert quickly threw off the tarpaulin. At long last the mystery float was unveiled to a waiting world. They were away.

There stood Danny in the middle of a huge improvised cage made of chicken wire. Old Danny was clad only in his mangy wolf skin and the white tennis slippers. A wreath of ground pine rested slightly askew on his perspiring bald head. One skinny leg rested on a cardboard rock. Danny's thin, powerful arms were folded across his chest as he stood gazing up sightlessly at the skies over Chippewa. He stood imperturbable, like something carved out of the native granite hills. His immobile calm was broken only by the milling and spitting, the clawing and hissing, of not one, not twenty, not fifty, but surely *all* of the stray cats in Chippewa. Twin signs on either side of the dray announced to a startled world the significance of this deathless tableau. "DANIEL IN THE LIONS' DEN" the legend proclaimed.

Never before had the people of Chippewa beheld such a spectacle. A chorus of "ahs" marked the progress of the mystery float down Main Street. Wonder had returned to the tired earth. Some of the onlookers appeared so moved by what they saw that they were helped away in the arms of others. Buller, in his borrowed hussar's hat, carefully guided Daniel and his den down Main Street, past Charlie's Place ("Hallo, Danny—dat's da bucko!") past Chief Booze-in-the-Face, across the railroad tracks, and alongside the judges' reviewing stand which stood at the bottom of Main Street hill. *"Whoa!"* Buller shouted, amidst the feline din, pulling the horses up abruptly. Statuesque Danny lurched a little, glancing ominously at Buller, but kept his balance. The startled judges peered and blinked at Danny in his cage and then at each other and then back at Danny.

Wink Vivian's borrowed horses, Cub and Dick, chose this moment to start playfully biting each other. Buller bathed them in a gentle shower of stealthy profanity, but this only seemed to whet their appetites. So he quietly reached under his feet for his trusty dray stake. He'd fix 'em. Leaning forward with the upraised stake, he flailed Cub and Dick mightily across their buttocks. The effect was electrical. Cub and Dick whinnied and reared and then suddenly plunged forward. With a splintering sigh and pursuant to certain inevitable laws of motion, Daniel's lions' den broke away from the dray, tilted up in the air, hung there poised for a frozen moment, and then tumbled over onto Main Street.

No two people agreed later on exactly how it happened. One thing was certain—old Danny had described a perfect parabola as he crashed headfirst through the chicken wire cage onto Main Street. From then on the picture was clouded by cats. Clawing and spitting, meowing and screeching, the entire cageful of cats headed for the hole formed by the passage of Danny. There were white cats, black cats, orange cats, mottled cats, a veritable rainbow of cats, pouring from the cage like Fourth of July pinwheels and streaking in all directions like shafts of varicolored lights.

Buller was abject. He ran back to Danny, but Danny had passed beyond all concern with the affairs of cats and men. Buller decently pulled the wolf pelt down, from over Danny's ears. He tried to fan Danny with his hussar's hat. The harried judges of the parade hurried down off their stand to assist in the revival. One of them whispered to Buller. Buller knelt beside Danny and shook him.

"Wake up, Danny, wake up! You won first prize, ol' man," Buller pleaded.

Danny's eyelids fluttered open. "Where'm I at?" he demanded, sitting up on Main Street.

"Here," Buller joyfully ran on, dumping three large hams on Danny's lap. "You won the first prize!"

Danny contemplated the three hams on his lap. "I thought it belonged to be a live pig," he demanded. He had grown to covet the live pig. "What's these here hams fer?"

"Fer the funniest goddam float," Buller answered proudly. "They jest tol' me. Boy, oh boy! They said the vote was u—u—unan— Aw hell, Danny—*the sons-a-bitches all agreed!*"

18

BULLER'S NEW SUIT

Buller had driven Wink Vivian's dray since early in June, thereby establishing an undisputed record at Hungry Hollow for continuous employment. He even began drinking less and saving money. The halo of respectability hovered uneasily over his head. It finally began to look as though he had forsaken the boys at Hungry Hollow—he seemed to avoid them when they came to town. Danny and the boys were perplexed and sore hurt. At length they constituted themselves an aggrieved delegation to come to town and find out if Buller had really resigned from Hungry Hollow. It was a Saturday night when Danny found him and accosted him on the subject in Charlie's Place.

"Look, Buller! What the hell's the matter? You ain't gone an' fallen in love?" Danny demanded.

"Nope," Buller said, hanging his head.

"Got religion then?" Danny said.

"Nope," Buller said, avoiding Danny's eyes.

"Ain't turned city slicker on us, have you?"

"Nope," Buller said, intently studying the ceiling.

"Then what's ailin' you? Why don't you come on

(206)

home?" Danny peered closely at Buller.

Buller plucked at the sleeve of Danny's plaid jumper and led him to Charlie's back room. They sat facing each other across the green poker table. Buller was opening and closing his mouth like a beached bass.

"Confess!" Danny said remorselessly.

"Look, Danny—" Buller was in labor. "Look! It's jest this—I'm buyin' a new suit. Two more weeks an' it's paid fer."

"A new suit!" Danny exclaimed sharply, his eyelids fluttering.

"Now don't git sore at me, Dan. I ain't had a hull new suit since—since I buried my maw." Buller sat blinking his little gray eyes. "Danny, I—I can't explain it clear. A fella's really got to own somethin' *good* once in a while. I jest got to git that there new suit."

Danny rose, rubbing his nose with his thumb, sniffing. "Why, of course you do, Buller. I understan' perfeck. Why'n hell didn't you tell me? Say! Le's go an' have a drink instead of moonin' aroun' back here. Hey, Charlie! Set 'em up!"

The suit itself, a glorious double-breasted powder blue creation with patch pockets and a pin stripe, was still being molded over at Jafet Moilanen's tailor shop on Pearl Street. Jafet's Finnish cronies dropped in every day to remark his progress on the vast garment. Some of them had started to rename the little old tailor "Jafet the Tentmaker." In the meantime Buller had quit the Chippewa House and had gone to live with his chum Chuck Woodlock, a local hero of a thousand drunks, in Chuck's tar-paper shack over by the French church; this so that he could save more money for the suit and thus sooner be released from the drudgery of Wink Vivian's dray.

For the first time in years he had money in the bank.

Well, not exactly in the bank, but in the iron safe in Charlie's Place right next door to the bank, which was practically the same thing. Each Saturday night when Wink Vivian paid him off, Buller would march over to Charlie's Place and hand Charlie a cash deposit on the suit. Obliging Charlie was always glad to help a friend, especially when that friend usually tarried and spent the rest of his week's pay over the battered mahogany bar.

On the Saturday night before Halloween, Buller came bustling into Charlie's Place with Chuck Woodlock and drew out all his money. The suit was finally paid for. Buller bought a round of drinks for the house. He then ostentatiously shook hands with Charlie, like a departing diplomat, and he and Chuck went over to Jafet's tailor shop. Jafet had finished the suit and had it on display in the front window for passing pedestrians to pause and marvel at.

"Dat's vunderful fit, Mister Buller," Jafet exclaimed ecstatically, in the tradition of tailors the world over, after Buller had wrestled himself into his new blue suit. "She fits you like a 'love.'"

Buller kept twisting and posturing before Jafet's swivel mirrors, beaming like an expectant young bridegroom. He somehow resembled the Aga Khan at an annual diamond weighing. He was enchanted by what he saw.

"It's wonderful!" he finally sighed, reluctantly turning away and counting out the money he owed Jafet.

"You got t'ree dollar dwenty cents coming back," Jafet said, reaching toward his wooden till.

"That's all right," Buller said airily, wheeling before the mirror again. "Keep the change, Jafet, keep the change." Buller was in no mood for fractions.

"Oh, dank you, Mister Buller. Do you vant to take

your ol' clo'es now or vill you call for dem some nudder days?"

Buller looked disdainfully down at his soiled and crumpled dray clothes. "Hell, give 'em to the pore, Jafet," he said, grandly waving them away.

"Here, give 'em to me. You never kin allus sometimes tell." Thus spake Chuck Woodlock, the voice of experience, as he gathered up Buller's old clothes and wrapped them in a newspaper. "You never kin allus tell what tomorrow will sometimes fetch."

To say that Buller's adventures of that Saturday night achieved epic proportions would smack of understatement. It would have taken a hardy soul to follow his meteoric double-breasted course. That night Buller was Falstaff, Prince Hal, and "Bet-a-Million" Gates all rolled into one. He had at last become a gentleman, a man of the world.

Accompanied by the faithful old family retainer, Chuck Woodlock, Buller managed to display his new suit in every saloon in town. It was a sensation. Toward midnight he and his wavering man Woodlock devoured two great dripping steaks over at Urho Pentamaki's Tiptop Café. They next paid a social call on Big Annie and her girls, where the new suit practically stopped all professional activity. Somewhat later Buller met his employer, Wink Vivian, back in Charlie's Place.

"Hello, Buller," Wink said, worriedly observing Buller's inflamed condition. "You plannin' to take the dray out Monday mornin'?"

This unfortunate and poorly timed reference to such mundane things as employment caused Buller to draw himself up haughtily, carefully rebutton his tight-fitting coat, and suggest to poor Wink where he might promptly proceed to drive Cub and Dick, either together or in single file. Buller fixed Wink with his reddened eyes. "Misther Vivian," he concluded with dignity, "I tender my reshignation—'fective 'mediately, sir. C'mon, Chuck, I detec' an odor of horshes in here. Charlie, ol' boy, pleash wrap up coupla quarsh Ol' Cordwood!"

Only another visit to the feminine comfort of Big Annie's could soothe Buller's ruffled feelings. At length, in the wee hours of Sunday morning, Rocco Pantalone drew up in front of Chuck Woodlock's shack in his old Cadillac taxicab. There he unceremoniously dumped Buller and his man Woodlock onto Chuck's creaking brass-knobbed bedstead. Rocco diligently searched in the pockets of Buller's new suit for his fare. He finally found and fished out a solitary wrinkled dollar bill.

"Gooda night, Meester Bull'," Rocco called from the door.

"Blub-wah," Buller answered, turning his face to the wall.

Sunday was the eve of All Saints' Day, more often known as Halloween, and the youth of Chippewa scampered about the frosty, wind-blown streets all morning on reconnaisance tours for the coming mischief of the evening. A successful practice rock aimed at Chuck's door finally aroused the sorry pair around noontime. Buller and Chuck lay blinking at each other for minutes before either of them dared utter a word.

"Wah," Buller finally said.

"Woof," shivering Chuck answered.

"I—I'd give anythin' fer a drink," Buller sighed.

There was a long silence. Then, "How about pawnin' your new soot?" Chuck craftily suggested.

By two o'clock Buller and Chuck, the former again clad in his old dray clothes, were hammering at the door of Jafet Moilanen's tailor shop. Buller was carrying a large bundle wrapped in newspaper. Jafet finally padded from the back room, where he lived, and admitted the quaking pair.

"Look, Jafet," Buller got right down to cases. "I'm sick—sicker'n any man's gotta right to be an' live. If I don't have a drink soon I'll up an' die. Will you buy back my new suit fer half price? Will you, Jafet?" Buller eagerly thrust the bundle at Jafet.

Jafet recoiled as though Buller were offering him a writhing cobra. "I knew for dat," he sighed. "I yust knew you vould be back." Jafet was sorely distressed. "But, Buller, I can't do for dat. Honest crossings my heart, I can't."

"Why?" Buller demanded, aghast.

"Look!" Jafet made a frank appeal to reason. "Even for da half prices I vould lose money." He held up two fingers. "You see, like a godtam fool I make really two suits for prices of vun in da first places—dat muts cloth you using up."

Buller and Chuck looked at each other incredulously. There was only one way out. The sacrifice must be made. They simply had to have whisky.

"Five dollars, then," Buller said resignedly.

Jafet was sorry but firm. "No, Buller. Use you common sense noodle. If you even *give* me dat suit back, what place I can sell it? What regular kind mens can ever vear dat godtam *tent*? Tell me dat?" Jafet threw out his hands.

Jafet's logic was devastating. Buller was cut to the quick. This was heaping insult on injury. And still there was no whisky in sight. "C'mon, Chuck, le's git out of this graspin' ol' miser's dump." Buller turned at the door. "All right for you, Jafet," he pouted. "In the future I'll take all my tailorin' business over to Rosenthal. You'll be sorry."

"I vish you vould," Jafet answered, wearily drawing the shade and turning the key in the lock.

Back at the cold shack thirsty Buller and Chuck built a roaring fire in the cast-iron stove and boiled up a pot of coffee. Buller carefully shook out his wrinkled new suit and lovingly hung it up at the head of the brass bed. Then the two sat on the tumbled bed and drank their steaming coffee.

"Hey there, Chuck!" Buller suddenly shouted. "You'll burn the goddam joint down. Check the bloody stove." He pointed up at the glowing stovepipe, which was red-hot clear up to where it went through the tar-paper ceiling.

"Naw. She won't burn down," Chuck answered languidly. At this point he felt little concern over the future. "Anyway, I don't give a tinker's damn if she does. I'm figgerin' to clear out, anyway. The hull bloody place ain't worth five bucks." To prove his point he got up and threw several more chunks of coal stolen from the L.S. & C. Railway onto the roaring fire. He glanced over at Buller. "Hey, what's up!" Chuck exclaimed.

Buller was sitting on the bed, wide-eyed, nodding his head, lips pursed, wearing the beatific expression of a man seized with a celestial vision. *"A fire!"* he kept repeating, as though to himself, his eyes getting wider and wider with the wonder of it all.

"Fire?" Chuck began.

"We need money fer whisky, don't we?" Buller demanded tensely.

"Sure, sure," Chuck agreed.

"An' we's both broke, ain't we?" Buller said.

"They ain't none broker," Chuck glumly admitted.

"Look," Buller said excitedly. "Does the Fire Department still pay eight bucks fer the first team of horses what shows up at the fire hall to haul the hose cart when the fire bell rings?"

"Sure," Chuck said, "only it's raised to ten dollars now."

"Spot cash?" Buller said.

"Soon as you git back from the fire."

Buller licked his lips and winked at mystified Chuck. "Well," he went on slowly, "I still got the key fer Wink Vivian's barn, where he keeps Cub and Dick."

"Yes?" Chuck said, faint streaks of dawn beginning to break.

"An' at four o'clock I could have 'em harnessed an' all waitin' an' ready behin' the billboard nex' to the fire hall." Buller paused craftily.

"Go—go on," Chuck whispered hoarsely.

"An' if a guy could fin' a real pal that'd turn in the fire alarm, say—le's see—from the alarm box at Doc Martin's corner up on Strawberry Hill"—Chuck was wordless before such genius—"then by five o'clock we could be back here with the price fer a supply of Ol' Cordwood to celebrate fer performin' our plain moonacipial dooty." Buller was carried away. "Hell, I could even wear my new suit tonight."

Chuck, still stricken dumb with delight, tossed some more coal on the blazing fire so that everything would be snug and shipshape when they returned for their party.

"C'mon," Buller called from the door. "We gotta git goin'!" He reached over and smoothed out a wrinkle in his new suit, hanging from the head of the brass bedstead. Buller patted the suit tenderly. "Boy, oh boy, what a garment! What a day!"

At 3:50 Buller was waiting with Cub and Dick, fully harnessed and whipple-treed, behind the billboard next to the fire hall. He kept his eyes glued to the clock in the bell tower. "Ten more minutes," he whispered, moistening his lips. "Whoa there, Cub, Dick!" At 3:55 Buller was whispering "Jest five minutes more," when the fire bell started clanging, bong . . . dong . . . bong— *bong, bong, bong, bong, bong!*

"He's five minutes early," Buller muttered to himself, bringing down the leather reins across the rumps of the startled horses. "Giddap, Cub, Dick! C'mon! Run like you never run before!" Out from behind the billboard plunged Cub and Dick, the whippletrees banging and clattering, with Buller making great elephantine bounds to keep up with them, all the time urging the frantic horses to even greater bursts of speed. The chariot race for the price of Old Cordwood was on.

The tall doors of the fire hall stood open. Men were running up and down, snatching helmets and boots and rubber coats from hooks. Other men were sliding down brass poles. Buller's horses clattered wildly into the hose-cart door. Lo! his was the first team. The Old Cordwood was in the bag.

In the next doorway the big new red hook-and-ladder truck was warming up, alternately sputtering and roaring. "Nice goin', Buller! Hook 'em up!" someone shouted in Buller's ear. Buller backed Cub and Dick around in front of the hose cart. "Gee there, Cub and Dick! Ha a little! Now back! Easy there, Cub!"

He quickly adjusted the tugs, tossed the reins up over the seat and, puffing mightily, clambered up to the cushioned seat where he grabbed the reins and vigorously clanged the foot bell. Then, without another backward glance, he lashed out at Cub and Dick, who promptly catapulted from the fire hall with a dozen or so startled firemen clinging to the sides of the rumbling hose cart.

"Clang, clang, clang!" went the foot bell, as Buller
made a reeling turn north towards Doc Martin's house.
"Giddap, Cub, Dick!" Buller shouted. "Don't worry,
Doc, we'll be right there!" *"Clang, clankety, clang!"*

"Hey!" shouted Barney Langley, the fire chief, bolt-
ing wildly from the fire hall after Buller. "You're goin'
the wrong bloody way! Hey, you bloody fool!" But
Buller paid no heed, so intent was he on saving the
threatened Martin home from flames. "Clang, clang,
clang!"

Buller was proudly seated, arms folded, on the hose
cart drawn up in front of Dr. Martin's house. Several
firemen were standing around on the Martin porch
talking with a perplexed Dr. Martin. "They ain't no
fire aroun' here!" one of them shouted at Buller.
"They ain't?" Buller echoed in wide-eyed wonder, biting his lower lip and shaking his head.

At this point the town fire bell sounded a second
alarm. *"Bong, bong, bong, bong, bong!"* came drifting
upon the crisp October air. The firemen left Dr.
Martin standing on his porch and raced back to the
hose cart. Some ten minutes later they were still standing around noisily debating what they should do when
the fire chief's little red coupe squealed around Doc's
corner. Mike Nolan, the chief of police, was sitting
beside Barney Langley, the fire chief. Barney parked
alongside Buller and slowly got out and put his foot
up on the hub of the hose cart, squinting one eye up at
Buller and slowly stroking his chin.

"Look, Buller," the fire chief said, with a sort of
deadly calm. "Would you mind jest tellin' Mike an' I
what in hell you're doin' up here? Who tole you to
come here in the first place? We was jest wonderin',
that's all."

Buller had had a rather full week end, and the pace was beginning to tell. His face had gone the color of a red-brick schoolhouse. "Why—I—you got an alarm turned in fer here, didn't you?" he inquired brightly.

"To be sure, Buller," the fire chief affably agreed. "Jest two minutes *after* you headed fer here!"

Buller gulped and meditated. "Musta been jest a prank. Mebbe some Halloween kids turned in a false alarm," he ventured politely.

"I'm thinkin' they was goddam big ones," Barney answered grimly, looking Buller straight in the eye. Buller swallowed and looked away.

"Y-you mean, B-Barney, I went to the w-wrong f-fire?" Buller tried again.

"Exactly!" Barney continued to beam falsely. "The alarm you should of ought to answered was Chuck Woodlock's shack over by the French church!"

Buller swayed on his tall seat. He closed his eyes and quickly shook his head, like a wet and discouraged St. Bernard. "Y-you put it out, of course?" he asked in a child's voice.

"Yeah—we saved the lot! How in hell could we put it out with you gallivantin' up here with all our goddam hose?"

"You mean you didn't save nothin', not even nothin' like a suit of clothes or nothin'?" Buller was swaying badly again.

"All we saved was Chuck Woodlock hisself. Guess he musta been half snaky. He kep' tryin' to run in there to rescue somethin'—somethin' for a frien', he kep' sayin'." Barney turned to the chief of Police. "Well, Mike. Enough of this clownin'. You heard it from Buller's own lips. Shall we take him over the jail now an' git it over with?"

Buller had turned from schoolhouse red to aquarium

green. He weakly held up a perspiring fat hand. "I'll go quiet," he said in a small voice. "But jest stan' clear fer a minute. I—I think I'm gonna be sick."

19

OLD ROCKING CHAIR

The first heavy snow had fallen. Winter had settled upon the waiting, obedient Northern earth. The November deer-hunting season was well advanced when Buller finished serving his twenty-day sentence in the county jail at Iron Bay. He caught a ride to Chippewa on a logging truck. The wintry afternoon was beginning to wane when he finally walked into the camp at Hungry Hollow. Timmy was alone, seated at the oilcloth-covered table, preparing his precious fly rods for winter storage.

Timmy looked up. "Hello, Buller," he said, turning again to his work. "Figuring to stay around for a while?"

Buller had lost weight. There was a sad and hungry look about him. His old dray clothes hung about him loosely, giving him a curiously Lincolnesque appearance. "I'm stayin' aroun'," he said. Then, after a pause, he casually asked, "Anythin' in the Mulligan kettle?" He glanced hungrily at the cookstove.

"Help yourself, Buller," Timmy said, deftly putting a touch of varnish on a new silk winding. "An' there's a new batch of Swan's bread in the cupboard."

Buller hurriedly dipped out a heaping plateful of vegetables and stewed rabbit from the big iron kettle. He sat at the table by Timmy and fell to eating like a famished wolf. Timmy glanced at him several times from under his brows. Buller was ready for another helping. "Where's the boys?" he asked from the stove as he dipped out another plateful.

"Taconite and Swan are out cutting wood," Timmy answered.

"Whew!" Buller blew as he sopped up the last of his second helping with the heel of a loaf of bread. "Where's ol' Danny? He's all right, ain't he?" Timmy did not answer. "I say—Danny's all right, ain't he?" Buller repeated anxiously.

"Who? Oh, Danny?" Timmy glanced up from his work abstractedly. "Hell, we ain't seen Danny since daybreak. He spotted Old Rocking Chair this morning, down by the Mulligan. From a distance. He came running back to camp for the .44 and took after him. He's been out tracking him ever since, I guess."

"Betcha he don't git him," Buller said, judiciously pursing his lips and nodding.

"O.K.," Timmy said. "What'll we bet?"

"Betcha a big drink of whisky he don't nail him." Buller was obviously motivated solely by a scientific interest in ballistics. "Betcha the drink right now—if I had a drink."

"Betcha!" Timmy said, grinning, moving quickly to Danny's latest hiding place, and bringing out a quart of Hungry Hollow moonshine. Buller grabbed the bottle with shaking hands. "Boy, oh boy!" He was home again.

They called him Old Rocking Chair.

The great white-tailed buck was so old—as deer go —that he had become almost legendary to the boys of Hungry Hollow. Six years had passed since Danny and the boys had first sighted this magnificent animal. It had been a cool October morning. Danny discovered him standing on the crest of the little birch ridge behind the camp, sniffing the crisp morning air, his wet muzzle and spreading rack of antlers glistening in the early autumn sunshine. One by one the boys had filed out of the camp to gaze at him. Swan came last, in his stocking feet. Then the fabulous deer had scented Danny and the boys. He stood there for a frozen instant with questioning ears forward, first one and then the other. Then he blew twice, "Whew!" tossing his great rack, wheeling, running easily and stiff-legged, disdainfully bouncing down into the swamp behind the ridge, his tall tail wigwagging a white farewell.

"Lookit them horns!" Danny had croaked. "Did you see them goddam horns! Jest like the rockers on my maw's ol' rockin' chair! Yep, yep! 'Ol' Rockin' Chair!' That's his name." Danny suddenly glared at Swan's plastered blond hair. "Sure, an' if you hadn't smeared yourself all over with that goddam she-bear grease, he wouldn't of smelt us." He grasped Swan's reluctant head in his two hands and took a deep whiff of Swan's latest scent. Danny dolefully shook his head. "Jest like a two-bit whore," he muttered.

After that the boys hadn't sighted Old Rocking Chair for two seasons. They had about concluded that either some lucky hunter had got him or that he had taken his masculine charms to some other section of the Peninsula. Then one morning Danny went down to the misty Big Dead pool to try for an unsuspecting trout— and there stood Old Rocking Chair, up to his belly on a sand bar in the middle of the river. "Whew!" he had blown again, splashing with great dignity to the opposite bank, shaking himself, impatiently stamping his right foreleg, blowing disgustedly once more, then indignantly tossing his great rack, which was still in velvet, and quietly moving into the protective cover of the woods.

"I coulda hit him with a goddam rock!" Danny excitedly explained to the boys.

Several more years had passed. It was the fall before, when Timmy had wired the Mulligan swamp for sound, and Old Rocking Chair had almost knocked him down, that Danny and the boys concluded that the great deer led a charmed life. "His maw musta been a gypsy an' his paw half ghost," Danny had solemnly announced at the time.

Old Rocking Chair's tracks took Danny clear down across the shallow Mulligan, up the other side, skirting the road to town for nearly a mile, always keeping to the woods for cover. There was about six inches of damp snow, ideal for tracking. The deer seemed to be walking slowly. His great splayed hoofprints told Danny that there was something wrong with his right foreleg. "Mebbe he's hurt hisself—or else he's gettin' rheumatism like ol' Danny," Danny whispered to himself, holding the .44 ready, cautiously edging forward.

Then the tracks veered abruptly east, keeping easterly, always in or near cover. The tracks were getting fresher. Danny saw where the deer had stopped and relieved himself. Then he had moved on, starting to climb the foothills of the Mulligan Range. He had stopped to paw and nuzzle some moss. The tracks were getting fresher.

"Whew!" Old Rocking Chair blew. Danny had the

rifle up, peering ahead. There was the sound of heavy running, a swishing in the thick spruce cover, and then there was silence—nothing but the tall spruces bent and clotted with their mounds of snow, nothing but the brooding, whispering stillness, the vast hush of winter.

Old Rocking Chair ran less than a quarter of a mile. His bad leg was obviously bothering him. Danny could see that he was favoring it. His fresh tracks kept climbing, out of the spruces, into the thin birches and maples. "Where the hell is he waltzin' me?" Danny muttered. "Up the goddam mountain?" There was no mistake. Up, up, led the tracks, up a narrow valley, then another, and yet another, twisting and turning for cover, toiling up, always up. First Rocking Chair would stop and blow, then old Danny would have to do likewise. It had become an endurance contest between the two old campaigners.

In all the years they had lived at Hungry Hollow, neither Danny nor the boys had ever actually climbed the Mulligan Mountains. To be sure, they were always going to. "Next summer, mebbe." "This fall for sure." And now Danny was really climbing them, lugging the heavy old .44, hot on the trail of fabulous Old Rocking Chair himself.

The great deer and Danny toiled up and around and up for nearly an hour. "Whew!" Danny blew, as he gained the top and rested, leaning the .44 against one of the towering Norway pines which fringed the crest. He mopped his forehead with the sleeve of his wool jumper. Then he fished in the game bag of his jumper and brought out a pint bottle of his own moonshine. "Here's to you, Ol' Rockin' Chair," he whispered, draining half of it in one splendidly sustained trumpet solo on the bottle.

He turned and looked down and across the vast

sweep of the Big Dead valley. The waning sun was a dull clot of red in the southwest. The distant Mulligan and Big Dead rivers made occasionally visible ribbons of quicksilver in the broad carpet of solid forest. Danny stood staring down at the silent spectacle.

"C'mon, Danny, ol' man, don't stan' here moonin' over the scenery like a bloody tourist. Let's git after this goddam deer," he petulantly complained to himself, grabbing up the .44.

Old Rocking Chair had rested less than a hundred yards from him. His limp was much worse. He was tiring rapidly. Danny put several more cartridges in the .44 and adjusted the rear sight for a short shot. He eagerly pressed forward. It wouldn't be long now.

The wavering tracks took Danny through a thin fringe of gnarled, wind-blown scrub pine. Then abruptly the pine opened on to a broad plateau, on top of the mountain. "My Gawd!" Danny exclaimed, lowering his rifle and looking in awe at the sight before him.

A great forest of full-grown white pine had once stood on the mountaintop. All of them had been up-rooted, mowed down, in some violent, far-off catas-trophe, the giant trunks jumbled and crossed like mighty matchsticks, mostly lying east, while the great gnarled roots lay west, reaching witch-fingered into the air, beseeching and rigid in the final agony of death. The scene was invested with a sense of nameless and infinite ruin. Danny stood staring at this mute evidence of a tail-lashing, angry Nature.

"My Gawd!" he repeated, "Ol' Ferguson'd turn over in his grave."

In the center of this vast graveyard was an open space, a shallow swale, devoid of cover save for a solitary low-branched spruce which grew in the center.

The dying sun glittered over the scene as Danny stood muttering to himself.

"Well, I'll be——!"

It was Old Rocking Chair, coming out from behind the bole of a fallen pine, from the side of the swale at Danny's right. Slowly he moved out into the open swale, sleepily blinking his soft velvet eyes, limping painfully as he trudged toward the protection of the spreading spruce in the center of the broad swale. Danny sighted him in the .44 and gently pulled back the hammer. The great antlers shone in the sun. No longer was the splendid head held erect, as always before; it was bent nearly to the ground, as though the sheer weight of the proud antlers had finally grown too great a burden to bear.

Danny sadly followed Old Rocking Chair through the rifle sights. It was a short, easy shot. He could see the gray hairs on the thick, powerful neck and broad withers as the aged buck headed for the lone spruce. Should he let him have it now? No, he'd better wait and let him get nearly to the spruce so that if, by some miracle, he *did* miss him on the first shot, he'd at least get another shot in before the deer reached cover.

Old Rocking Chair gained the spruce. "Now!" Danny breathed. "When he comes out from the other side of that there spruce I'll let him have it." He knelt in the snow on one knee, squinting along the .44. A minute passed, two minutes . . . Danny lowered his rifle. "Now don't tell me that sleepy ol' codger has gone an' bunked down right there." Danny twisted and craned, trying to look under the spruce, but it was set too low in the swale. He raised the rifle, carefully sighted, and waited once again. Still the deer did not appear.

Danny glanced over his shoulder at the sun. It had

disappeared and dusk was rapidly falling. He stood up. He'd have to hurry to bleed him and dress him out and hang him up before dark. "Yep, yep. I guess I'll have to go in an' root him out. I never assassinated a goddam sleepin' deer yet so far!"

He cautiously worked forward, the rifle held ready, hammer back, alert to fire whichever way the animal bolted. Five feet, another ten feet, another twenty feet. Danny kept edging toward the spruce, and still no Old Rocking Chair. Ten, twenty feet more. Danny was at the spruce. He edged rapidly around the left side of the spruce, tense and ready, the rifle sighted.

"Well, I'm a goddam sidehill gouger!"

There, limping painfully over the edge of the swale, some forty yards away, was Old Rocking Chair. He had sensed Danny's presence when he had got out into the swale but had given no sign, knowing he was beyond retreat. The wily old buck had made a right-angle turn when he had got behind the tree, and had made a bee line for his escape, keeping the spreading spruce squarely between him and his tormentor. Danny quickly fell to one knee and again sighted along the .44. It was still a comparatively easy shot.

"But I gotta shoot him through the rear valve," he whispered, grimacing and shaking his head. He lowered the rifle, then raised it again. Suddenly he lowered the hammer to safety and stood up chuckling, flinging the rifle from him into the snow. "Not by a goddam sight!" he shouted. "Hey, Rockin' Chair! Look! Here's bumps!"

Old Rocking Chair turned in the fading afterglow, his large eyes luminous and liquid. Danny whipped out his pint bottle and stood there gurgling until he had drained the last drop.

"So long, Rockin' Chair!" he shouted, flinging the

empty bottle after his rifle. "Good luck, ol' boy! See you nex' fall, I hope!"

"Whew!" Old Rocking Chair blew, proudly tossing his great head as he turned and hobbled painfully over the ridge and out of sight.

20

THE MIDNIGHT RIDE OF HEINRICH WERTHER

Under the magic therapy of Swan's cooking and Danny's moonshine Buller soon became his old self again. His lips gradually resumed their moist rosebud pout; he slowly took up the slack in his old dray clothes; he even got so that he could refer to his misadventures of the past summer without too many grimaces of pain. Then at the dinner table on Thanksgiving Day, as though to celebrate the completeness of his recovery, Buller gave the boys their first blow-by-blow account of the saga of his new suit, from its glorious inception in little Jafet's tailor shop to its final incineration in Chuck Woodlock's burning shack. Danny and the boys, at once sympathetic and curiously embarrassed by Buller's confession, listened with rapt attention, occasionally darting quick glances at each other over the mounds of venison, rabbit, and partridge bones piled high on the long Thanksgiving table.

"There," Buller concluded, reaching for a bit of partridge breast that had so far miraculously escaped his attention, "that's why in the future an' from now on I'm layin' off that Jafet Moilanen in partic'lar an' all tailors in general—they's nothin' but a bunch of graspin' robbers." He sighed. "If only I just hadn't of seen that beautiful piece of cloth in his goddam window," he regretfully concluded.

Old Danny had sat in brooding silence during Buller's recital, meditatively raising vast clouds of Peerless smoke from his corncob pipe. Now he spoke up. "Lissen, Buller," he said quietly, "talkin' about tailors, did you ever hear tell the story of the little ol' German tailor, 'way back in the white pine days, what really got his comeuppance?"

"No," Buller breathed, swiftly rising to the fly. "Let's have it. Tell us the story about the little ol' German tailor what really got his."

"Hm," Danny said, glancing doubtfully at the camp clock, craftily sparring for advance royalties on his story, "I ain't sure as if I'll have time. You see, damned if today ain't my turn to wash the goddam dishes." He tugged at the slack on his neck and gazed thoughtfully at Buller. "But I'll tell you what," he generously conceded, "I'll tell this here story about the little ol' German tailor if you'll take my turn washin' all these Thanksgivin' dishes." He spread his hands out benevolently over the littered table. "Ol' Danny don't feel up to doin' both, so take your pick. Buller no dishes, Danny no story."

Poor Buller writhed in his dilemma but found himself more concerned with learning the plight of the little German tailor than in relieving his own. "All right, all right, you tell the story an' I'll do the bloody dishes," he pouted. "But it sure better be good. As fer you—you should ought to of been a tailor yourself, you connivin' ol' goat."

"His name was Heinie Werther," Danny hastily began, before Buller could change his mind. "He was a chubby little ol' fella—he looked like an assistant Santy Claus—what landed in Chippewa from Germany long before I did. He was awful nearsighted, too, an' wore square silver specs as thick as opera glasses. An' talk about a German accent! He had an accent as thick as a man what's swallowed a big chunk of salt pork. *Ach!* Fer a long time he was a high-class tailor with a big shop near what's now Big Annie's on Pearl Street. On Sundays he'd drive to church with his team of prancin' bays pullin' a fine big rubber-tired Studebaker carriage. I remember his carriage had silk tassels, too. Well sir, for years he made oodles of money tailorin' all the fancy suits an' coats fer the minin' crowd an' all the big lumbermen—but he had one weakness." Danny paused and lit his pipe. "Yep, yep"—he sadly shook his head—"the pore little fella had one bad weakness."

"What's that?" Buller asked, innocently eager to learn of one chink in the moral armor of any tailor that breathed.

"He *drank!*" Danny declared, glaring at Buller. "All his troubles—like others I could name—came straight from strong drink!"

Buller sought to hide his confusion over this shaft by hastily spooning up a few crumbs of partridge dressing. Danny composed his ruffled dignity and went on with his story.

"By an' by little Heinie's drinkin' got so bad that all his swell customers started to commence leavin' him. They discovered the suits he was makin' 'em was gettin' either too big or too small. His customers all begun lookin' like they was aimin' to win first prize at a masquerade. Natcherly they up an' quit him. So ol' Heinie finally got down to just makin' plain blue serge suits fer the miners an' lumberjacks an' folks like us— it seems that the likes of them weren't so partic'lar about the fit."

"An' did he up an' die in the porehouse?" Buller charitably inquired.

"Not exackly," Danny said. "But ol' Heinie finally lost his Studebaker carriage an' his team of prancin' bays to ol' demon rum. At last he took to drivin' aroun' to all the lumber camps in winter moochin' meals an' takin' orders fer blue serge suits. He traveled in a little red sled pulled by a big yellow dog." Danny lingered over the memory of the big yellow dog. "Yep, yep, that there mongrel dog of his was big enough to skid logs with. I remember like it was yesterday—his name was called Bismarck." Danny, always a keen student of semantics, appealed to Buller's sense of linguistic fitness. "Now ain't that a hell of a funny name fer a big yellow dog?"

"Fergit the goddam dog—what about the drunken tailor?" Buller petulantly demanded.

"Heinie an' Bismarck'd travel from camp to camp, like I says, showin' samples an' measurin' up the lumberjacks fer their blue serge suits. His terms was five dollars down an' the balance upon delivery of the suit when the spring drive was over."

"Well, what happened to this little nearsighted tailor?" Buller doggedly persisted.

"Then the very winter before I went to work fer ol' Ferguson—t'was right where we're livin' now—ol' Heinie come on his rounds with his dog Bismarck an'— would you believe it?—measured up forty-seven suits for spring delivery at this one camp alone—at five dollars a head. Hm . . . When the lumberjacks come to town that spring they all piled straight over to Heinie's place to git their new suits before they started blowin' their money on whisky an' wimmen. When they stomped into Heinie's place in their caulked boots I give you one guess what shape they found their little ol' tailor in."

"Dead?" Buller hopefully ventured.

"Dead drunk, more like," Danny glibly rolled on. "An' nary hide nor hair of a blue serge suit or even a sample or so much as a yellow tape measure to be found in the hull bloody shop. The place was jest clankin' with empty whisky bottles—an' there was little ol' Heinie wallowin' an' snorin' in the midst of 'em. Yep, yep, the boys at Ferguson's camp alone lost—le's see— five fours is twenty—over two hunnert an' some odd dollars. My, my, if it wasn't that ol' Ferguson himself happened to be along with them, holdin' stakes fer the balance on the suits, them jacks was so mad they'd like to of up an' kilt little Heinie." Danny clucked his tongue over the memory of Heinie's close shave.

"You don't mean they let him get away with it?" Buller demanded.

"Not so fast, chum," Danny warned. "Jest keep your britches on. Now let's see, where was I at? Oh, yes! The next winter ol' Heinie an' his big yellow dog arrived at camp as usual fer to take the new suit orders fer the followin' spring. I was workin' fer Ferguson by then—it was jest before the big storm what snowed us in. Say, did I ever tell you boys about that there big blizzard?"

"Not today—yet," Buller replied with infinite sarcasm.

But Danny, with the problem of the Thanksgiving

dishes neatly out of the way, refused to be ruffled. "Little Heinie an' Bismarck arrived jest aroun' supper time," he continued placidly. "It was kinda odd the way he allus managed to hit all the camps jest at mealtimes. Anyway, Paddy Belden, the barn boss, unhitched Heinie's big yellow dog and stabled him in with the horses whilst Heinie took his packsack of suit samples an' order books an' tramped up to the bunkhouse jest in the nick of time fer supper. The cook was jest bangin' his triangle."

"They didn't feed the rascal, did they?" Buller wanted to know.

"Sumptuously," Danny replied. "Yes, they all et supper, an' after supper they goes over to the bunkhouse an' commences their usual card games an' dancin' an' singin' to the accordion—all the while ignorin' poor little Heinie an' his samples. Then Heinie up an' promised faithful he'd apply their ol' five dollars from the winter before as down payments on their new suits. But the boys kept right on ignorin' him. Heinie then played his trump card: with tears mistin' his specs he reaches in his packsack an' drug out six quarts of Ol' Cordwood—*full* quarts, mind—an' sets 'em on the long bunkhouse table."

Buller was incredulous. "You mean he jest up an' *give* you boys all that whisky?"

"Yep, yep. 'Dring idt up, poys,' is all Heinie said in that katzenjammer lingo of his. Then Red Murray, Gawd bless 'im, ran out to the cook shanty fer to fetch me an' the cook—an' inside an hour every mother's son of us was toastin' little Heinie an' orderin' suits like we was one of them rich old-country dukes settin' out on a worl' tour. The cook ordered a high silk hat. Red Murray even ordered a fine opera cloak with red silk linin'."

"Damn fools," Buller muttered.

"Little Heinie was hoppin' aroun' like a hen on a hot griddle, measurin' suits an' markin' down orders an' drinkin' an' singin' German songs an' measurin' an' drinkin' an' markin'—an' pretty soon all of us was half shot, what with that bein' the first whisky we'd tasted in months an' the heat from the big bunkhouse stove an' all. Lucky fer Heinie an' us that ol' Ferguson was in town busy with his own drinkin' or he'd of skinned us alive. All the lumber camps in them days had strick rules ag'in drinkin'. Thinks I, we need such a rule today in *this* camp. Anyway, pretty soon Paddy Belden come up from the barn an' takes out his silver watch an' says it's near midnight an' time fer bed."

"What then?" Buller asked, scowling and hitching forward in his chair. It was plain that the little tailor had not yet suffered appropriate enough tortures to please him.

"Little Heinie asked Paddy would he first please hitch up his yellow dog Bismarck to his red sled for him. 'Poys, Heinie's liddle dronk,' he said. So Paddy give us the wink private, an' we knew somethin' was up. Paddy had a few quick drinks an' ordered a coupla three suits an' said, 'Heinie, your big yellow dog is down in the barn all hitched up an' ready to go, pointed straight up the sleigh haul toward Chippewa.'

" 'Donk you,' Heinie said, smilin' sleepy-like an' takin' another big hooker of Ol' Cordwood.

"Then we floored the rest of Heinie's whisky an' Paddy and Red an' me an' pretty near all the rest of the jacks waltzed Heinie down from the bunkhouse to the barn to see him off to town. All but the cook, who never could hold his likker anyway, an' who stood outside in his underwear hammerin' an' bangin' away at his triangle. It was a fine clear night, near to zero, an' the full moon on the snow was gleamin' blue all over everythin'.

"It was kinda dark in the barn an' Heinie was commencin' to wobble pretty bad, so we helped put him an' his samples in his sleigh an' tuck the robe aroun' him whilst Paddy stood at the dog's head so's he wouldn't bolt.

" '*Ach*, mine dog Bismarck, it iss vell you doan dring, too,' Heinie said.

" 'Whoa there, Bismarck, whoa,' Paddy kept repeatin', winkin' at us. An' those what could still see, not includin' nearsighted Heinie, fer the first time saw that it weren't no big yellow dog hitched up to Heinie's sled. No sir, it weren't no dog a-tall." Danny paused and with aggravating slowness filled, tamped, and relit his pipe.

Buller could stand the suspense no longer. "My Gawd, man," he shouted, "what *was* it then hitched up to the goddam sled!"

"Why Paddy's pet deer, a young spike buck called Prancer, what'd been hangin' aroun' the camp ever since he was jest a little spotted fawn. Yep, yep, Prancer'd never been put to harness before an' he was buckin' an' plungin' somethin' awful."

"A goddam deer?" Buller whispered, awe-struck.

"A goddam deer," Danny solemnly answered.

"What happened then?" Buller said, wiping his brow.

" '*Gute nacht*, mine friendts,' little Heinie said, wavin' his fur mitten an' commencin' to sing a new German song. 'Good night, Heinie,' the boys said. 'Good luck on your trip home to Chippewa.' "

"Then what happened?" Buller breathed, leaning forward tensely.

"Then Red Murray quick thrun open the barn doors

an' Paddy give Prancer a smart whack over the rump. 'They're off!' Red Murray hollered—an' away dashed Prancer an' Heinie an' his red sled up the icy sleigh haul in the moonlight. Yep, yep, that was the fastest goddam ride what any tailor ever got up to that there very night."

"An' then what?" Buller muttered.

"Us jacks stood down by the barn an' cheered Prancer an' little Heinie on. In the meantime the cook kept poundin' away at his triangle. In nothin' flat Prancer was up to the first curve, near a quarter mile away—but instead of takin' the curve like he should ought to of he kept goin' straight, plungin' clear over the high snowbank in one leap, slick an' clean, sled an' all, dumpin' off little ol' Heinie ass over tin cups— an', so help me, scatterin' samples an' orders fer blue serge suits an' opera cloaks half way 'cross township 49. Yep, yep, that little ol' drunken tailor sure musta thought he'd been hitched to Halley's comet that night. Yep, yep!"

Danny glanced at the camp alarm clock and turned to Buller, yawning elaborately. "Well, there's your tailor story, chum, like I promised. Me, I'm takin' a snooze." He gestured at the littered dinner table. "Now how about bein' real quiet, Buller, when you wash up all them dirty dishes?"

Buller sat purple with glee, convulsed with gales of silent mirth, shaking his head, slapping his thigh, turning and appealing wordlessly to the others. "Boy, oh boy, what a whale of a story," he managed to gasp. "Oh me, oh my! What ever happened to little ol' Heinie? Did he high-tail straight back fer Germany?"

"Wellsir," Danny said, "we natcherly had to rescue him an' bed him down with us fer the night. Elsewise he'd of froze stiff. The next mornin' we went out on

snowshoes an' finally foun' his sled an' harness—minus
the deer. Paddy rescued his big yellow dog where he'd
hid him in the oat bin—an' once again we waved the
little tailor off for Chippewa."

"Did he make home that time?" Buller asked.

"Twas the last time we ever laid eyes on little ol'
Heinie or his big yellow dog—or even our pet deer,
Prancer, fer that bloody matter."

Little Timmy suddenly got up from the dinner table
and hurried across the room and stood sulking by the
window, frowning darkly.

"What's eatin' you, Timmy?" Danny demanded. "It
ain't your turn to do the goddam dishes, is it? Or did
you run clean outa them damn crossword puzzles?"

Timmy wheeled on Danny, shouting hotly, "I think
it was a damn shame the way you big bullies treated
that little ol' drunken tailor. I jest wished I'd of been
there. It was a damn dirty shame!" Outraged, Timmy
stood glowering at old Dan.

Danny was remarkably reasonable. "P'raps it was,
Timmy," he admitted. "P'raps it was. I 'spect it's all
in your point of view. Now if a man of your fine inten-
tions an' high character'd been there you'd a saved
Heinie all right—an' Heinie'd of jest went on bein' a
little drunken ol' tailor. That's how all you reformers
an' snoopers manage to save folks. But under our
special lumberjack treatment what do you think really
happened? Hm . . . Heinie got so damn scared that
first of all he up an' quit drinkin' jest like that"—
Danny snapped his fingers—"an' then he sold his big
yellow dog, an' in a few months he was back makin'
dress suits an' fancy togs ag'in fer the big loggers an'
minin' crowd—even employin' seven young German
tailors." Danny sniffed virtuously and reached for his
pipe. "Yessir, we really deserved a gold medal fer

savin' him from the demon rum. An' would you believe it—when he died, as we all must—an' this I have on the best authority—in three days little Heinie was busy up yonder makin' opera cloaks exclusive fer St. Peter hisself." Danny rolled his eyes up to heaven. "Yep, yep, Timmy—it's as true as I'm settin' here."

21

FROM OLD NICK TO
ST. NICK

It was the week before Christmas.

In the Chippewa city hall the young mayor and city council were sitting in extraordinary session, wrestling with a grave problem. Here it was past mid-December and they had not yet found a Santa Claus. What to do?

Every year at Christmas Santa Claus paid a visit to Chippewa. During these annual visits, Santa made his headquarters at the fire hall. On the afternoon before Christmas he would ride in state to the municipal Christmas tree on the big red fire truck. There he would distribute oranges, popcorn balls, and candy to the delighted children, receive their wishful little letters, and even kiss those children that insisted upon this final beatification.

Unfortunately, just the Saturday night before, sly Santa had paid a premature visit to town. Traveling incognito, he had wandered into Charlie's Place. During the subsequent enthusiasm of the evening, waggish

Santa had mistaken the entrance to Charlie's steep basement stairs for that to the latrine. He was presently languishing in the Chippewa hospital, still incognito, and with a broken leg suspended from a unique series of pulleys. There were those who darkly hinted that Santa had been hitting the bottle. But they were the incorrigible town cynics and Yuletide agnostics. They were vastly outnumbered. At any rate, this year there was as yet no Santa Claus available for the visit to the Christmas tree.

"How about you, Ole?" In desperation the harried young mayor appealed to Councilman Sodergren.

"Dat ver gude yoke," big Ole guffawed, slapping his knee. "Ded Mester Mayor ever hare a Santeh say 'Merra Chrastmiss' vit' a Svedish ac-sant?"

"I guess you're right, Ole," His Honor gloomily agreed, staring out the window down Main Street. Suddenly he turned to the assembled councilmen. "Who's that?" he exclaimed. "Who's that big fat fellow walking into Charlie's Place with Danny McGinnis?"

"Why that's Buller Beaudin," the city clerk said. "Everybody knows Buller. Why? You don't mean—?"

"Why not—" the Mayor began to say.

Councilman Sodergren leapt to his feet. "Ay make a motion dat Mester Mayor be otterized to amploy Mester Buller for Santeh—not to axceed fafty dollar!" moved Councilman Sodergren.

"Me, I secca da mosh," quickly agreed Councilman Luigi Purgatorio. The motion carried unanimously. The assembly sighed with relief and swiftly adjourned.

"I'll make it thirty-five, then," the Mayor said to Buller, placing another ten-dollar bill on the green-cloth-covered poker table in Charlie's back room. Perspiring Buller stared hard at the money, then shut his eyes tightly to blot out the alluring vision, puckering out his lips and extravagantly wagging his head like a petulant child.

"Forty, then," the Mayor said grimly, adding a crinkly five-dollar bill.

"No—*ouch!*" Buller glared at Danny who was threshing his legs around under the table. "Lissen, Your Honor," Buller went on, glancing quickly at the bills on the table, "I've done a lotta queer things in my day fer money—but I ain't never yet took up with deceivin' little kids. Surely, fer all that dough you should ought to be able to get the genuwine produck down from the Nort' Pole."

"Fifty," the Mayor said doggedly, tossing out a crisp new bill. "That's the very limit. Take it or leave it."

Buller mopped his brow and stole a look at Danny. Danny was sitting back staring up at the ceiling, trying hard to pull out one of his mustaches by the roots. A storm was brewing.

Buller gulped. "I—I'll take it," he said, reaching out for the money only to find that Danny was there first. Danny carefully counted and folded the bills and, daintily extracting a wrinkled five spot, tossed it over to Buller, sinking the rest away in his buckskin wallet. Danny patted the wallet.

"That there's on account," he said to Buller. "There's many a slip 'tween here an' the moonacipial Christmas tree!"

"There's only one more thing," the Mayor said to Buller. "I don't mean to infer anything, but we'd like it if Mr. McGinnis here came in with you to the fire hall on the morning of the twenty-fourth." The young mayor was obviously embarrassed to suggest even remotely that Buller might go and get drunk. "What I mean is—just to—to be a sort of chaperon like. Is it a deal?"

Buller and Danny and His Honor arose and solemnly shook hands across Charlie's poker table. The pact was made. There was no backing out now.

"*Charlie!*" Danny shouted at the top of his lungs.

"Wat's dat?" Charlie shouted back.

"Fetch back three boilermakers—on the double!"

"Yes-sirree, Mister Danny," Charlie shouted. "Coming up like a yiffy!"

On the morning of December twenty-fourth a morose Buller, along with Danny and the boys, rode into Chippewa in Matti's big sleigh. They put the horses in Burke's livery stable and resolutely marched past a dozen saloons, getting to Mrs. Smedburg's hotel for breakfast. After breakfast Danny locked his arm in Buller's and firmly towed him out the door toward the fire hall.

"Meet you in Charlie's after the doin's," Buller's jailer called over his shoulder to Matti and the boys.

At the fire hall Danny casually drew Assistant Fire Chief Tug Cooney to one side. "Lissen, Tug," he whispered, "where's a safe *dry* place we can lock that buzzard Buller till it's time to wrassle him into his unee-form? We want to make sure he don't step on his Santa Claus whiskers durin' the big doin's."

Tug got the point. He winked elaborately at Danny. "Hm . . . Shure an' even Buller can't git dhrunk on stoker coal. Lave it to me. I'll kape him sober."

Tug drew Buller aside and whispered to him confidentially. "If you'd moind to wet your whistle a wee bit before you put on them hot whishkers—jist you slip down to the b'iler room there when ol' Danny ain't lookin'." Tug winked at Buller. "You'll foind the bottle hid behint the stame gauge on the furnace, that you will." Buller nervously wet his pursed lips like a trumpet player making his debut at Carnegie Hall. He winked back at Tug and earnestly gripped his hand. "Thanks, Tug," he said. "You're a real pal."

Tug slyly suggested a cribbage game to while away the time. After all, the ceremonies didn't start till two, and Buller needn't start changing until one.

Buller found himself rather restless and, no thanks, he didn't want to play. So Danny and Tug and Firemen Skinner McKittrick and Sliver Anderson cut for partners and were soon deep in their "fifteen-two's" and "fifteen-four's." Buller sidled over to the boiler-room door, blithely whistling "Jingle Bells" to show his Yuletide resignation and vast unconcern. But Danny didn't even look up. Stalking Buller studied a flyblown advertisement of fire hose which was tacked on the boiler-room door. He stood back and nodded appraisingly. Damn nice hose. Glancing back at Danny, he gently opened the door and ever so gently tiptoed down the stairs, closing the door softly behind him. How in hell could a man go in for this Santa Claus stuff on a dry battery?

"There," said Tug, winking at Danny and triumphantly turning the key in the lock after Buller. "That'll hold ol' St. Nick 'till we're after playing our game. Whose dale is it, now?"

Oddly enough, trapped Buller seemed quite content to sulk alone down in the boiler-room. There was no mad bellowing or railing or wild lunging at the door. Buller was completely beaten. The cribbage game ran on and on.

"—an' eight is twelve an' out," Danny said, just as the clock in the fire-hall tower boomed one.

Tug unlocked the boiler-room door. "O.K. it is now,

Buller. It's toime fer you to be gettin' on your fake whishkers!" he called down into the basement. There was a hollow echo but no reply. Tug looked wonderingly at Danny.

"Oh, my Gawd!" Danny moaned, frantically clattering down the boiler-room stairs. Buller was stretched out on his back in front of the furnace, with the cement floor for a pillow, his plump right hand clasping an empty quart bottle of Old Cordwood. The heat from the furnace had done the rest. Tug vainly tried to shake and roll Buller awake, but Buller just oscillated to and fro, slowly coming back to rest like a huge, soft, gyroscopic toy.

Skinner McKittrick hurriedly tiptoed over and looked behind the large dusty face of the steam gauge. "I knowed it," he mumbled, ruefully biting his lip. "I jest knowed it would happen to me."

"Fireman McKittrick!" Tug said sternly, pointing accusingly at his subordinate. "Was you the laverick what planted that there quart of whisky behind that steam gauge!"

Fireman McKittrick hung his head and explored the cement floor with his toe, peeking up at Tug from under his troubled brows.

"I'll tind to you later, you pantry-drinkin' knave." Tug turned to Danny. "This leprechaun of a Skinner's gone an' found the hiding place I used to use before I became assistant chief. Honest, Danny, I didn't know there was a bottle hid down here. By all the saints I didn't, that I did not." Buller began to snore. "Oh, the Lord save us," Tug moaned, "'Tis twinty after one —an' we got no Santy Claws a-tall a-tall!"

When the town clock struck two it seemed that every child in Chippewa was milling around the decorated municipal Christmas tree. His Honor the Mayor and the members of the common council stood around in various attitudes of chilled municipal rectitude, stamping their cold feet on the tall pine platform which stood beside the lofty tinseled spruce tree. They were flanked by baskets and cartons of oranges and candies. Here they would officially greet dear old Santa, present him with the keys to the city, and help him dispense the Christmas goodies to the dear little tots of the sterling mothers and fathers—and voters —of Chippewa.

Down Main Street and along Bank Street as far as the fire hall, the official route was crowded with people: mothers, fathers, cynically dubious older children; miners, lumberjacks, farmers—even Big Annie and her girls. Matti and the boys had taken up their stand at the fountain. They wanted a good look at Buller in his new role. Agile Timmy had managed to scramble up alongside Chief Booze-in-the-Face, the better to witness the public triumph of one of the boys from Hungry Hollow.

Back on the platform the mayor and council members stirred uneasily. Here it was quarter past two and still no Santa. "Where's Santa Claus?" "We want Santa!" childish voices began piping up around them. The distraught Mayor and his council fell into a whispered huddle from which they emerged and returned like members of a stupid backfield.

"Boo-hoo! If I can'th thee Thanta Cloth I won't take my cough medithin, Mama."

At this unhappy juncture there was a prolonged cheer from down Main Street. "There he comes! Here comes Santa!" The Mayor and council hastily resumed their broken ranks, bowing and smiling benignly at themselves and at everyone. Everything had turned out all right, just as they had known it would, all along.

Sliver Anderson slowly drove the big red fire truck out of the fire hall, with Tug Cooney and Skinner Mc-Kittrick standing on each running board at rigid blue-coated attention. Tug and Skinner served as Santa's guard of honor—and also to keep overzealous juveniles from clambering up into Santa's lap, if not into his very whiskers. And there on the very top of the fire truck, in regal splendor, sat enthroned the twinklingest, plumpest, jolliest, merriest Santa Claus that Chippewa had ever seen.

Santa Claus was indeed in rare form. He bowed and chuckled his way down Bank Street, keeping up a running fire of sally and quaint comment along the way. "Yep, yep, yep." As Santa passed by the public fountain he gaily winked and waved at Big Annie and the boys, tugging fiercely at his flowing mustaches as if to show the whole world that at last *this* was the real McCoy.

With a little sigh Timmy slipped from the side of Chief Booze-in-the-Face and landed on the snow-packed street next to Matti. Dreamy-eyed Matti wanted company and was pleased. "Wat's matter you, Teemy? You be li'l 'runk too?" Matti confidentially inquired.

Timmy kept staring up at the bowing and gesticulating Santa Claus. "My Gawd, my Gawd, it's the ol' man—it's ol' Danny hisself," he said in an awed voice.

Everyone agreed later that never before had Chippewa been visited by such a wonderful Santa Claus. From the time old Santa climbed down from his fire truck and made his chuckling way up to the platform and heartily pumped the limp hands of a bewildered Mayor and common council, to the final moment when he joyfully passed out the last orange, took the last letter, and resoundingly kissed the last child—*this* was a

Santa Claus that warmed the heart, gladdened the soul, and removed the last lingering doubt from the mind. Nobody minded that Santa, amidst the general confusion and in his jolly zeal, occasionally planted a resounding kiss on some of the comelier mothers instead of their offspring. It was with a collective sigh of genuine regret that the crowd watched old Santa finally clamber back on his throne and drive triumphantly back to the fire hall, where the tall wooden doors majestically swung closed behind him.

22

DEATH AND
RESURRECTION

Danny was so swollen with pride over his howling
success as Santa Claus that he stayed on in Chippewa
celebrating his new role until well into January. As
usual he established himself in the bridal suite at the
Chippewa House. The old brick hotel was his main base
of operations, being centrally located in his favorite
tavern district.

Finally, one morning Danny came slowly down the
creaking hotel stairs and appeared before Mrs. Smedburg with his packsack and snowshoes. His hands were
shaking violently as he paid his bill. After serving a
generation of carousing miners, lumberjacks, and trap-
pers, this phenomenon did not unduly impress Mrs.
Smedburg. Alcoholic jitters were an old story to her.
But she had never seen Danny or any of her customers
grow quite so plump and puffy during their bouts with
John Barleycorn. It was most remarkable.

"Vat's da matter, Danial?" Mrs. Smedburg peered

(247)

at him. "You vere all svelled oop like a poisoned pup. Yust take vun gude look at yourself!"

Danny peered into the rippled mirror over the lobby desk. "Oh, my Gawd!" he exclaimed, feeling his pouched round cheeks. "I guess I went to the well wunst too often," he moaned, staring at himself in awed fascination. "If I wasn't so ol' I'd swear I was goin' to have a baby." He felt his forehead. "Oh, my Gawd! I'm burnin' up with fever. Take holt of my head, Missus Smedburg."

Terror filled Danny's eyes as the Widow Smedburg tenderly placed her toil-roughened palm across his brow. Her maternal instincts were immediately aroused. "By golly, Danial, you *do* have vun terrible fever. Better you go back oopstairs to bed an' Ay vill call a doctor."

"No, no," Danny exclaimed, hoisting his packsack over his shoulders. "If I'm gonna up an' die it's goin' to be out to the Hollow. I don't belong to d-d-die no other place." He took a farewell peek at himself in the mirror. "If I ever git out of this here alive I'm goin' to take the pledge—an' sell my goddam still fer junk to Ruttenberg." Danny was at the door. "An' if I don't come through, Missus Smedburg"—Danny gulped —"I want you to know that I-I thank you a hull lot fer puttin' up with all my divilment an' hell-raisin' fer all these years. It was mighty fine of you. Mighty fine."

Mrs. Smedburg blinked and sniffed and removed her spectacles to wipe the mist away.

"There's jest one more thing I want to tell you, Missus Smedburg," Danny began, a seizure of confession being upon him.

"Vat's dat?" Mrs. Smedburg asked.

"I was the one what stole the Gideon Bible that

there time. Do you mind the time?" Danny said, hanging his swollen head in shame.

Mrs. Smedburg blinked her pale blue eyes at Dan. "Ay knew it, Danial," she said quietly. "Ay knew it all along. Ay will give you half-dozen Bibles if dey'll pull you t'rough dis hare awful ailness."

"No thank you, ma'am," Danny said, gently closing the hotel door.

The boys were at supper. Buller noticed Dan's swollen condition as soon as the old man dragged himself into camp. Danny stood swaying in the light.

"Danny," Buller exclaimed, "how many poun's of Peerless are you chewin', man? My Gawd, where you been at?"

"My Gawd, where ain't I been at?" Danny said. Buller caught him just as he started to fall. He and the boys tenderly laid the old man out on the bunk. Taconite and Swan quickly undressed him as Timmy got out the nightshirt and tasseled cap from Danny's packsack. Buller mixed up a double hot toddy and brought it over to the bunk.

"Danny," he said gently. "Danny, wake up, ol' man, an' take this here hot drink."

Danny opened one eye. "Take it away," he said in a muffled whisper. "Take that goddam vile fluid away." Danny closed his eyes and relapsed into troubled, ratchety slumber.

Buller and the boys stared round-eyed at each other. When Danny refused a drink of whisky the end could not be far away. "Shall we go git Doc Gourdeau?" Buller whispered in an awed voice. The boys nodded their heads solemnly. Doc Gourdeau was nominated.

Since Doc Gourdeau was a rheumatic old practitioner who lived in Chippewa, this meant the boys had to pull him into camp from Matti's farm on the toboggan. The plowed road ended at Matti's. Buller and Taconite and Swan quickly got into their rubber boots and woolen jumpers. Timmy lit them out with the long flashlight as they adjusted their snowshoes in front of the camp. It was snowing hard and the wind was rising.

"You gotta save him till we git back with the Doc," Buller said hoarsely, raising his mittened hand to Timmy in bleak farewell.

"It shall be done!" Timmy answered, squaring his jaw as he shut the camp door against the swirling storm. Danny still lay in deep slumber, his breathing troubled and difficult. And his cheeks seemed to be getting fatter by the minute. Timmy hovered over him helplessly, tucking in the covers, arranging the tassel of his nightcap. Then he shaded the lamp and sat at the oilcloth table, working on one of his crossword puzzles. The restless wind searched and pried at the logs of the camp, moaning and whistling. Timmy had dozed over his puzzle. It was midnight.

"Timmy!"

It was Danny, sitting up in his bunk, his eyes bright and feverish, his face swollen into fantastic proportions. Timmy hurried to his side.

"What is it, Danny?" Timmy said anxiously.

"Gimme a drink." Danny mouthed his words as though indeed he had a monstrous chew of tobacco in each cheek. "Gimme a drink!" he repeated.

"Whisky?" Timmy hopefully inquired.

"Water," Danny said, "an' lots of it. I'm burnin' up!"

After his drink Danny seemed to rest easier.

"You'll be all right soon, Dan," Timmy volunteered. Danny shook his swollen head. In the swelling process his droopy mustaches had been drawn up into a brisk, military aspect, faintly reminiscent of Von Hindenburg. Danny kept shaking his head.

"I'm not the man I used to be," he said sadly. "What's more, I never was."

"You'll be all right," Timmy repeated.

" 'Cept fer my goddam head, I feel four poun's lighter'n an ol' straw hat," Danny said.

"You'll be all right," Timmy said doggedly, as though the phrase possessed some magic properties.

Danny shook his head dolefully. "I'm afraid this is the last of the ol' man." He was in the reflective mood which is said to possess some men as the end draws near. "It's a funny thing, Timmy—las' week I felt as strong as a hull team of horses with a little dog runnin' behin'. My poor ol' mother—Gawd bless her, she's dead now—lived to be ninety-four. An' here I'm up an' dyin' afore I even git my growth. Yep, yep. It's a goddam funny thing."

Timmy turned away and fumbled in the medicine cabinet. He surreptitiously wiped the mist from his eyes. He rattled the bottles and jars and came over and placed a bottle of Sloan's liniment and Grover's mange cure on the chair beside Danny's bunk.

"Kin I rub you, Danny?" he said, ever solicitous.

But Danny did not want to be rubbed. He wanted to talk. Mouthing his words through his puffed cheeks he rambled on about his childhood in Canada, of the girl he should have married back there, of how he wanted to be buried on the birch ridge in back of the camp, of how he wanted Timmy and the boys and Bessie to carry on the same as before, just as though nothing had happened. Danny was nodding over his pillow.

"There's jest one more thing I want," he mumbled.

"What's that?" Timmy asked, swallowing the lump in his throat.

"Pervided I las' the night out—I want jest one more look at good ol' Bessie." Danny's head slumped over on his pillow. Once again he had fallen into a deep and troubled sleep.

The next morning a little after daybreak Buller and Matti and the boys arrived with old Dr. Gourdeau sitting huddled on the toboggan. It had stopped snowing. Timmy was just leading a disconsolate Bessie away from the camp door. Her bell tinkled dolefully. Danny had had his last look. The boys kicked off their snowshoes and tugged old Doc to his feet.

"Ee's still alive?" Dr. Gourdeau asked Timmy in his guttural French-Canadian voice.

Timmy, pale, tight-lipped, and on the verge of tears, grimly nodded his head.

Old Doc Gourdeau had come to Chippewa years before as a dewy-eyed young medical student fresh out of McGill. Since then he had been through mine disasters, riots, and strikes; fire, famine, and flood. Still it saddened him that he must now attend the passing of that old pine knot, his fellow Canadian, Danny McGinnis.

Danny was sitting up in bed, his eyes bright and watchful as Dr. Gourdeau and little Matti and the boys gathered silently around his bunk. Doc placed his satchel on the floor beside him and threw off his big buffalo coat—the same one he had brought with him from Canada years before.

" 'Ello, Danny. W'as all dis foolish talk I 'ear 'bout you gwan to die?" Doc asked, as waggish physicians have ever been prone to do.

Danny's feverish eyes were darting birdlike about the room. His cheeks were swollen to enormous proportions. "Hello, Doc," he mumbled listlessly. "I guess you heared it correc'."

Dr. Gourdeau, with his oily black mustache which partially hid his pendulous wet lip, was the composite picture of all the weary, baggy-eyed elder statesmen of old France. He rolled up his shirt sleeves and took Danny's pulse. Matti and the boys pressed closer.

"Hm," Doc said.

He took Danny's temperature and read it carefully. "Hm," he said, jutting out his lower lip.

"Le's see your tong'," old Doc said to Danny.

Danny opened his swollen cheeks and stuck out his tongue. It had the hue and general aspect of a soiled Turkish towel.

"Hm," Doc said.

Danny sat up in bed. He wanted to make a statement. This was the end. Why hold back now?

"Lissen boys—Doc, you're a witness—when I'm gone I want you to put a quart of whisky—a *full* quart, mind—on the lid of my coffin. If it's still there the nex' mornin', nail down the goddam lid! *I'm dead!*"

"Hm," Doc said, pouting out his fat lower lip and slowly shaking his head. With great deliberation he reached into his satchel and brought forth a quart of Old Cordwood. He placed the bottle on the chair beside the liniment and the mange cure. He looked around at the boys and then down at Danny, counting.

"Brang seven glasses, please," he said.

"What's he got, Doc?" the boys said in one voice.

Doc Gourdeau turned his veinous brown eyes to the boys. They waited eagerly for the verdict.

"Hm," Doc said. "Wat you dink?"

"For Gawd's sake, tell us!" Buller said.

"Ee's sofferin' from 'angover, plos," Doc said.

"Plus what?"

"Plos momps," Doc said quietly.

"Mumps!" the boys cried in unison.

Doc nodded his head in assent.

"Momps!" he repeated firmly, wearily reaching for the bottle.